THE WORKSHOP OF FILTHY CREATION

Richard Gadz

Deixis Press

First published in 2021 by Deixis Press
www.deixis.press
ISBN 978-1-8384987-4-0

Cover design by Libby Alderman
paperyfeelings.co.uk
Typeset using Crimson Text

THE WORKSHOP OF FILTHY CREATION

Richard Gadz

Deixis Press

BOOK THE FIRST

CHAPTER I

London – Tuesday 18th January 1803

Gentlemen, ladies," called Dr Keate, above the low throb of voices. "Signore Aldini is ready to begin his experiments."

Dozens of faces turned towards the pair of stout wooden tables that had been set up in the centre of the room. Arranged on one of them were three devices, thin columns of metal discs held in rigid frames. Around both tables were tall candle stands capped with reflectors, to throw a yellowish, shimmering light down upon the proceedings.

The room itself was very large, but its extremities and its ornately decorated ceiling were lost in the gloom beyond the candlelight. Outside the building, bitter cold gripped Lincoln's Inn Fields and the rest of the city, but the room was warmed by the press of bodies: doctors and surgeons from various London hospitals, some of their wives and mistresses, friends and hangers-on, a scattering of curiosity seekers and journalists. Their second and third rows stood on long refectory benches to get a better view. The room was thick with their breath and a musty, acrid odour hung in the air, a churning mixture of human beings and dead tissue.

Dr Keate, president of the Royal College of Surgeons, beckoned the visitor forward. Giovanni Aldini stepped into the glow of light, smiling in response to a polite patter of applause.

Aldini had sharp, hawkish features, with a shock of dark hair and a tall, stiffly starched collar. His bright, hooded eyes confidently scanned his audience—the men exhibiting the gradations of their status in the quality of their cloth coats, their knotted linen cravats, their round-hats and tie-wigs, the women in high-waisted dresses, their hair spilling fashionably from beneath feathered bonnets.

Aldini's confidence was a result of his having given demonstrations such as this many times before, always with the same result. He nodded acknowledgement and the applause died down.

Dr Keate snapped his fingers at a couple of ragged assistants as he spoke, pointing them to fetch items from an adjoining room. "Signore Aldini is professor of experimental philosophy at the university in Bologna and a member of the medical and galvanic societies of Paris. We are tonight promised a series of interesting experiments, illustrative of the power of electrical galvanism."

Keate nodded to a familiar face in the crowd, a thin man with his arms around two plump women he'd tonight been introducing to people as his wards. "I see Dr Ettis from St Saviour's is among our number this evening, I know he attended Signore Aldini's demonstration there last week and has spoken of it with enthusiasm."

Dr Ettis grinned warmly and hugged at his companions. Neither of them appeared comfortable with either their brand new clothes or their august surroundings.

"Signore Aldini will be aided by our college beadle, Mr Pass," said Dr Keate, who then withdrew into the audience.

Aldini's voice was high, almost musical, his accent showing only in its Italian intonations. "My friends, I have travelled throughout Europe showing distinguished persons like yourselves the remarkable results achievable through the techniques I have developed."

As Aldini spoke, the short, small-eyed beadle Mr Pass, accompanied by one of the ragged assistants, carried a long, heavy bundle up to the empty table. It was wrapped in grimy sacking, spotted here and there with dark stains. Once it was heaved into place, Mr Pass dabbed nervously at his face with a cloth.

"The application of electrical currents," said Aldini, "has already proven to have marked therapeutic effects in the medical treatment of ailments of many kinds. I myself have achieved complete and lasting cures in patients suffering disturbances of the mind of the most acute and distressing nature. The sponsors of my journey to England, the Humane Society, are interested in the application of galvanism for revivification in cases of drowning. I will show you tonight that this, and far more, is indeed possible."

At his cue, Pass hopped forward and removed the sacking. Left on the table, lying naked on its back in the yellow candlelight, was the dead body of a man in his twenties.

"I began my experiments using the legs of dead frogs, replicating and advancing the work of my own uncle, the respected professor of anatomy Luigi Galvani, from whom the process of galvanism derives its name. I then moved on to the bodies of oxen, showing that the same techniques can be applied to larger animals and now, as you will see, to the human body itself."

The audience's attention was fixed and silent. Ettis's plump wards stared, their cheeks pink. Mr Pass fetched a large wooden tray, on which were a selection of sharp surgical knives and long, thin metal rods.

"Here," declared Aldini, indicating the table in a smoothly flowing gesture, "is the corpse of a man executed by hanging at Newgate Prison only a matter of hours ago, a man named George Forster. Yesterday, he was tried and found guilty of the murders of his wife and child, and of the disposing of their bodies in the

Paddington Canal. As you can see, no life remains. The body, although fresh, is quite dead."

Aldini took a knife from the tray. With a theatrical flourish, he jabbed the point into the corpse's skin at several points along its side, then spread his hands towards the audience. See? Dead.

George Forster's motionless eyes faced up into the light, sightless and unblinking. The onlookers were gripped with anticipation. Mr Pass felt his heart pulse in his ears.

"My first experiment begins with an incision into the nape of the neck, close below the occiput."

Grasping the corpse's hair, Aldini pulled the head to one side and cut into the area at the base of the skull, making a rectangular hole that quickly exposed the top of the spinal column. His hands were thick with residual blood as Pass handed him an instrument resembling a pair of pincers.

"I use the bone forceps to remove the posterior section of the atlas vertebra."

His face pinched as he forced the bone apart. There was a splitting sound and a gush of fluid spread across the table and pattered onto the floor. Among the onlookers, necks were craned for a better view. Several non-medical members of the audience discreetly took handkerchiefs from their pockets and pressed them to their noses. The cheeks of Dr Ettis's wards turned even pinker.

Aldini moved to the corpse's thigh and cut out a section of flesh. "Then I make an incision in the muscle at the hip, to expose the sciatic nerve." He moved to the ankles. "And a smaller incision into the heel, like so."

Dropping the bloodied knife onto the tray, he picked up two of the long metal rods and used one of them to point towards the three tall column-like devices on the other table. Mr Pass busied himself running narrow wires from the devices to the metal rods in Aldini's hands.

"These three mechanisms are Voltaic piles, which generate electrical charge by chemical means. Each one contains forty discs of copper and forty of zinc. Their design is based on the recent work of my compatriot, Signore Alessandro Volta." Casually and without pausing, Aldini touched the end of one rod to the exposed spinal tissue, and the other to the corpse's dissected hip.

Instantly, the corpse twitched violently. The entire audience gasped with shock. Aldini turned the rods slightly, pushing them deeper.

The corpse jerked suddenly, its arms and legs folding tightly, its fingers balled into fists, its back arched. Every muscle tensed and shook.

The onlookers broke into a murmur of terrified voices. Aldini nodded to Mr Pass, who stepped forward, pulling on a pair of gloves. Aldini withdrew the rod from the corpse's thigh and the body went limp. "Notice now the variation in response." He inserted the rod into the heel incision. The body kicked sharply, its leg thrust out, juddering. Brushing the sweat from his eyes with his arm, Mr Pass took hold of the leg and tried to bend it at the knee, without success.

"The muscular force thus produced is greater than that possible in life," declared Aldini. He plucked both rods free and the body of George Forster sagged back into stillness. "Here is the conclusion of my first experiment. My second demonstrates the revivification of the musculature in sequence."

A man in the front row fainted, crumpling slowly to his knees before those either side of him grasped him beneath his shoulders and dragged him aside. Every onlooker was in a state of agitation, many quietly expressing their astonishment, some visibly trembling with nervous shock. A metallic smell of blood and heated skin had been added to the room's miasma. Dr Ettis's wards had their hands to their faces, while Ettis swung his gaze gleefully between the two of them. Dr Keate stood quiet and pale, struggling to retain his composure.

Paying no attention to all this, Aldini cut a small section of flesh from the corpse's forehead. Smaller rods were slid into the tissue, and back into the exposed heel. The larger ones were embedded through the corpse's sides into the chest cavity. Mr Pass, his hands shaking, took a few minutes to install a different set of wires between the rods and the Voltaic piles.

Aldini raised a wire in one hand and gestured towards the table with the other. The audience hushed. "You will observe a fresh arrangement of the electrical connections. I will complete the necessary connection using this length of copper, varying the galvanic effect as I do so."

He stood beside one of the Voltaic piles. He reached out and gently brushed the exposed end of the wire up and down the column of metal discs, which crackled and spat sparks.

The corpse shuddered. Its chest began to rise and fall. Its dead eyes suddenly opened wide and its face jerked into motion, the jaw and lips chattering as if trying to form words.

Screams from throughout the audience suddenly cut the air. Voices rose in terror. One cried out, "For the love of God, the man is returned to life!"

The face twitched, its expression unmistakably shifting from agony to horror to pain. The chest breathed spasmodically. The corpse's hands rose from the surface of the table, twitching, upturned, in supplication.

Dr Keate stepped back in shock, almost tripping over those behind him. A few onlookers fled, their footsteps clattering against the wooden floor. Mr Pass looked away, his eyes pressed shut. One of Dr Ettis's wards turned to leave but didn't get more than a couple of paces before vomiting. The other stared, aghast, tears running down her flushed cheeks, watching as the corpse mouthed piteously.

Aldini, unperturbed by the reaction, proceeded to his third experiment, severing the head of the corpse with a saw and galvanising the head and torso separately. After a little over an hour, the demonstration ended and the meeting broke up. Some left without a word, others grimly congratulated Aldini on his remarkable and extraordinary results. Dr Keate calmed himself by directing the reorganisation of the room. Dr Ettis's wards left without him.

Three men, who'd been standing to one side, hung back a while. They approached Aldini once Dr Keate was out of the room and asked him a series of questions which told Aldini they had a knowledge of his subject that was at least the equal of his own. Adjourning to a nearby coffee house, the four of them spoke together long into the evening.

CHAPTER II

Friday 10th October 1879

The young woman—or so she appeared to be, to judge by her bearing—made her way down the gangplank and stepped ashore at the Millwall Docks. From the moment she did so, she was an object of curiosity. It may have been the air of mystery which surrounded her: the dark cloak, the hood pulled low over her face. It may have been her shape or the way she moved: tall and slender, walking with an oddly flowing, almost rocking gait. It may have been her long, thin fingers, pale and nail-less, gripping the edges of her cloak together. It may have been the man who walked beside her, cautiously, his hands fluttering at her sides almost as if he was herding geese. He seemed concerned not only that nobody should bump into her, but also that he should avoid any kind of contact with her himself.

The man was stocky and middle-aged, but at that moment looked older than his years. His face, with its slightly beak-like nose and straight line mouth, was sallow and lined. His matted hair and side whiskers merged into the heavy stubble across his rounded chin, unshaven for days. His clothes, which had clearly once been smart and well-tailored, were dishevelled and grubby from the long journey that he and the young woman had just undertaken. His name was Professor George Hobson.

As the two of them moved forward, his expression wrestled with itself, at one moment attentive and alert, the next filled with an uncomfortable introspection. He seemed as if ice water was slowly dripping through his veins. If the attention of observers had strayed away from his companion, they would quickly have realised that he was afraid of her.

Behind them, the battered old cargo ship on which they'd arrived from Ostend, the *Freya*, was preparing to unload. The captain bellowed orders to his crew in French, his long moustaches flapping like curtains as he spoke.

It was almost six o'clock in the evening, and the docks were crowded and noisy. London was beginning to breathe out its workers, just as it had breathed them all in twelve hours earlier. From home to work, work to home, in and out, inhaling and exhaling the industry and economy of the city. A steady flow of people pulsed through the capital's streets and alleys, blood flowing through the veins of a living creature.

Above the city, dense, yellowish clouds circled with an aching slowness. The belching fumes of a hundred thousand chimneys clotted into a thick, sluggish blanket which spanned the sky and blocked out most of the remains of the daylight. At ground level the air felt thick, used so many times and heaved through so many lungs that it was heavy and exhausted, reeking and throat-scratching. The air, as everything else, was choked with grime and soot, the combined oil and filth of machinery, factories and more than three million human beings.

The dampened pollution in the atmosphere made the outlines of the city hazy and grey. From the docks, to the south across the Thames, there was a low horizon of roofs. To the west, a forest of ships' masts on the tea clippers berthed downriver at the East India wharfs, a mass of gently waving vertical lines set against the simmering clouds.

The river snaked away in a wide arc, boats of every size and shape struggling along it. Just visible, in the middle of the irregular cut-out of the skyline, was the Palace of Westminster. To its right, the dome of St. Paul's, blackened with soot smuts and smoke, the tallest building for many miles.

There were about two hundred people scurrying around the Millwall Docks. Dozens of steamers and sailing vessels were being loaded and unloaded. A small commuter ferry was heading for the opposite bank, filled with neatly dressed men. Beggars huddled in corners, or were sent packing by boatmen. A newspaper seller yelled at the quayside, flipping out large, thin sheets to customers as they passed. Street vendors, come to catch the late afternoon trade, called out their wares.

"Penny slice o'pineapple!"

"Bootlaces! Fastenings!"

"Rat poisons and fly papers here!"

The river was restless, unusually choppy, slopping up against the sides of all the sea vessels. The surface of the water was oily with vegetable and animal matter, industrial and human wastes. Its putrid smell was at its worst here.

Professor Hobson pressed the back of his hand to his face. He'd lived in London for most of his adult life but had never got used to the stomach-turning stench of the river. On most days, the stink drifted for miles.

"We'll catch a cab on the road," he said to the woman, raising his voice above the shouts and noise. "At the top of the bank, up the steps, over there. Do you see?"

Her pulled-down hood turned, then nodded.

The professor was getting steadily more anxious as the crowds around them were getting thicker. They were jostled as people bottlenecked the only path that ran parallel to the road.

Behind them, a young man in a hurry spotted a gap and put on a sudden burst of speed. He pushed his way through, nudging several others towards the edge of the quay.

The ripple of movement pressed against a haggard-looking woman, dressed in rags and grime, who was standing on the lip of a wooden loading platform which jutted out over the brown, swirling water. An equally dirty and fearful toddler clutched at her skirts. Around her neck hung a tray of matchboxes which she held out at passers-by, silently, her face pleading.

The shove of the crowd made her take a sudden step back. The child at her feet let out a sharp, startled cry as she lost her balance, glancing down into the filthy river below, matchboxes tumbling. She let out a hoarse shriek.

The cloaked woman suddenly sprang away from the professor's side. A single, sharp motion took her to the toppling woman's side and with one hand she lifted both the matchbox seller and her child clear of the water before they fell, just as the yelping child's bare feet broke the river's cold surface.

There was a collective gasp from those around them. The steady flow of people all but stopped. The hood and sleeve of the young woman's cloak had flown back, leaving her to look openly at those around her, an expression of nervous defiance on her face. The small crowd stared back at her with baffled shock. Fearful whispers asked who or what she was.

She was pale, almost to the point of translucence. Her skin was delicately mottled and veined, as if she was made of living marble. The features of her odd, vaguely unsettling face were large but very slightly uneven, the bone structure beneath appearing to be a little off-centre. She had eyes that were a clear blue, icy and piercing, and the set of her mouth gave her a look halfway between smile and sneer. Straight, copper-shaded hair fell around her shoulders. She had a strangely macabre presence, her intense gaze flitting from person to person like a searchlight.

For a few seconds, there was silence. Professor Hobson, momentarily frozen in dread, finally hurried back to her side.

An old lady at the front of the crowd, bent with age, shuffled back from the strange young woman. She clutched at her neckerchief, strands of greasy grey hair swinging over her gnarled fingers. "Oo's this?" she breathed, to nobody in particular. Her watery eyes remained fixed on the stranger. "She's lik' a ragdoll, she's lik' a little wax dolly. Wha's 'appened to 'er, then? I not seen nothin' like that face in all my puff!"

Her words seemed to break the tension that was holding the crowd still. Voices became louder. Fingers plucked at the strange woman's cloak and she flinched.

The professor, regaining his composure, raised his hands quickly. "Please, please, all of you, there is nothing to see here." His voice was cracked with nerves. "I assure you all, there is no need for alarm. I am a scientist and ... er, I am escorting her ... to, er, a hospital."

He indicated for the young woman to replace her hood. She did so and he ushered her forward. The crowd made a wide parting, watching both of them with suspicion.

"Hey," cried the old lady, "she's not got no pox, 'as she?"

A sharp ripple went through the crowd. The professor swiftly turned and raised his hands again. "No, oh no, I do assure you. She has no disease. You are at no risk, you have my solemn word. She has ... er, a medical condition, sensitive to light, hence the hood. Simply, er, a form of advanced anaemia. Treatment will quickly restore her to full health, thank you."

He hurried her away. The old lady's voice tailed after them. "Poor luv. I seen it all now. Bless you, Mister Scientist, it's a miracle what they can do these days."

The professor hurried his companion up the stone steps at the end of the quay. At the top, close to the road, he looked back. The flow of people appeared to have returned to normal. The momentary side-show was over.

Relief turned his nerves into anger. "Maria, did you not listen to me?" he hissed. "Did I not stress the importance of secrecy."

The young woman fixed her blue eyes on him. "You did. Many times," she said irritably. Her voice was as oddly unsettling as her face. "Although why remains a mystery."

As they made their way up to the road, Maria's mood softened. "I don't know why I saved them," she said suddenly. "It didn't make sense. I'm sorry, you're right, it was a stupid thing to do."

The professor ran a hand through his wavy hair. "I'm not saying that. It was—brave. I'm sure they're grateful to you, but ... " His words tailed off.

The sky was growing darker and a night-time smog was beginning to curl itself around the city's extremities. On the other side of the road were rows of tall warehouses, the names of shipping companies painted in white above sets of gates. Cabs were being picked up from a long line which stretched the length of the docks.

The professor led the way to a compact four-wheeler. The cabbie, muffled against the cold in a thick woollen scarf and bowler hat, broke off from brushing down his horses and vaulted up into the driving seat as they climbed aboard.

"Kensington," called the professor. "Wenham Gardens."

The cabbie called back something that was halfway between 'righto' and 'giddyup.' With a snap of the reins, the horses clopped into a steady pace. Inside, Maria and the professor rocked and juddered with the motion of the cab.

The professor caught sight of his reflection in the window of the cab's door. He was suddenly shocked at how aged he looked, how tired and drawn. He was used to seeing a well-fed face but he looked thin and lank, his eyes glazed and distant. He longed for sleep, but knew he couldn't rest.

He turned to look at Maria as the cab rattled westward, through London's thickly mudded streets. Londoners flashed in and out of sight. With a flush of renewed fear, the professor wondered what all of them would think, if they knew exactly what was being carried past them at that moment.

Maria was intent on watching the city go by, taking in every detail of people and buildings glimpsed in the shadows or in oases of gaslight. She spoke softly, without taking her eyes off the road. "Professor, I know my head has been clear for little more than a day, but something is already weighing on my mind. On the ship, when we were sitting on the deck, I knew perfectly well that I was looking out to sea, that I'd experienced that sensation many times before, that I'd smelt salt in the air. Yet I also knew that I'd never seen a sea before in my life. Ever." Her fingers strayed along the window sill beside her. "And now I know this material, that lines this cab, is called silk and that I've worn garments made from it. Yet, I know *for certain* that I've never before touched anything like it. It's an extremely unsettling feeling, and I have no way to explain it."

She paused for a couple of minutes, gathering her thoughts, her attention remaining focussed outside. The professor sat silently, feeling his heart race.

"Our encounter back there at the docks," said Maria, "has shown me beyond doubt what I already suspected, that I am abnormal." She paused again. "Profoundly abnormal, in mind and body. Those people were afraid of me. You are afraid of me—I'd like to know why."

Professor Hobson was glad that her gaze remained on the street because he couldn't have looked her in the eye. Instead, he turned away in shame-faced embarrassment. A flood of sadness nearly set his jaw shaking. He tightly pressed his teeth together. He felt exhausted and drained, and wanted no shameful display of emotion.

After a while, Maria said, "This is a very old city."

"Yes." The professor cleared his throat. "Yes, that's right, it is."

Maria glanced up as the cab passed an imposing Georgian building. "There's such a mixture. You can see where some things were fitted in around others, much later."

"Indeed."

They rode on in silence. At last, the cab turned a sharp left into Wenham Gardens and came to a stop halfway down a long terrace. The tall houses were almost identical, a solid bulwark of respectability—clean bay windows, steeply pitched roofs, painted front doors and freshly whitewashed doorsteps. The trees that faced them, on the opposite side of the street, swished gently in the twilight.

The professor paid the cabbie, grumbling about the fares charged at this time of day. Maria stood looking up at the house as the cab clopped away. The professor took hold of the iron railings above the steps leading down to the basement level.

"This is my home," he said. "I hope you'll, er—well, hope that you'll consider this, in time, your home, too." He fumbled in his pockets. "Fortunately, I still have my key. The blackguards left me that, at least."

Moments later, they were standing in a narrow entrance hallway. A yellowish gas light flickered on one wall, throwing dancing shadows across the tiled floor and up along the bannisters on the stairway. Maria shrugged off her hood and ran the tip of her middle finger over the patterned wallpaper and wood panelling.

Struggling out of his travel-soiled coat, the professor called up the stairs. "Millie! Millie!" He turned to Maria. "Millie is my maid-of-all-work." He was flustered, shifting his weight from foot to foot. He was a bachelor, set in his ways, unused to having house guests at the best of times, and the macabre oddity of having this one to stay was only now beginning to sink in. "Millie lives in. My housekeeper lives a few streets away. Mrs Sewell. As I haven't been home for a while, she's probably left for the night." After a moment's awkward silence, he leaned over to shout up the stairs again. "Millie!"

A girl of about seventeen appeared, running up from the kitchen and scullery in the basement, flattening her apron against her plain green dress as she trotted along the passageway. "Sir!" she exclaimed. "You're safe! Sir, we were so worried about you, Mrs Sewell got a bill from your hotel in Paris, she went to the police she was so worried, the hotel said you'd vanished!"

He patted his hands in mid-air. "Thank you, Millie, I'm very glad to be home at long last but, as you can see, we have a visitor."

He stepped aside and Millie had a clear view of Maria for the first time. She blinked, confusion clouding her freckled face for a moment.

"Yessir," she said, bobbing a curtsey to Maria. "Please to meet you, ma'am. Miss. Ma'am."

"This is Maria," said the professor. "She is, er, under my care. She will be staying with us for, er, a while."

Millie's eyes never left their guest. "Yessir, may I ask, sir, what's been happening? You've been gone for more than three weeks, sir, and begging your pardon but you look done in, and I don't quite—"

"I'm sorry, Millie," said the professor, more sharply than he intended. "There will be time for explanations. I take it Mrs Sewell has gone home?"

"Yessir."

"Very well. The moment she arrives in the morning, the two of you are to come straight to me. Is that clear? Straight to me."

"Yessir."

"There is important business to discuss with you both, tomorrow. However, from this moment on, Millie, you are under one very strict instruction. You are not to mention the presence of Maria in this house to anyone. To anyone at all. Do you understand?" He held up a finger for emphasis.

"Yessir."

"Not next door's cook. Not the butcher's boy. I've seen you gossiping."

"Sir," blushed Millie.

"And I'll be saying the same to Mrs Sewell." He took a long breath. "Now then, Millie, we've all had an extremely troubling few days. Please settle Maria into the spare room and arrange a cold supper for her from, er, whatever we have in the larder."

He looked back and forth between the two women. "She may also appreciate a bath. Once all that is sorted out, I'd like some hot water myself, if you'd place it on my night stand, please. Er, for some reason I'm not terribly hungry, I'll fetch myself some whiskey and I'll be in my study for a while."

Millie nodded. "Sir."

The professor turned to Maria. "Er, well—goodnight. I would say 'sleep well' but of course you—the spare room is where I store part of my library and back numbers of various periodicals, so please feel free to, er—"

Maria sensed his discomfort. "Thank you, professor," she said quietly.

The professor nodded and retreated to his study, further along the passageway. Millie lit an oil lamp and, suppressing her own disquiet at their guest's odd appearance, led Maria upstairs. Beneath the well-worn stair carpeting, the wooden boards creaked. With his study door open, the professor heard the nerves in Millie's voice.

"I'll fetch you the bath from the downstairs, Miss," she said. She dropped into a stage whisper. "We still use a tin one. We don't have one of those bathrooms yet, the professor says it's a needless expense. He pinches the pennies, Mrs Sewell joshes him over it."

For the first time in many days, the professor smiled.

CHAPTER III

Wednesday 15th October
from the journal of Prof. George Hobson

It is now five days since I returned from the Continent. I've had time to rest and reflect, and to regain my senses a little. The simple pleasures of clean clothes, clean sheets and decent food have, I'm relieved to say, done much to dispel the darkest thoughts that plagued my mind.

I am calmed, yet I remain deeply afraid. Of her, of Maria. I know I must record, here, my thoughts as dispassionately as I'm able, yet the haunting fear of the circumstances in which I find myself, of the responsibility which has fallen upon my shoulders, still runs like ice through my veins. A dispassionate appraisal seems impossible.

Having Maria in the house is both unnerving and fascinating, rather like studying some deadly reptile at close quarters.

No, that is not fair. And not accurate. My fear is certainly not a fear of bodily harm. Maria does not pose a physical threat to anyone in this house. My terror is a chilling sensation of the mind, nothing less than a sense of dread, of almost spiritual horror. Horror, I must confess, at what she represents.

I flatter myself that I am a man accomplished in the biological and natural sciences, but none of my studies, none of my readings in the philosophical disciplines, seem to be of any use to me now. I try to apply what I have read about materialism and vitalism to this situation, but I can come to no conclusions. Is her life the product of mere skin and bone? If not, then where is the divine spark? What cascade of questions does she pose to the human condition, to the human soul?

Even as I write these words, I can feel a fresh nervous tremor plucking at my heart! I will regain my calm with an account of more practical matters.

On the morning following my return home, Millie and Mrs Sewell attended me in my study, as requested. I made sure that Maria was fully occupied, exploring my bookshelves at her leisure, something she seemed very happy to do.

Mrs Sewell, her white-grey curls as flamboyant as ever, came bustling over to me, her skirts creaking. Her dark, mouse-like eyes were a-glitter as she patted my hand between her old, bony fingers. "Sir, the Lord be praised that you're safe," she squeaked softly. "We were so worried on your behalf, especially after we heard word from Paris. I sent Millie down to the police station, didn't I, Millie?—"

Millie nodded quickly.

"—But they said that, since you were out of the country, you were out of their jurisdiction. They proposed to do nothing, nothing at all, not a thing. A disgraceful attitude. A gentleman of your eminence and learning! I prayed for that police sergeant, I did."

I smiled and thanked them both for their concern. Then, as steadily and as succinctly as I could, I relayed to them the facts of where I had been and what I had encountered, of my abduction and short imprisonment in Germany.

I told them who Maria is and why she is living here with us. Obviously, I omitted the more repulsive and shocking details of the whole affair, giving them only such information as was necessary to fully appreciate the situation. Naturally, I wished to avoid any offence to their femininity, but also I wished to minimise any possibility of information being—albeit inadvertently—divulged either to a third party or to Maria herself, before I've devised a longer-term strategy.

Even so, both of them were visibly upset by what I had to say. Millie swatted at her eyes, her lips pressed tightly together. Mrs Sewell, having plucked the handkerchief from her sleeve, kneaded it incessantly while her head gave little shakes, sending her curls into a dance. "That poor creature," she muttered, more than once. "Poor little mite."

At last I sat forward in my chair and said, "Do you both understand the need for secrecy? Whatever our private fears or concerns may be, Maria is relying upon us to keep her safe. I cannot even begin to guess how she herself feels at the moment. Frightened, bewildered, almost certainly alone. We must, at least until further decisions are made, present her with as normal a life as possible."

"Yessir," said Millie. She sniffed, dabbed at her eyes and forced a smile and a nod.

Our interview ended and I sent them back to their duties. Before she went, Mrs Sewell approached me again, a mix of emotions playing across her wrinkled face. "God bless you, professor," she whispered, the edges of her mouth fluttering. "You are a good man. A kind-hearted man. You have no idea. The Lord protect you, sir."

She patted the back of my hand once more and bustled away to supervise the midday meal. I've always known my housekeeper to be a sincerely religious woman, but I'd never before heard her speak in such terms. Despite myself, I felt rather moved.

The household quickly returned to its regular working routine. Of course, I remained—and remain—unsettled. Perhaps if I was less a creature of habit … ? However, I've now had ample opportunity to observe my new house guest under less trying conditions than during our harrowing journey back to London.

I had already suspected that, for her size and build, Maria is unusually strong, and this has been confirmed by the sight of her moving objects, including a very large bucket filled with water, without any apparent effort whatsoever. I stated that she poses no physical threat, but it's clear that she could easily hold her own against any prize-fighter who might dare to challenge her! She also exhibits a natural agility which is equally remarkable. Twice I have seen her ascend the stairs in three preternatural bounds, something which seems to amuse Millie no end.

Her mind is even more robust. Quite apart from those mental faculties I've already witnessed, Maria's capacities for learning and reasoning are extraordinary. She deduced that Millie has an invalid mother living in the suburbs, simply by watching the girl fuss about in the hallway for less than a minute! She inferred the existence of this very journal by noting the state of the two candlesticks that sit on top of my desk!

So far, Maria has divided her time between two activities, the predominant one of which is reading. She is working her way through my library at speed. I had assumed that her sleeping for less than an hour a night was down to disturbance caused by our travels, but apparently I was wrong. She spends all night devouring one volume after another. The majority of my books are related to my work, but she seems equally taken with the limited range of fiction on my shelves. She has already read works by Messrs Dickens, Verne and Scott. I've had to send out for the latest numbers of various magazines, and have been forced to double the household expenditure on newspapers to accommodate her intellectual pursuits.

For the few hours of the day during which her head is not in a book, she accompanies Millie about the house and shares all the maid's fetching and carrying. She appears to have attached herself to Millie and follows the girl from kitchen to attic. For her part, Millie is delighted to have a helpmate and has completely overcome her initial wariness of Maria. Poor Mrs Sewell, on the other hand, is most vocal in her disapproval of a guest sharing the housework. "Not proper," she mutters under her breath.

Watching Maria shadow Millie in this way is rather like watching a nervous child cling to its mother's apron strings, desperate to please and afraid of getting lost. It's behaviour that's strangely contrary to the sophistication of every other aspect of her demeanour, as if beneath her surface stir more fundamental instincts. As if, deep inside her, her infantile nature—for, surely, she is literally an infant—struggles to find expression.

At the same time, and in odd juxtaposition, she is developing a rather austere, one might say haughty, persona. She increasingly exhibits a character that is politely but insistently opinionated, both disarmingly blunt and engagingly enquiring. On the morning following her arrival, I sent Mrs Sewell out to replace the cloak and ragged peasant's dress, in which she'd travelled, with—at no slight expense!—a selection of more suitable attire. Maria shunned almost all of it, insisting on adopting trousers and a button-up sack coat. Mrs Sewell muttered her disapproval once more. "Not proper at all."

Maria's personality mostly clearly shows itself over dinner each evening. On Saturday, Mrs Sewell placed our main course before us and, with a new potato poised half-way to my mouth, I noticed to my embarrassment that Maria was staring at the contents of her plate with undisguised revulsion.

"Maria?" I said, putting down my fork. "Is something wrong?"

"This—is animal flesh?" she asked in a low voice.

"It's a lamb cutlet," I said. "You, er, had something similar in Munich."

She gazed at me with those piercingly blue eyes. "I did?"

I nodded. She looked down at her plate. "This was alive. Now it is dead."

"The, er, same applies to the potatoes and the carrots," I said. "Ah, I see, has this London Vegetable Society been in the papers again? No, what's the word? Vegetarian. I wouldn't want you to get the wrong impression, such views are rather to the fringe."

She shook her head. "No, it's not that. It's something I rem—" She broke off mid-word, frowning, staring down at the meat. Her long, pale fingers touched at her temples for a moment. Her voice hardened. "I don't want it," she said firmly. "It's obscene!"

I reached over and speared the cutlet with my fork. "Well, let's not waste it," I said. "Would you like some extra potatoes?"

On Sunday, over a simple vegetable pie, which we both enjoyed, she asked me all manner of questions relating to politics and the organisation of society: by what authority do the rich control the poor? What did I think of Mr Disraeli's recent factory legislation? Why don't Millie and Mrs Sewell eat their dinner with us?

I answered her as best I could. At one point, she held forth on universal suffrage and the inadequacies of the '67 Reform Act! I have the anxious suspicion she may have been reading about the Paris Commune.

On Monday, the topic was history. Last night, sensational literature, of all things.

This evening, religion. At the end of our conversation—and here I feel my nerves asserting themselves once more!—she made a remark that chilled me to the core. It is the reason I have scurried into my study, to this journal, in order to organise my thoughts.

Before she said it, she asked me why people attend places of religious worship. "You yourself are a colleague of Thomas Huxley, are you not? Haven't the Darwinists now disproved the ancient mythologies?"

I gave a soft grunt of amusement. "Don't let Mrs Sewell hear you talk that way, you'll upset her terribly."

"Why?" said Maria. "She's as intelligent as you or I."

"People like believing in something greater than themselves," I said, dabbing a napkin to my lips. "It's not a matter of being rational but of, well, faith."

"Really, professor," said Maria, arching an eyebrow, "you're supposed to be a scientist. This is the nineteenth century." Then she added the words that froze my blood: "Surely it's time to throw away such medieval superstitions."

That phrase was a precise echo of one spoken to me not a fortnight ago. Those exact words.

I tried not to betray my discomfort. She had clearly spoken in all innocence, entirely unconscious of how these words would affect me.

Was she merely thinking along similar lines? Simply expressing a similar thought? Or was it something more? Was this proof of the processes that were so meticulously described to me in Germany? I see my pen shaking slightly in my hand!

I remember taking Mrs Sewell, Millie, and Millie's friend Emily to the Egyptian Hall a few years ago—early '75 if memory serves—to see Maskelyne and Cooke show their Magical Automata. A small mechanical man correctly picked playing cards from a rack in a manner that was quite uncanny.

I recall the expressions of wonder on the faces in the audience. I shared a thrilling sense of unworldliness, watching those little people made of wood and metal, glimpsing—just for a moment—apparently thinking beings in non-human form.

All done with tubes and air pressure, I understand. All a clever illusion.

Those automata were mindless, the simulation of intelligence. Maria's actual intelligence is all too real. This is why guilt stops me answering her other questions, those she has asked me tonight, and last night, and the night before, and the night before that: "Why am I different? Where have I come from? Why can't I remember past the last few days?"

The words dry up in my mouth. How can I tell her the truth? A simple automaton could not recoil at it, but Maria will. How long can I expect her to confine herself to this house, and to trust me, on vague promises of "soon" and "in due course"?

No! Vapid indecision is a luxury I cannot afford. If I cannot decide on a course of action for myself, then I will seek advice.

I have a distinct feeling that, for better or worse, the next days and weeks will reveal Maria's destiny in no uncertain terms, whatever that destiny may turn out to be.

CHAPTER IV

A large, bulky atlas was open on the thick counterpane that covered Maria's bed. Trembling gaslight shone across its pages, glowing fitfully from the little fan-shaped tongues of flame that shuddered on the wall fitting overhead. Tall bookshelves and a massive, gloomy wardrobe stood to either side. The curtains at the window were undrawn, but the feeble, pre-dawn moonlight outside threw no shadows in the room.

Maria sat, her legs crossed beneath her, examining a double-page diagram in the atlas. There, set out in detail, the entire world. The territories of the British Empire, large and small, were coloured red, scattered across the globe like a sudden spattering of blood.

Her thin finger traced the outlines of continents. All that land and water, she thought, all those thousands upon thousands of miles of plains and mountains, valleys, rivers, cities, forests, teeming with life, and here she was, on this little island to the north. London, a tiny pinpoint of ink, and herself a microscopic speck inside that tiny point; a single drop in a vast, rolling, unstoppable ocean. She felt despair at the vast bulk of the world, and her vanishing insignificance beside it.

A breath of wind rattled the window and she glanced up. The bedsheet she'd draped over the oval, wood-framed mirror on the dressing table had fallen askew. Part of the mirror was visible again. She slid from the bed and re-covered it hurriedly.

She didn't like seeing herself. When she looked at her reflection, her off-centre face and copper hair, she experienced the creeping, prickly sensation that was rapidly becoming familiar to her, a sensation of *knowing* and *not knowing* at the same time. This was her face, this had always been her face, yet she had never seen it before.

Easier not to look at all. She felt like a stranger in her own skin, as if the face in the mirror was real and the one she wore was fake, as if she was a perfect copy of herself and the genuine her was gone forever.

She wanted to scratch her face away, tear at the skin, pull out its mocking eyeballs and break the bones beneath.

She flipped the pages of the atlas, trying to distract herself, blankly watching the world go by. Perhaps if she went back to her stories—? She looked down at the heaped pile of books and newspapers beside the bed.

She told herself that she was tired, that's all. She'd need some sleep soon. Only a few minutes of it, but even a few minutes was long enough for the nightmares to come and eat her alive, as they did every time her eyes closed.

Perhaps, when she had some answers—? Soon. In due course. For days, and nights, she had struggled with the professor's failure to give her the only information she really wanted. She'd tied her mind in knots trying to work out if he really knew the truth or not, if he had some ulterior motive, if he was stalling for time or plotting in secret.

She knew that her frustration was growing a hardened shell around her. She didn't like how sharp she was becoming. Eventually, she'd decided that Professor Hobson was exactly what he appeared to be, a conclusion she'd reached for one reason only: his obvious fear of her.

He tried so hard to hide it, to spare her feelings, but it was clear and genuine. It was what prevented her from getting angry with him. It was what prevented her from demanding, shouting, running from the house. What hideous truth could have caused it? She simultaneously craved answers and shrank from them. That creeping, prickly sensation.

Over the past few days, she'd thought his fear of her had waned a little, but it had suddenly shown itself again the previous evening. They had been eating together in the ill-lit but cosy dining room which overlooked the narrow kitchen garden at the back of the house. The room was a little musty, and a little crowded with oddments and furniture that had overflowed from other rooms, but the small, crackling fireplace sent out a comforting warmth and Mrs Sewell was an excellent cook.

They'd been discussing religion. The professor suddenly baulked at her words, something about medieval superstitions, and the atmosphere in the room had instantly changed. The professor momentarily paused, mid-movement, his expression freezing over. With forced cheeriness, he had steered the conversation into a description of famous cathedrals, finished his meal and called for Mrs Sewell to clear away the plates.

At first, Maria thought her opinion had offended him in some way, but it was obvious that his reaction wasn't one of offence, but of fright. She had no idea what had triggered it and was sure she'd said nothing untoward. Lost in thought, trying to unpick the cause of it, she accidentally drifted into sleep.

The nightmare always took the same form.

She was enclosed, in a cramped and sparsely furnished room. She had to leave it, at once, since it was deep underground and the air in the room was rapidly becoming dank and fetid. She opened the door and walked through into a second room, exactly the same. Turning ninety degrees, she left that room and entered an identical third. Turning ninety degrees, into a fourth, a fifth, a sixth.

Gradually, the floorboards beneath her feet began to curve and twist. She needed to rush, to escape before the weight of earth brought down the ceilings and she'd be pinned beneath tonnes of soil, but the warping of the floorboards prevented her from hurrying. She had to pick her way, to avoid tripping.

The rooms became smaller. Each one seemed to fold back in on itself. The ambient light, a flickering yellow pool from elegant candelabras, grew steadily dimmer. She knew she was heading in the wrong direction, moving deeper into the ground with each successive room instead of closer to the surface. The rooms narrowed into passageways, claustrophobic and confining, sloping down.

Down, into smaller and smaller spaces. Soon she was crawling on hands and knees, then on her belly, pulling herself along, twisting around, from space to space, tighter and tighter. She was going in circles, feeling her feet and then her legs curve around at an impossible angle that should have met her clawing fingers.

Darker and darker, deeper into the earth, smelling the worm-filled slime that strained to burst through the wooden boards that pressed hard against her sides and back.

Arms flung ahead of her, her fingers clawed at a tiny gap, the only source of air, the only escape. Two fingertips wide. She pulled and squeezed, suffocating, knowing she was stuck, knowing she was helpless.

And out of her mouth came a scream. A shaking howl of terror.

And out of the scream came people. Swarming out of her, biting through her skin to escape her in the same way she'd tried to escape her underground prison. They tore her flesh, bursting out between her ribs, her knuckles, her vertebrae. Hundreds upon hundreds. Legs, teeth, nails.

Her face split. Hands clawed at her. Mouths wailed. A gush of human beings crawled out of the disintegrating remains of her body. She felt herself dissolve, unable to cry out. They wept, they gibbered, they laughed in hysteria.

And there! Watching her suffer, from the first moment of the nightmare to its end, the Eye Above. Huge and unblinking, dark and shining, its iris a black, bottomless well.

Staring. Accusing her. Judging her. Gloating and delighting in her death, so richly deserved.

The nightmare always left her drained and tearful. She curled up on the counterpane, grimly staring at the daylight arriving at her window.

CHAPTER V

At 10am, after Professor Hobson had sent Millie out with an urgent note and instructions to call a cab, he went into the formally-appointed living room beside the front door. Maria looked up from her magazine and *The Mystery of Sasassa Valley*.

"Would, um, would you like to take a short cab ride with me?" said the professor. "I'd like you to meet an old friend of mine."

Maria blinked. "Yes. Yes, very much."

The professor grinned and nodded. "Good. Excellent—I thought perhaps a hat and a scarf? It's, er, quite chilly out."

Shortly before eleven o'clock, the two of them climbed into a four-wheeler. The professor plucked a pocket watch from his waistcoat. "We have time to spare, Maria, er, perhaps you'd like to see something of the local area before our appointment? Now that we're, um, out and about? Yes?" He leaned out of the cab slightly. "Circle the Hyde Park area for twenty minutes, then on to Cromwell Road, if you please."

The cab jerked into motion, diffused autumnal daylight faintly dappling its interior through the trees. After a few minutes they were skirting the park, close to the Serpentine. Maria looked out on a large social gathering spread across a broad grassy area, being held beneath long, ribbon-like Temperance League banners suspended from tree branches.

All kinds of itinerants and tradesmen had gathered at the edges to cash in. It was past the normal fairground season and an event such as this was a useful bonus before the long, income-less winter ahead.

To one side, an assortment of small wooden caravans and larger, elaborately decorated wagons were huddled into a semi-circle. All were weather-worn and mud-spattered, their colours chipped and drained by time. Beside them, a grubby green canvas tent was surrounded by hastily-erected stands and awnings, like a faded monarch attended by courtiers. A painted sign, in intricate lettering, was strung between one corner of the tent and the nearest caravan, declaring JEMMISON'S SPECTACULAR MENAGERIE.

A round, squat man with bushy moustaches stood under it, on top of an upturned crate. His threadbare suit was loudly check-patterned and his face was garishly made up with oversized eyebrows and lips. In a clipped boom, he regaled the milling crowd, his hands sweeping theatrically from the lapels of his coat to the tent, to you charming ladies and gentlemen, to the gently swinging sign above him.

"Rooooll up! Rooooll up! Come one, come all! See! An exhibition like no other your eyes have ever beheld! See! Fearsome freakish fantasticals from the four corners of the world! See the bearded lady, she's as fat as a suet puddin' and as hairy as a coconut! Ladies, gentlemen and children, gather round! See the sensational skeleton man, the thinnest human being alive! He'll turn the strongest stomach! See, preserved under glass, a gallery of ghastly grotesques, a diorama of diabolical deformity! The two-headed baby and the famous lizard boy of Southampton! Kiddies half price! Rooooll up!"

A knot of grimy toddlers ferreted about around the wheels of the caravans, laughing and chasing and pushing each other over into the mud. Beside the semi-circle of wagons, a brazier had been lit, sending a narrow, twirling column of smoke up into the low, churning and sulphurous clouds.

Maria stared at the tent, her eyes alert and her expression blank. One or two of the crowd had been enticed in. The stout man held open a flap of canvas for them and they stepped into the darkness beyond. Maria's thin fingertips touched the glass of the cab's window.

Professor Hobson sniffed his disapproval at the caravans and wagons. "Vagabonds and diddiki, the lot of them," he muttered.

The cab turned into Rotten Row, wheels crunching on the wide, stony road. They passed a well-heeled group walking in the opposite direction, the women in voluminous skirts, the men in starched collars, all absorbed in conversation.

To the side of the path was an organ grinder, his painted hurdy-gurdy hefted on a thick strap around his neck. A reedy, melancholy tune wheezed and chimed from it, the sound drifting on the chilly air of the park. An undernourished monkey, scrappy-haired and wearing a miniature Napoleon hat, hopped at the organ grinder's shoulders, holding out an old tea cup to passers-by.

Coffee stalls and meat pie vendors were strung out along the road. A large, rosy-cheeked woman strode up and down carrying a tray of live sparrows, their legs tied to lengths of string, selling them as playthings for little children.

Maria's attention was caught by a photographer, who'd set up his pitch a short distance back from the others, on an open patch of grass where the daylight was slightly clearer. A tall barrow, displaying some of his work and containing his portable darkroom, was propped beside him. He had his camera on top of a spindly wooden tripod, pointed at a young couple about ten feet away. He was exhorting them to stand absolutely straight and still, just there, stay there, thanking you kindly, here we go. The couple were grim-faced and formal, he in bowler hat and she with her best shawl tied in a bow at her neck. Their hands were clasped tightly together.

The professor noticed Maria's interest. "I let Mrs Sewell talk me into having my photograph taken last year," he said. "Rather uncomfortable having to sit there like that, but it's a fascinating business. Expensive, though."

"Can I see it?" smiled Maria.

The professor shrugged. "If you wish. I think I put it in a drawer somewhere." He peered through the window to check their progress. "We'll be at the museum in a few minutes. As you'll see, the building is still under construction. It won't be finished for a year or two yet, but the section in which I work is almost complete. All the labourers will be elsewhere and I'm currently the only one with an office on my particular corridor. It makes for a nicely peaceful workplace, but having it all but deserted for the time being can be a nuisance. My department seems to be spread across half a dozen buildings at the moment, dreadfully inconvenient, but Owen insisted the new place should be occupied as soon as possible. We were overflowing from our rooms at the British Museum."

"Mr Owen is the curator?" said Maria, keeping her gaze on the passing scene outside.

"That's right."

The cab turned into Cromwell Road and the huge, slab-like shape of the Natural Sciences Museum came into view. The horses clattered to a stop at the gate.

"They were to call it the Natural History, but Sciences won the vote in the end."

Maria, her breath misting around her face in the damp chill, stood looking up at the symmetrical arrangement of arches and towers, the whole building surrounded by sparse stretches of freshly planted saplings. High above, from parapets and ornate edges, lines of gargoyles looked back at her, beasts of reality and imagination caught in stone.

"Beautiful," she said softly.

"You think so?" said the professor, counting his change from the cab. "I find the style a bit fussy, myself."

He led her through the building's main entrance and across the echoing emptiness of the huge, vaulted hall inside. Maria took off her hat and scarf as they ascended one stone staircase after another, their steady footsteps reverberating.

On each successive floor, the walkways became narrower and the ceilings lower. By the time they reached the long corridor where the professor's workroom stood, at the top of the building, the massive proportions of the ground floor had become more domestic, although the heavy doors and arches wouldn't have looked out of place in a castle.

The professor's room was large and cluttered. The cold, stone echo that characterised the rest of the museum was absorbed in the furniture and patterned Turkish rug. The bookcases were filled to capacity. Apart from its size, the only feature which distinguished this room from the professor's cramped study at home was a long rack of shelves on which were crowded many tall, sealed jars containing a range of biological specimens.

Maria walked past them slowly. Dozens of dead creatures looked back at her from inside their yellowish ethanol and formaldehyde. Fins, gills, scales, curled tentacles and open mouths.

"This is a collection I've been gradually assembling for over twenty years," said the professor proudly. "As you know, my chief area of study is aquatic life, and you'll find a broad assortment of saltwater and freshwater species here. I could describe some of the more interesting for you, if you wish?"

"Thank you, no," said Maria. She moved on to the bookshelves and spent a few minutes examining some of the expensively leather-bound reference volumes, taking as much interest in their form as their contents, the heavy smoothness and dusty smell of their pages.

Her reverie was suddenly interrupted by a firm knocking at the door. She flinched in alarm and the professor held up a hand to calm her. He checked his pocket watch. "He's slightly early," he muttered to himself.

The door was opened to reveal a slim, frock-coated man, a few years younger than the professor, and an equally elegant woman dressed in a fashionable cream dress and bustle. Its flat front was interrupted by a fourth-month pregnancy bump. Her long, blonde hair, pulled high at the back, fell in ribboned twists around her neckline.

"Delighted to see you, old chap." The man thrust a hand towards Hobson and the professor shook it. "Apologies, I did what you expressly asked me not to, and told Sophia. When I got your note I simply couldn't contain myself."

"Hardly the first time," said the professor. He nodded a greeting to the woman. "You're most welcome, Sophia."

The woman smiled broadly at him. "We're relieved to find that you're safe and sound, George," she said.

"Is she here?" asked the man, his expression filled with puppyish enthusiasm.

"Er, yes, indeed," said the professor. He stepped aside for the two visitors to enter the room and closed it behind them.

Maria spun on her heels as they came in, fixing them with her penetrating gaze. The man's expression washed over with undisguised curiosity, the woman's with equally undisguised shock. Maria took an instant dislike to the pair of them.

"Maria," said the professor, "these are my old friends Thomas and Sophia Meers. I trust them both entirely, and you can place the same confidence in them as you can in me. Thomas is a doctor at St Saviour's charitable hospital. I wanted him to meet you because he is a biological scientist like myself. Thomas, Sophia, this is Maria."

Dr Meers took a step forward, while Sophia stayed beside the door, her back pressed gently to the wall. Maria was impassive.

Dr Meers stood directly in front of Maria, stooping slightly so that his face was level with hers. His eyes were small and his features boyish, framed by narrow muttonchop whiskers. There was a scattering of premature grey in his dark mop of hair. "Will she understand what I say, George?"

"Of course I will," snapped Maria. At the sharp sound of her voice, Dr Meers's eyes widened and Sophia blanched, visibly alarmed. Her gloved hands pressed tightly into each other.

"Forgive me," smiled Dr Meers. "George has told me very little about you."

"That makes two of us," said Maria. Dr Meers let out a short laugh. Professor Hobson shifted uncomfortably.

"I'll examine you, if I may?" said Dr Meers. His eyes shone with fascination.

Maria nodded guardedly. Meers held up a forefinger. "Would you follow the shape I outline, please?" He traced a large rectangle in the air which Maria's eyes tracked. "Good." He took a match from his pocket and lit it, watching Maria blink and her irises contract. Blowing out the match, Meers picked up a book from the professor's desk, stepped back a little and spun it across the room for Maria to catch. She snatched it neatly from mid-air and placed it back on the desk.

"Excellent," smiled Meers. "I wonder—would you be able to describe yourself to me? Tell me something about your life?"

Maria's eyes narrowed slightly. When she finally spoke, her tone was icy. "I had a boiled egg for breakfast."

Dr Meers drew closer to her again and held out his palms, indicating for Maria to place her hands in his. He turned them over, feeling the pale, slightly marbled skin, the bone structure beneath, the nail-less finger tips. His touch was gentle and delicate.

"The flesh is unlined," he muttered, seemingly more to himself than to his wife or his friend, "nothing for a fortune teller to read here, I fancy. The skin over the knuckles isn't puckered in the usual way. The metacarpal joints are narrower, too. Extremely interesting."

He dropped her hands. "Are you in any pain, at all?"

"Pain?" said Maria. "No."

Dr Meers nodded. "Would you raise your head for me, please, look up at the ceiling?" Maria lifted her chin and Dr Meers leaned closer. She could smell coal tar soap and the morning's activity on his collar.

He scrunched his eyes a little to focus, then with the end of his little finger held an inch from her neck, he followed a path along her jawline and down her neck, curving back in the direction of her left shoulder. "If you look closely, there are subcutaneous lesions of some kind. Not creases in the skin, but indentations deep in the flesh. It's almost like the joining point of two sections, as if the assembling of a jigsaw puzzle—"

Suddenly, Maria slapped his hand away and drew back.

"That's enough!" she snarled. "I am not an exhibit in a freak show!"

Dr Meers held up his hands and declined his head. The professor opened his mouth to speak but changed his mind, folding his arms and pursing his lips. Sophia stood unmoving, one hand held splayed against her rounded belly.

"I'm sorry," said Dr Meers, "I was simply trying to understand you—"

"As a butcher understands a turkey," said Maria. Her anger subsided when she saw that his remorse was genuine.

Dr Meers cleared his throat and indicated the door. "George, perhaps I could have a word with you in private?

"Er, yes, of course," said the professor.

Meers turned to Maria. "Once again, my sincere apologies. It's been the most extraordinary pleasure to meet you and I do hope we meet again soon. Sophia, do you—?"

"No, my dear, thank you," said Sophia quickly, her voice trembling at the edges. Maria's gaze flicked to her and Sophia felt her body become a mass of pins and needles. In those eyes and that vaguely peculiar face were an alien otherness that Sophia had never even dreamed existed.

Maria's expression shone a mixture of pity and irritation at her. Sophia blinked, embarrassed, and looked away. She hurriedly followed Dr Meers out of the room. The professor paused in the doorway. "I'll be back in a moment, Maria."

The door shut and Maria was left in silence. She let out a long breath, her lips beginning to wrinkle as an aching, unfocussed loneliness seeped into her. She quickly returned to the reference books laying higgledy-piggledy on the shelves.

Out in the echoey corridor, Sophia Meers pressed a hand to her racing heart. "George," she hissed in a strained whisper, "what is that creature? She's not human. What is she?"

Before the professor could answer, Dr Meers took hold of her shoulders and gently directed her towards the staircase. "Please, go down and wait in the carriage. Believe me, I am every bit as shaken as you."

Her face in motion, Sophia paused for a moment then complied, her skirts rustling as they dragged down the stone steps. Dr Meers watched her go, then bustled his friend to the far end of the corridor, well away from the professor's office. They stood in the shadow of a gothic arch.

"For God's sake, man," whispered Meers, "that … young woman is the scientific discovery of the age!"

"You think I am unaware of that?" protested the professor in a suppressed voice.

"Keeping her shut away and out of contact with the world is not only impossible but immoral. That is clearly a thinking, intelligent being!"

"I know that only too well!" hissed the professor impatiently. "But the moment the wider scientific community gets to know about her is the moment that she becomes no more than an object of research and curiosity. A fairground sideshow, as she herself has just pointed out! I will not be responsible for turning her life into a humiliating public circus."

"And what marvellous freedoms does she enjoy right now?" hissed Meers. "Like it or not, old chap, you are responsible, she's in your care. And partly mine, now, I would suppose. For once, George, lift yourself out of your narrow academic burrow and face facts. Where did you find her? Where does she come from? What precisely is she? You have no right to keep these things to yourself, and you certainly have no right keeping her in ignorance! Denying her the truth is simply cruel, man!"

"You may have a different opinion, Thomas, when you know what that truth is," muttered the professor. "She herself may wish she'd been less enquiring!"

Dr Meers flung his arms wide in frustration. "Be that as it may, the truth will out." For a moment or two he rocked on his heels, his fingers drumming at his sides, his lips pulled tight in thought. "I appreciate your dilemma, George, I really do, but why not call a meeting? A select few, perhaps some of your colleagues from here at the museum? Or go and see Huxley?"

The professor sighed. "I'm not sure there are many of my colleagues I'd trust not to exploit the situation for their own ends. Huxley is unlikely to be discreet."

"Then a meeting of our own circle. The two of us, Charles Barré, maybe Jabez Pell. They're practical, well-connected people, with resources at their disposal, surely between us we can handle the matter? Make long-term plans? What do you say?"

Meers had regained much of his puppyish enthusiasm. Professor Hobson rubbed his chin and nodded. "Perhaps you're right. When I return home, I'll make arrangements and let you know. Would tomorrow night be convenient?"

42

At dinner that evening, Maria noticed that the professor's mood had lightened. A weight seemed to have gone from his shoulders.

For a few minutes, she considered catching him off guard and asking him, unexpectedly, when his meeting was going to be held. In the end, she decided against it.

An hour after they'd returned from the museum, three small thin envelopes had been on the hallway table waiting for Millie to put them in the post. They were addressed in the professor's handwriting, one to Dr Meers at St Saviour's, one to a police inspector, one to someone at a factory on the other side of the city, and all clearly written at the same time. The thinness of the envelopes indicated short notes rather than documents, and their done-at-once uniformity suggested a single topic of conversation. The unusual assortment of people implied personal friends rather than a business arrangement, and the inclusion of Dr Meers among them implied a consequence to earlier events.

The planning of a meeting, to discuss her future, was Maria's rapid conclusion. She decided to keep her mouth closed and her eyes open.

-💫-

CHAPTER VI

Friday 17th October

As twilight approached, Charing Cross railway station was filled with the hiss of steam and the boiled-kettle smell of locomotives, the clattering of train carriage doors and the chatter of voices. At that time in the late afternoon, the station was busy with travellers coming and going, greeting and parting.

The steam swirled in thick clouds above the parallel platforms, almost hiding the station's huge glass roof from view. Even the oversized clock, high up on the wall at the back of the platforms, was hard to read through the billowing grey haze.

With a grinding, metallic screech, the boat train from Dover pulled noisily into Platform 2. Doors were flung open all along its side before the train's engine had clanked and snorted to a halt. Passengers began to flow out, either setting themselves down from the carriages in a single hop or watching their feet as they stepped carefully from step to platform.

Nearby, a dozen or more uniformed porters sped into action to offer their services, stubbing out cigarettes underfoot and wheeling hand trolleys ahead of them. The passengers and porters met, from opposite directions, like minor armies clashing on the platform battlefield.

There was a flurry of movement. Porters tugged the peaks of their caps in deference, passengers wagged fingers at suitcases and boxes. The broad, sliding hatch of the train's baggage compartment rumbled open and guardsmen began to unload heavier baggage onto the platform. Luggage was heaved and stacked, pennies were dropped into porters' hands, passengers craned their necks to spot loved ones waiting for them or to look for the nearest exit.

One of the porters, a slim young man with tightly cropped hair and a generous face, found himself without a customer. His gloved hands weaved his trolley around various colleagues who were already halfway through loading up. The others were swifter on their feet, pushier in the scrum. He kept wheeling and weaving, keeping an eye out, looking busy. He was sweating and nervous, mindful of the fact that, after six hours on duty, the tips accumulated in his pocket were barely going to cover the cost of his supper.

He was about to hurry back to Platform 1, where the next train was due in a matter of minutes, when he noticed a figure emerging from the thick swirl of steam up ahead. Other porters were now starting to head for the main gates or the rank of taxis, pushing piled-high stacks and followed by customers who marched to keep up. This figure remained on his own, watching over the last of his trunks and boxes being taken off the train.

The young porter grinned to himself. Not too late, one left, might be a bob or two coming his way after all! He doubled his speed and the metal wheels of his trolley rumbled against the tiled surface of the platform. Posh, this one, by the look of him. Posh meant bother, but beggars could not be choosers, eh?

The figure was of average height and wore a voluminous, dark overcoat with the collar turned up. His hat was in the continental style and had an unusually broad brim. The glow from the overhead gas lights threw deep shadows under that brim, and it was only as the young porter drew closer that he realised the stranger's face was almost completely covered by the folds of a plain white cotton scarf. Darkened spectacles obscured the man's eyes, and he leaned heavily on a thick, ornate walking stick.

Despite himself, the porter hesitated for a second, unsure what to make of it. However, the obvious expense of the man's clothes—look at them shiny boots!—quickly overcame any nagging qualms. He adopted the broader smile and more refined tone he reserved for well-to-do customers. "G'd'evenin' to you, Sir, may I help you with your luggage?"

The stranger paused, looking him up and down, then tapped at the nearest of his trunks with the end of his walking stick.

"Thank you, Sir, right you are." The porter gave a sharp nod and started dragging the stranger's belongings onto his trolley. He chatted cheerily while he worked.

"The name's Smith, Sir, Edward Smith, and you're in safe hands this evenin' wi' me, Sir, if you don't mind me takin' the liberty of sayin' so. Have you travelled to London from the continent of Europe, if I may ask, Sir?"

The stranger nodded. Bending to haul a large, wooden crate, Smith noticed that the man's right hand was covered in a soft, tan suede glove while the other, which gripped his walking stick in heavily bony fingers, was bare.

"I thought as much, Sir, judging from the elegant style of your dress. I'm one for noticing—whuuuf, this one's a heavy load, Sir, you got a dead body in there, Sir?" He chuckled loudly, swiping the sweat from his brow with a sleeve. "Not really, Sir, that's a humorous thing we porters say when encountering a weighty item, Sir, another one being to wish as we had an extra arm to help bear the strain, Sir. To tell you the truth, we shouldn't josh, seeing as how they did find a murdered body in a trunk, Sir, over at Paddington, a couple of years ago. The Paddington Trunk Murder, the papers called it."

Smith finished loading, making a few remarks about the weather and about the bumpiness of the railway tracks on the line south of the city. "That's the last one, Sir," he said, out of breath, "now if you'd be so kind as to follow me."

He pushed the trolley carefully, its centre of gravity now at chest height. The stranger walked slowly and awkwardly, as if his legs and back were extremely painful. His knuckles whitened as his weight shifted onto his stick. Behind them, the emptied train hissed steam and began to reverse out.

"Might you be a visitor to London, Sir, or are you now returning home?"

The man's voice was cracked and scratchy, and he spoke with a heavy accent. "I am a visitor."

"I see, Sir, then might I offer my additional services, Sir, as unofficial guide? Should you be needing an introduction to the best hotels, or to any other form of accommodation, Sir, then I'm your man, happy to suggest suitable roomings for any gentleman such as your good self."

"No," breathed the stranger, "I have a specific destination. I may be lodging with friends."

They were walking beside low railings, approaching the tall iron gates which led out onto the main concourse of the station. Twice, Smith had to pause to allow for the stranger's slow progress. The stranger, his breath rasping, touched the back of his gloved hand to the railings here and there, to steady himself.

"I wonder if I might enquire, Sir," said Smith, feeling he was earning himself a decent tip and wondering if he'd have time to meet the train on Platform 1, "if you've travelled here from one of the *German* provinces, Sir?"

The stranger's covered face turned slightly towards the young man. "I have."

Smith grinned and cocked his head. "I thought as much, Sir, I'm one for noticing things and your accent is most distinctive, if I may be so bold, Sir. O'course, we get all sorts through here, Sir, this being the terminus for the Dover train. Germans, Dutch, French, far and wide. The other week, we had a whole family of Russians, if you please, all fur hats and brass buttons, Sir, with half a dozen children in tow, of descending height, thus prompting a humorous comment from a colleague, Sir, on the subject of Russian dolls."

At that moment, a commotion from the other side of the paved concourse drew the attention of Smith and everyone else within earshot. Two police constables were manhandling a whip-thin, violently wriggling woman, one of them holding her tightly around her shoulders, the other trying in vain to contain her legs. The woman, dressed in a frayed tea gown, bucked and twisted, her face red with fury.

"Gerrof me, y'fuckers!" she screamed. "I done nothing!"

"A painted judy like you ain't never up to nothing," growled the constable at her shoulders. A respectable-looking couple, the man carrying a pair of valises, quickly scuttled out of the way. With affronted expressions on their faces, they hurried off.

"I done nothing wrong!" screeched the wriggling woman, her voice suddenly breaking with emotion. "He was goin' to buy me dinner!"

"Not in the Golden Cross, he wasn't. Stop making a bleeding fuss! Frank, 'old her, will yer?"

A kick sent the other constable's helmet flying. Smith rocked his trolley upright and took a few steps forward, intending to help. Another porter beat him to it, running over and grabbing the woman's flailing leg.

Smith turned back to the stranger, to find him leaning with his back against the gate's heavy ironwork. His head was bowed slightly and his breath came in erratic gasps.

"All sorts, you see, Sir?" said Smith with enforced jollity. He felt the prospects of a decent tip were rapidly falling from his grasp. "May I fetch you a cab, Sir?"

The stranger looked up at him. In the smoky light from the nearest lamp post, Smith thought he caught the shadow of a large, round eye behind the stranger's darkened lenses.

"Yes, but first, Mr Edward Smith, I have questions for you."

"Sir?"

"You are healthy?"

A frown blinked across Smith's face. "I—I don't quite catch your meaning, Sir."

"You appear to be young and healthy," said the stranger. "Are you physically fit and active?"

"Oh, that I am, indeed, Sir, this job keeps you on your toes in more ways than one, Sir. I don't entirely—"

"Do you have family? Children? A wife?"

"Ah … in actual fact, Sir, no. My old mum and I, Sir, came down here some years ago, following the sad passing of my late father, Sir, since time she herself has—Sir, might I ask—"

"You are not married?"

Smith gave an uneasy grin. "Lady Luck has not yet smiled upon me in that particular aspect, Sir. If I'm not—"

"Good, that is most convenient. Are you a popular figure among your colleagues?"

"Sir? I—well, Sir, truth be told, I'm still learning the ropes of portering, as you might say, since the—"

"Good. How much money would you require to remain in my service for the next few hours? To load my belongings into a cab, travel with me, unload, then be free to return. How far is the East End of the city from here?"

"That'd be three miles, Sir, or a little more. In a cab, something in excess of one half of an hour, at this time of the day."

"Then no more than two hours, or less. I have only goldmarks with me, but their value should be equal to at least £50."

"Ff—fifty?" In his mind, and across his face, the money wrestled with the ringing of alarm bells. He felt his heart in his chest and a glistening uncertainty in his stomach. He glanced around, across the concourse. The constables were long gone.

"Answer me," said the stranger, with a note of irritation. "I have medical requirements that I must attend to. We must be on our way. If you don't want this brief, simple job, then find me a porter who does."

Smith grasped the handles of his trolley. "No, Sir, I'm your man! Come this way, Sir, the procurement of a cab will be the work of a moment, Sir."

A few minutes later, the stranger was huddled inside a four-wheeler that rocked and creaked as Smith and a grumbling cabbie tied heavy trunks to the cab's rear and roof. Propping his stick against the seat opposite, the stranger reached inside his overcoat with his ungloved hand. He drew out a 25cl phial and eased the stopper from its neck. He delicately pulled down the edge of his cotton scarf and, with a shaky hand, tipped some of the almost-clear liquid from the bottle onto his tongue. With a wheezing breath, he felt it trickle down into his throat and slowly returned the phial to his pocket.

Edward Smith and the cabbie climbed up onto the driver's bench and the cab set off. The young railway porter had no idea that he would be dead before daybreak.

CHAPTER VII

Meanwhile, on the other side of St James's Park and past Sloane Square, Thomas Meers was the first to arrive for the meeting at Hobson's house in Wenham Gardens, about half an hour before the time Hobson had specified in his note. Sophia had voiced no desire to accompany him this time.

He and Hobson arranged four chairs in front of a freshly-banked fire. Its bright, orange-yellow flicker was the only light in the living room. The walls were lined with paintings that the professor had gathered over the years, both portraits and landscapes, so many of them that they almost hid the patterned wallpaper. On the mantelpiece above the fire were plaster busts of figures from the ancient world, their faces white and unsmiling, their eyes blank. They, and the portraits on the walls, looked down upon the room and the professor, a silent audience of the past, an assembly of the eminent and distinguished from beyond the grave.

"Is Maria in the house?" asked Meers in a subdued voice.

"She is," said the professor. "I've told her that my visitors tonight are concerned with membership of a charity committee that's associated with your work at St Saviour's. I've asked her to remain in her room, or with Millie. She doesn't suspect our real purpose."

Meers nodded grimly. The two of them sat in silence for a few minutes, looking into the flames and their own thoughts.

The front bell rang and Mrs Sewell showed the caller in. "Mr Pell, professor."

"Thank you, Mrs Sewell. As soon as Inspector Barré arrives, you may go."

Jabez Pell was a rotund man, with a thinning pate of sandy hair which he'd long ago given up trying to control. He had a slightly lumpy, slightly pock-marked face, with a bulbous nose and grey eyes which sat glassily behind round, wire-framed glasses.

He was the proprietor of Pell & Blight Ltd, "Purveyors of Tonics & Healing Curatives, Medicinal Supplies & Sundries." The company had come into his sole ownership in 1868 after his erstwhile business partner, who was also his brother-in-law, had died after a brief illness brought on by the eating of a spoiled herring, according to the official report. Pell's wife had been killed in a horse-riding accident the following year. He now lived in rooms above the company's factory in Whitechapel and had a reputation in the London business community as a solidly prudent industrialist. The London business community had entirely the wrong impression of him.

The buttons on his waistcoat strained as he huffed his way to an armchair. "Intrigued to discover what this is all about, George," he wheezed, flopping himself down heavily. He glanced around for signs of a bottle or decanter, but saw none. "Charles said you'd vanished to the continent for weeks, asked if I knew where you'd gone."

"That's part of this, er, problem," said the professor.

The bell rang again and Mrs Sewell ushered in Inspector Charles Barré. He was tall and hawk-like, wearing a crisp dark suit and monocle, a precise and dapper man whose movements were as clipped as the moustaches which concealed his narrow lips. He looked far more like a City clerk than a Scotland Yard policeman, something his colleagues quietly joked about behind his back. They also considered him snobbish and plodding, an unfair assessment of someone who'd simply developed a cautious nature. His family had once been a wealthy one, of French Huguenot descent, but had lost every penny in the railway mania stock crash of '46. Sudden destitution had left an indelible mark on Charles Barré's early life. He and George Hobson had known each other for over twenty years.

As the four of them settled down, Jabez Pell produced a large hip flask from his jacket. "Brandy, anyone?" There was a general murmur of agreement and Mrs Sewell was asked to fetch four glasses before she left for the night.

It had been some months since they'd last met together and they talked for a minute or two, in the light of the fire, about the burgeoning careers of Barré's two daughters and his recent successful apprehension of Lesterson, the notorious Surrey Poisoner. Pell lit a meerschaum and the smoke merged with the dancing firelight shadows beyond the semi-circle of armchairs.

Meers noticed Hobson's quiet nervousness and, throwing back the last of his brandy, asked the professor to begin his account of why he'd gathered them that evening. "I've been told something of the story, gentlemen," said Dr Meers, "and I can assure you that even the little I already know has made me doubt my own senses."

Pell and Barré looked at each other, then at the professor. The grim expression on Hobson's face told them that Meers wasn't, for once, letting his words carry him away in exaggeration.

"I've called you here," said the professor, "to help make a decision. Perhaps, a series of decisions, relating to nothing less than a scientific marvel. Decisions I cannot make alone."

"Have your researches led to some new discovery?" said Barré.

"Not exactly," said Hobson. He reached across to a nearby table and fetched a sheaf of tightly handwritten sheets which he clutched to his lap. "You may remember, back in July, I was invited to speak at a conference on the biological sciences, to be held in Paris over four dates of last month. I was particularly keen to attend, since the major topic under discussion was one in which I've been interested for years and on which I've written several well-received papers, namely those rare animal species which are able to hold electrical charges in their bodies, notably of course the electric eel. I was led to believe that a number of prominent theorists would be in attendance, including one or two I've wished to meet for some time. All the expenses of the conference, I should say, were to be met by a philanthropic American businessman, keen to promote the sciences. Naturally, in retrospect, perhaps I should have paid more attention to the fact that none of my colleagues at the museum received a similar invitation. However, I was to be something of a guest of honour, and—well, I can tell you now, gentlemen, that the invitation was a fake."

"There was no conference?" said Pell.

"None at all," said the professor. "I arrived at my hotel. A reservation had been made for me, but the concierge, when questioned, had no knowledge of other guests arriving for a scientific gathering of any kind."

"Peculiar," said Barré, polishing his monocle with a handkerchief. "Why would anyone want to lure you to Paris?"

"Exactly my thought, at that moment," said the professor. "I stood there, uncertain of what to do, realising with shock that I had been royally duped and that my foolishness would probably come at considerable expense. However, there was no prospect of my starting a return journey to London at that hour, so I resolved to spend the night at the hotel, make what enquiries I could the next morning and book passage home as soon as possible. I took a meagre supper in the hotel's crowded dining room and was shown to my room, sure that I wouldn't get so much as a moment's rest. And so it proved. No sooner did I set foot in my hotel room than I was set upon by ruffians."

"Good grief," muttered Jabez Pell.

Inspector Barré sat forward slightly. "They robbed you?"

"Not exactly," said the professor. "I was knocked to the floor and trussed up like a goose."

"Did you get a look at them?" said Barré.

"Unfortunately not. There were three of them, though, I could tell that. Sacking was pulled over my head and I was lifted into some sort of hammock affair in which I was carried. I was too astonished and afraid to even think clearly, let alone fight the blackguards. I struggled but quickly saw this was futile. I was taken outside and put into a carriage."

"Through a crowded hotel?" said Barré. "There must have been witnesses."

The professor shook his head. "I heard echoing footsteps on stone. I think I was carried via back stairs or staff quarters."

"Where on earth did they take you?" breathed Dr Meers.

The professor raised the papers in his lap. "I've written a full account out on paper, principally so that I could get the whole horrible business organised in my own head, omitting nothing. A statement, if you will. Once you've heard it, I'll incorporate it into my journal. I'll read it to you, and it will explain the agitated and febrile state in which I currently find myself."

-❦-

CHAPTER VIII

from the journal of Prof. George Hobson

My journey lasted three days, travelling solely by carriage. During the hours of daylight, the coach stopped only to change horses. At night, the three ruffians would find some remote spot and settle under canvas, leaving me securely tied. I was fed, largely with bread and cured meats, by having the sacking pulled up above my mouth. At no point did I see anything of my surroundings, apart from the daylight that filtered through the hood over my face, neither did I leave the confines of the carriage. The personal discomforts of such confinement were every bit as undignified as you might imagine.

I learned almost nothing from my captors. For the first few hours of the journey, I made loud and vehement demands, but eventually gave up. I doubt any of them understood English; from overheard snatches of conversation I judged one to be French and the others German.

At one point, in the evening of the first day, there was an altercation outside. One of the ruffians climbed into the carriage with me and held a blade to my throat, saying something in a low voice that was clearly a threat. After a few minutes of raised voices outside and a series of sounds I could not identify, we continued on our way and the blade was removed.

By the time the sacking was plucked off my head, I was exhausted, disoriented and dirty. A sudden flood of light made me turn my head and squeeze shut my eyes. As they grew accustomed to the glare, I saw that it was in fact only the low glow of candles, fixed into three ornate candelabras placed on a long, heavy refectory table in front of me. I was seated in an equally robust wooden chair, chains firmly attached to my ankles.

As I was to discover, this was the main hall of a large mansion, originally medieval but added to several times over the centuries, built into the side of a mountain in the Hanover province of Germany, not very far from the border with Austria-Hungary. The mansion was tall and turreted, jutting upwards like sharp fangs from the thickly wooded area which surrounded it, overlooking a deep, narrow valley. At the foot of this valley nestled a few small villages, the only other signs of civilisation in this stark, remote countryside.

I sat chained in that chair, trying to get my bearings and to quieten the racing fear in my heart, when I suddenly started as I perceived a man's face appearing out of the darkness on the other side of the table. A sharply-featured, energetic face, squarely sculptured and topped with an overgrown thatch of hair. The face rose as the man stood up. He was dressed with dark, old-fashioned extravagance, in silk cuffs and a pinned cravat.

He grinned as he spoke in a sibilant, heavily-accented voice. "Good evening, Professor Hobson. I hope your journey wasn't too trying. I'm delighted to meet you at last, my name is Wilhelm von Frakken. Welcome to my home."

I'd never heard of him. "Whoever you are, sir," I said as forcefully as I was able, which was with no force at all, "I demand you release me."

Von Frakken smiled and nodded, spreading his long arms. "This house is efficiently guarded. You won't be able to escape it. Provided you are willing to admit this fact and settle down as my guest, then all restraints can be lifted and you will be free to move about as you wish. I'm sure you would like to clean up before dinner? Yes?"

Feeling dazed, all I could do was nod. The chains were removed by unseen hands and I was escorted to a comfortable bedroom on an upper floor, where there was a lavish four-poster and a night stand complete with soap and hot water. When the stealthy valet who'd accompanied me departed with a quick nod, I noticed—to my relief—that my travelling bag of fresh clothes had been brought from Paris along with my coat, although the brand new top hat which Mrs Sewell had insisted I buy was clearly now lost forever.

Half an hour later, feeling more myself and consequently fuelled by righteous anger, I returned downstairs to find a sumptuous meal laid out on the refectory table. Von Frakken ushered me to a seat, poured me some wine into a sparkling crystal goblet and sat himself at one end of the table directing various servants. The man was clearly determined to prove himself a congenial host!

Again, I began to protest at my kidnap and imprisonment, this time in the strongest possible terms. With shameless effrontery, Von Frakken simply deflected my every outburst with vacuous small-talk. More than once, I determined to leap to my feet and march from the room, but at the arched entrance was a hefty, bearded guard with a rifle slung at his shoulder.

In the end, sheer helplessness—not to mention hunger!—overcame me. A plate of stew, with dumplings, was placed before me and I ate greedily. While I ate, von Frakken asked me about my work, displaying a surprisingly detailed knowledge of both biochemistry and ichthyology.

When my stomach was full, I could assess my situation more calmly. I reasoned that I would more effectively learn about this scoundrel if I appeared compliant. As soon as he realised that

I was willing to talk on equal terms, he began to speak freely, albeit displaying the swaggering snobbishness and sense of entitlement that one finds in a born Junker.

From this—and subsequent—conversations, I was able to piece together a good deal of information about his disgraceful family history:

The von Frakkens, originally from Prussia, had been major landowners for hundreds of years, although this Wilhelm von Frakken was himself a scientist and medic. He was wealthy and extremely well-connected—so well-connected, indeed, that he claimed to have the ear of Chancellor Bismarck! His reputation among the elite of the new Germany had been assured when, six years ago, he cured the withered arm of his namesake, the crown Prince Wilhelm, on the occasion of the Prince's fourteenth birthday. Any form of physical impairment is taken as a sign of weakness in those circles—one can only wonder at the improved prospects that lad must now have, when eventually he becomes Kaiser.

Von Frakken claimed to have effected this cure by replacing the entire arm with that of another young member of the royal family who was put forward as a suitable donor. I utterly dismissed the claim as boastful nonsense, scientifically impossible, until I discovered more about the von Frakkens.

In the early years of the present century, one Victor von Frakken—inspired by the work of the Italians Galvani and Aldini, amongst others—was a medical student in Geneva and, at that time, heir to the title of Reichsgraf, or Count. He was thrown out of the university there in 1812, after conducting researches into the reanimation of dead tissue through the use of electricity. His stated aim was to—ridiculous as it sounds—create new life in defiance of Nature, in order to place Mankind (and presumably himself) above and beyond the natural world order. To this end, he is said to have constructed an original human body from limbs and organs taken from corpses, and to have somehow imbued this body with life!

This disgusting and bizarre experiment ended in disaster. The resulting monstrosity died in agony, but not before claiming the lives of several persons. Victor von Frakken was tried and executed in 1815. The von Frakkens had records of the trial destroyed.

I understand that, a year or two later, a shocking account of Victor's actions was written by the young wife of the poet Shelley, following a holiday beside Lake Geneva during which she had spoken to witnesses, as both Shelley and his disreputable friend Lord Byron had an interest in galvanism. Mrs Shelley's attempt to disguise the facts with deliberate inaccuracies—such as changing Victor's name to Frankenstein—wasn't enough for the von Frakkens. They used their wealth and influence to have the book suppressed and all copies burnt.

Victor's daughter, Ilsa—still a child at the time of her father's death—took up his research sometime in the 1820s. By then, similarly unethical and grotesque lines of enquiry were being pursued by others: a Dr Hügelgrun in Germany; small groups in Stockholm and New York; some medics in England calling themselves the Promethean Society. Although they communicated with each other, in a limited way, they all kept their work hidden from official scrutiny, collectively fearing the same outraged reaction which had greeted Victor's efforts. Ilsa von Frakken set up a laboratory at the family retreat in Bavaria, the same house in which I now found myself held prisoner.

In her remote location, and under the protection of her powerful family, she could conduct the vilest experiments with impunity. Over the years, when villagers went missing, or when strange things were seen and heard, fearful rumours would circulate in the valley. Nothing ever came to the attention of the wider world.

Given such lack of restraint, Ilsa's researches quickly raced far ahead of the field and she made enormous progress in her quest to create artificial life. By the end of the 1850s, she had all but abandoned Victor's original emphasis on the revivification of the dead. Instead, she developed various means of growing synthetic flesh in glass tanks. Through electrical and chemical processes, she discovered that this basic biological material could be deliberately adapted to form muscle tissue, bones, eyes, any organ of the body that may be required. She set out theoretical plans by which an entire body could be grown in sections, then stitched together to create a single inanimate creature, ready to be imbued with consciousness.

However, she never saw this hideous conception to completion. She died, in mysterious circumstances, in 1860. Although von Frakken wouldn't speak of the details, it was clear that her demise was a violent one, just like her father's.

It was left to her own son, Wilhelm, Victor's grandson and the man who had arranged my kidnap, to build upon her repellent legacy. Wilhelm von Frakken proved to be every bit as intellectually gifted—and as arrogantly insane—as his forebears. He refined and perfected Ilsa's process for creating artificial flesh, from which branched his own contribution to the grisly von Frakken project, namely the study of electrical transference in the human brain. He planned to produce not only a man-made body but a man-made mind to go with it! His objective was the extraction of thoughts from living brains using mechanical apparatus, an idea with its roots in those same experiments by Giovanni Aldini which had partly inspired Victor years before. Aldini had, it seems, successfully treated forms of mental illness using electrical currents, and Wilhelm von Frakken sought to pinpoint the physiological events by which the manipulation of consciousness might be achieved.

Naturally, his macabre ambitions eventually overtook even his skills as a scientist and surgeon. He found that, in order to progress, he needed expert help. However, to gain it he would inevitably risk his work being exposed to the scientific community at large. He had not even shared his more radical findings with those few persons already mentioned as following similar lines of research. Von Frakken's own hubris made it intolerable to contemplate the notion that his work might be superseded by others, so he decided to solve his dilemma by a method that, in its high-handedness, could only have been judged feasible following his years of isolation and secrecy—he resorted to kidnapping!

I was not the first scientist he had abducted. Three others had been snatched over the course of the preceding five years, including a Norwegian surgeon and an expert in miniature hydraulics from Russia. All were taken using the same method that had ensnared me, namely the luring of them into unfamiliar territory, from which they 'disappeared.' One strongly suspects, once again, the influential hand of the von Frakkens in concealing such outrages!

He described these others to me in a casual and matter-of-fact way that I found deeply chilling. It was at that precise moment it occurred to me that my own incarceration was, at the very least, intended to last for quite some time. I struggled to conceal the wave of unutterable fear that swept over me, and I cursed my own naivety and fatigue for not coming to this obvious conclusion sooner!

Von Frakken talked on into the night, his expression and gestures filled with glee as he described the accumulated horrors of his ancestral line. At that point, I still considered most of what he was telling me to be sheer poppycock.

The servants had cleared the table more than an hour before. One remained, at a discreet distance, ready to refill the crystal goblet that von Frakken spun rhythmically by its delicate stem. The candles had oozed wax in long rivulets and their yellowing light swam between us.

"You are required, professor," said von Frakken, "to assist me in relation to certain apparatus of my own devising."

"You assume my co-operation," I muttered. I kept my hands firmly on the arms of my chair, to prevent them from visibly shaking. My voice, I had less control over.

He flashed a frown of disappointment at me and thrust out a hand in my direction. "I think you will change your mind when you see the full potential of my work and the remarkable successes I have achieved. No? You remain sceptical?"

"Of course I remain sceptical, I'm a scientist," I said testily. "All this talk of artificial life, it's more black magic mumbo-jumbo than science."

Von Frakken growled and shook his head. "Professor! I expected a more progressive attitude." He sat motionless for a moment or two, then suddenly snapped his fingers as if coming to a decision. "The night is yet young! You must see the conclusion of my greatest experiment. That will convince you. I was going to leave this until tomorrow, when we are both refreshed, but why wait? Come with me, you will be witness to something truly remarkable. Something wonderful."

With a sudden rush of emotion, I rose to my feet swiftly, the movement noisily pushing my chair back across the flagstone floor of the hall. "Herr von Frakken, I refuse to—"

At the periphery of my vision, the guard at the door took a step forward. My defiance instantly melted and I felt weak and foolish. I was shamefully cowed into silence.

Von Frakken's tone was one of indulgent admonishment at a naughty child. "Please, professor, are we not civilised men? Come along now, come to my laboratory. You won't regret it, I can promise you that."

He grinned at me and picked up one of the candelabras from the table. He held it up high and I followed him across the echoing room. He led me, alone, through a series of rooms and passages, our footsteps clattering in the gloom. As we walked, he talked about the history of the mansion and described—as if recalling amusing anecdotes—some of the more antic, failed grotesques which had been created within its walls. I felt I was listening to the weird fictions of a raving lunatic.

At last we descended into the cellars of the building. The steps beneath our feet were undulating and shiny, worn away by the occupation of centuries.

We arrived at a large door, almost as wide as it was tall, heavily reinforced with metal strips and clearly of great age. Von Frakken unlocked it with a key clipped to his waist and it heaved open with a deep, metallic, scraping sound. A damp, chemical stench came from the pitch darkness beyond. A smell of decay, of meat and mould, of old blood and rotting bones.

Inside, gas lamps were bolted to the walls at regular intervals, fed by a tangle of snaking pipes. As von Frakken lit them, one by one, the cellars were gradually revealed to me.

They were a succession of broad, vaulted chambers, their low ceilings criss-crossed by stone arches which rose up from massive supporting pillars. As I looked up at them, I could almost sense our depth below the ground, the gigantic bulk of the mansion above us, the weight of wood and stone bearing down on this dark and furtive place.

The walls and floor seeped with a dank, stinking moisture. The air was heavy with a near-visible miasma, a palpable taste of rot.

Like sharpened teeth, the truth of what von Frakken had been telling me slowly sunk in. Here was, indeed, the foul beating heart of his inheritance, this workshop of filthy creation.

All around the laboratory were machines, bottles, jars, tubes, a vast array of equipment of various kinds. The purposes of some of it I could identify; the rest was a mystery. A portion of it, placed over to one side of the furthermost chamber, had clearly been discarded over the years and left to gather a festering layer of mildew. Much of the working machinery appeared to have been adapted from standard items, while the rest had been constructed from scratch.

To one side of the entrance, arranged along a series of shelves, were papers, files and notebooks. Many were battered and dusty with age, others recently consulted. Contained in this written archive, I assumed, was the full history of von Frakken's vile project, right back to the days of his grandfather Victor.

Von Frakken, having completed a circuit of the cellars, lit the last of the gas lamps. In the eerie glow that now bathed the whole of the laboratory, I turned to see a set of three narrow glass tanks, standing on end, arranged opposite the bookshelves, to the other side of the door through which we had entered. Each tank was taller than a man and filled with a brownish fluid. Each contained a human corpse, floating at the top of the liquid. All were missing limbs and organs. One was without its eyes, another without its left arm and leg.

I pressed my jaw together tightly in an effort not to cry out. These, I reasoned—with a jolt of horror that cut through me like a blade—were the remains of those scientists previously kidnapped by von Frakken. With my hands pressed tightly into fists, I attempted to calm my disintegrating nerves by controlling my breath, but the fetid odour in the air, of preservatives and flesh, made it difficult not to give in to panic. I told myself, over and over again, that I could not afford to lose my senses and must react in as rational and objective a way as possible.

There were many other preserved specimens, in smaller containers, dozens of them arranged haphazardly on wooden racking, on the floor, on the top surfaces of machines. They were a nauseating exhibition of experiments left half-finished or abandoned: bulging, staring eyes; distorted limbs; strange growths with outcrops of hair and teeth; livid organs mapped with veins. I looked away, at the greasy, uneven stone slabs beneath my feet, forcing the notion into my head that I had not—

had not!—seen movement in several of them. Nothing more than fear-ridden imagination!

Von Frakken was effusive. "Over here, professor. I wish to show you the devices which need your expert attention." He was standing beside a row of low, box-like objects. In the front of each was a glass panel, through which I could see what appeared to be white organic tissue, tightly packed in folds and held in a clear liquid suspension. He patted the nearest one as he spoke. "These are for controlling and containing high voltage charges. Due to the nature of this work, great strides have, of necessity, been made in both the construction of electrical batteries and in the science of refrigeration. Little is achieved in my field of enquiry without reliable methods of keeping dead organs fresh or of re-infusing them with power!"

He let out a braying laugh. "I am here indebted to those few fellow researchers with whom I am in correspondence, especially those in London and New York. Between us, we have moved these fields forward by decades, many years ahead of where they might otherwise have been. In refrigeration, we have developed large, air-sealed containers kept cool by the use of compressed gasses. The batteries which power them have, naturally, come a long way from the early days of simple voltaic piles, but our work goes beyond even the modern acidic cells of Bunsen and Poggendorf. We use nickel and manganese in alkaline electrolytes, and are experimenting with lithium."

Here, he once more tapped the glass-panelled box beside him. "This is an invention of my own which combines these advances. Organic tissue, cooled to minimise electrical resistance, which can generate massive electrical current at a steady voltage! You see the connection with your own work on the electric eel and the electric ray? Bioelectrogenesis, tamed in a simple container!"

Despite my fear, I could not help but be impressed by his achievement. I took a step forward, peering through the glass panel. "This creates a difference in potential between the intracellular and extracellular spaces?"

"Exactly," beamed von Frakken. "However! The current only holds steady when several cells are used in parallel, as they are here. Used alone, a cell's power cuts out at random intervals, a fault for which I can find no explanation. The perfection of this device is to be your task."

"What on earth is it designed to power?" I muttered.

"My greatest triumph," breathed von Frakken, "the experiment I have brought you down here to witness." He stepped around a tall rack of jars and beckoned to me. I followed, my heartbeat pounding in my ears, and for the first time saw his most bizarre and disturbing creation.

Surrounded by a sprawl of machinery that was festooned in levers and dials stood a huge, rectangular wooden frame. This frame was set at an angle, rather like a telescope in an observatory. Held inside it was a massive glass cylinder, not unlike those beside the entrance containing corpses. Tubes and wires were connected to various sections of the glass, all linked to the surrounding apparatus. The lower part of the cylinder ended in a flat base, into which was set a hatch and a release mechanism. The cylinder itself was filled with a thick, pale greenish substance.

Ghoulish curiosity drew me closer. With a start, I perceived a figure suspended inside!

Closer still, and I could see that the figure was that of an unclothed woman. Even through the slime which enveloped her and the distorting effect of the curved glass, I could make out the oddity of her features, the ghostly pallor of her skin. Her overall form was that of a normal human being, although somewhat delicate, with long limbs and fingers. However, she bore no signs of either papillae mammariae or of reproductive organs.

The body was motionless, with long hair slicked around her scalp and neck. Without any doubt, she was dead. At that moment—I cannot say why—I felt an intense pity for her. Before I was aware of my own actions, I had reached out and gently touched the cold surface of the glass.

"Good God, man," I whispered. "What have you done?"

Von Frakken's voice was low and steady, but triumphant. "I have made life. From nothing. Not from an array of corpses, not by forcing dead organs back into functioning, but by assembling flesh grown in this very laboratory. The pinnacle of eight decades' research. Every inch of skin, every bone, every muscle, every blood vessel. Built by my own hands."

"But ... she is not alive," I stammered.

Von Frakken grinned, his eyes alight. "Not yet."

I could barely breathe, torn between wonder and horror. "I will not play any part in this unholy nightmare."

"'Unholy'? Don't be such a cringing coward, professor! Surely it's time to throw away such medieval superstitions! This creature surpasses Nature in both body and mind."

The man's arrogance chilled me to the bone. He pulled a hefty lever at the back of one of the organic power cells and it began to emit a loud hum. Through the glass panel in the front, the folded organic tissue inside began to glow.

"In mind too?" I said. "I don't understand."

He moved along the line of cells, activating each in turn. "As you are aware, my own work has built upon that of my forebears. I have successfully stored the electrical activity of the human brain, enabling it to be transferred from one body to another. Not consciousness—so far!—but factual knowledge, isolated experiences, physical sensations. Millions of individual thoughts, all pulled from living minds."

He marched over to the glass cylinder and tapped at the glass directly above the head of his creation. "Placed, in this case, upon a fresh, blank canvas. The artificially cultured brain in this artificially cultured skull contains the sum of a dozen or more human brains, now re-moulded into an entirely new mind.

There are even many of my own brain impulses in there! You have to concede, professor—you have to concede—that what you see before you represents the absolute subjugation of Nature."

"I concede nothing," I breathed.

"This flesh, my creation, a creation by a mortal man, utterly overthrows the tyranny of Nature and the narrow-mindedness of Darwinism," declared von Frakken, his mood now tipping towards anger and irritation. "The skin and bone I have created is of a quality which puts Nature to shame! To produce this quantity of flesh alone, enough to make one body, has been the task of years. It repairs itself, at the cellular level, more quickly than human tissue, thanks to the reactive enzyme in which it is grown. This body and this mind might last a thousand years, its ageing slowed a hundred-fold. And you dare to say you will play no part in this wonderful enterprise?"

"I will not." My voice was a hoarse whisper.

Von Frakken fixed me with a piercing gaze for a moment, then busied himself at a bank of controls, pulling switches and tapping at bulbous voltage meters. "Be under no illusion," he said flatly, "if you will not give me your expertise willingly, it can be taken from you by force. Your knowledge is nothing more than chemicals and electricity. It can be extracted and then duplicated in the mind of the creature you see before you, almost as easily as a teacher might impart information to a pupil. All you have to be is alive."

I glanced at the hideous specimens beside the door, his earlier victims of abduction. I had no doubt whatsoever that he meant every word.

By now, the power cells were sending a steady, pulsing throb through the heavy air of the laboratory. The apparatus which von Frakken was operating was similarly alive with electricity. He lifted his hands from it, like a pianist finishing a symphony, and turned his attention to the massive cylinder of glass.

The greenish liquid inside it began to stir. Sluggishly at first, but soon a definite, circulating current had been set in motion. It flowed in a smooth, circular movement. The liquid began to vibrate, then to shine. Within seconds, a dim glow bathed the cylinder.

"Here is life perfected," cried von Frakken. "Free of disease, free of weakness. The forces of evolution are beaten!"

Surging fear prevented me from speaking. The greenish glow in the cylinder grew brighter, quickly eclipsing the light from the gas lamps on the walls. The swirl of the liquid increased in speed. The dead body inside was buffeted by the movement. The cylinder seemed to radiate an intense, concentrated energy.

Suddenly, I caught my breath. The creature's hand had twitched! No sooner had I convinced myself that this had been caused only by the flow of the liquid around it, than the hand twitched again! It gave a spasm, its long fingers first contracting then stretching.

Involuntarily, I took a step back in sheer fright. This thing had been dead flesh, now its limbs were shuddering with life! Its arms and legs juddered and jerked as the power cells throbbed and von Frakken stood over it with the greenish glow flickering across his rictus features.

The creature's neck suddenly arched. Spasmodic tremors shook it from head to foot, the liquid around it now racing in a suppressed whirlpool. Its arms reached out, twisting and flexing. A hand slapped against the inside of the glass, fingers splayed, then felt along the inner surface like a scuttling spider. Its body thrashed wildly inside the confines of the cylinder.

With a triumphant yell of joy, von Frakken hurried to release the seal at the base of the cylinder. He heaved at the clanking lock mechanism. The hatch burst open, swinging aside on loose hinges. The green liquid gushed across the cold, dark flagstones of the laboratory floor.

The creature slid out along with it, in a torrent of slime, its limbs convulsing. It suddenly gaped and gasped for air, then from its throat came a long, wailing cry, a scream so tortured and inhuman that I almost clapped my hands to my ears. The horrible sound echoed off the stone walls.

Its eyes snapped open. For the first time, I saw their sharp, luminous blue. The creature transfixed me, staring directly, I felt, into my very soul.

These were not the eyes of a monster. They were filled with intelligence and with pain, with pleading and with the bitterest distress. They stared up at me from her pale, shivering form. She howled and gibbered loudly, dripping the green liquid from her hair and fingers.

Without thinking, I instantly grasped von Frakken by the collar of his coat. A boiling anger filled my every nerve. "You maniac! What have you done?"

Furiously, he flung me back and I careened into a table piled with notebooks, which scattered across the floor. He must have been as strong as an ox, for I was physically the more imposing.

His action only goaded me into an even greater rage. I hurled myself at him and we struggled. With an angry grunt, he dashed me against one of the massive pillars that supported the chamber and I slumped to the ground, winded.

He turned his back on me, to attend to the electrical apparatus. Staggering to my feet, I barrelled into him once more. He pitched forward onto the power cells, knocking over a long, interconnected series of machines in a deafening smash.

One of the power cells burst open, sending a chain of blinding sparks into the air. Von Frakken rolled to one side, snatching up a section of broken cable which he raised above his head like a whip, and faced me with a murderous fury. His blow would have struck me across the face, but at that moment several more of the power cells disgorged a fiery mass of electrically charged growth which sputtered and spat across the laboratory.

The wooden frame that encased the cylinder burst into flame. Von Frakken spun on his heels. Before he could react, his coat-tails were alight too. He hurriedly tore off his jacket and used it to beat at the rising flames, but they were spreading rapidly.

I acted purely on instinct. No doubt, had I been in proper command of myself, I would have helped von Frakken to stifle the blaze. Instead, I scooped up his shivering creation. My feet almost slipped on the slime-drenched flagstones. Quickly retreating from the heat—which was expanding with frightening speed—I carried her towards the heavy laboratory door, her fingers grasping wildly at my neck and shoulders.

Behind us, the intensity of the flames caused several of von Frakken's specimen jars to rupture. Shards of glass exploded across the chamber. Von Frakken emitted a thunderous scream, half of agony and half of anger. In the doorway I paused and turned. He was surrounded by fire and one side of his body was already engulfed in flame. I saw him drop, bodily, into the shattered, sparking remains of his ugly experiment.

I carried the shuddering young woman up several flights of steps, chased by black, choking clouds. Summoned by the noise and the billowing smoke, a number of servants passed us, heading back the way we had come. When we reached the mansion's cavernous dining hall—I know not how—I dashed the white cotton cloth from the table and wrapped the poor creature in it, like a shroud, before hoisting her up into my arms once more. Of the armed guards, there was no sign.

From that house and from those terrors, I fled. Outside, night had fallen and rain was beginning to teem from the starless sky. Although the young woman was surprisingly light in weight, I struggled, my breath coming in gasps, along the unlit, muddy track which snaked its way all the way down into the valley.

At several points, I stopped to look over my shoulder. The first time, I could see smoke gushing from two of the lower windows of the house. By the time we reached the nearest habitation, over an hour later, it was gone and the mansion was as dark and quiet as a grave.

Freezing cold and wet through, we took shelter at the inn in the small village of Kliegsbad. Our sudden appearance caused immediate curiosity and it was impossible to avoid being connected with the smoke which had been observed coming from the von Frakken mansion. When I informed the innkeepers that the master of that house was dead—without, of course, informing them as to why—the news was met with a certain amount of quiet satisfaction. Perhaps because of this, my privacy was respected from then on.

Fortunately, I was still in possession of the money I had taken with me, safely stored in a bespoke pocket in the lining of my waistcoat. A worthwhile haberdashery expense! I was able to secure proper clothing for my strange travelling companion, along with food and beds for the night. However, I was fearful that the enduring influence of the von Frakkens might quickly place retribution at our heels, and we left the inn the following morning. We travelled north, as swiftly as possible but avoiding larger towns and cities wherever we could, although a short stop in Munich proved unavoidable.

The young woman remained in a confused and unfocussed state for several days, burbling incoherently here and there and having sudden periods of both agitation and calm. More than once, she suddenly began to speak in German, then Italian and what I took to be Norwegian until, hearing my responses, she settled upon English. She asked me who and where she was, and I—although, even now, I'm not sure why—told her that her name was Maria and that she was to consider herself in my care for the time being. Her blurred senses were such that she took me at my word.

For my own part, my nerves were utterly gone. The terrifying implications of Maria's existence pressed down upon me as if

I was Atlas transferred to modern times. All I wanted was to return home, as swiftly as possible.

We arrived at the coast and made our way to Ostend. There, we booked passage—at an exorbitant sum!—on a cargo vessel bound for London. We docked on the afternoon of 10th October.

CHAPTER IX

Professor Hobson turned the final page of his statement face down on his lap. He sat back in his armchair, his hands shaking slightly. Silently, he accepted more of the contents of Jabez Pell's hip flask, while Dr Meers brought Pell and Inspector Barré up to date on Maria's presence in Hobson's house, on her extraordinary nature and on the dilemmas regarding her which now plagued their friend the professor.

For a minute or more, nobody spoke, the four men peering thoughtfully into the crackling fireplace. At last, Charles Barré cleared his throat.

"You now intend to tell ... Maria the story you've just told us?" he said.

The professor nodded. "That is, if the three of you agree with me that she should be told? She deserves answers, no matter how unpleasant those answers may be."

"Does she?" muttered Pell. "Well, now, I wonder."

"How can you doubt it?" said Dr Meers.

Pell shifted in his armchair, his waistcoat buttons straining and his spectacles glistening in the firelight. "You're speaking as if this ... creature is a human being. It is not. Was it born like us? No. Does it grow and change like us? No. Does it share our physical limitations, abilities, or features? Apparently not. I believe the phrase von Frakken used was 'life improved'? Life debased, more like. Life mocked, life poked fun at. If its physiology is as described to us, then to refer to it as 'she' is an utter nonsense. And, for pity's sake, George, to give it the same name as our grieving sovereign's late grandchild is in the most appalling of poor taste!"

"What might you suggest?" said Dr Meers, throwing up his hands. "A name more appropriate for a pet? Whatever else she may or may not be, she is a thinking, intelligent being."

"So is a monkey," said Pell. "At best, we can consider this thing some sort of freak. And not even a freak of nature! Good heavens, George, it contradicts the very principles by which you work. Is it part of the natural order? No. Does it fit into any biological classification? No."

"Come now, Jabez," said Meers, "where's your scientific curiosity? Her origins may be, admittedly, macabre in the extreme but she's here, now. Surely we can learn from her?"

Pell nodded wholeheartedly. "I agree; we should hand it over to the vivisectionists and see what makes it tick. Excellent idea."

Meers bristled with exasperation. "Are you proposing that she be murdered?"

"Do we murder insects when we swat them? Hardly," blustered Pell. "No more than we murder a cow before it reaches the table."

Professor Hobson said quietly, "I know someone who'd disagree with you, there."

"The concept of murder," said Pell, "applies to human beings. And to human beings alone. I say again, this abomination is not a human being. If someone gave a pig the power of speech, has it suddenly become a man?"

"No," muttered the professor, "but it might object to being eaten for supper."

"Jabez, you're being ridiculous," said Meers. "What separates us from other animals is our reasoning, our self-awareness. Maria has both these qualities."

"As might the talking pig!" said Pell, warming to his theme. "At least such a horror would have a physical form which was normal for its species. At least it would still look like a pig. This monstrosity is, we are led to understand, pieced together from artificially farmed body parts! Just because it resembles a person, does not mean that it *is* a person! Suppose I were to take a child's doll, an inanimate plaything, and give it a clockwork brain. Suppose it could walk and talk and tell a funny story. Is that a person? I say it is not."

"But if it could think for itself?"

"I say no! Not even if it could play cards and debate Euclid! It would not be a natural thing, therefore not a person!"

Dr Meers let out a snort of frustration. He turned to Inspector Barré, appealing to the detective with outstretched palms. "Charles, we can always rely on you to be the voice of reason. You've been silent so far. What do you make of this?"

Barré drew in a long, slow breath. More than ever, he seemed veiled in the cloak of caution which had been his habit for so many years. "As you know," he said, in his clipped and un-policeman-like tones, "my instinct is to weigh evidence carefully before taking any course of action. In this case, decisions concerning this—well, 'person,' let's refer to her as that for the time being—decisions concerning her are needing to be made as a matter of urgency. Whether or not she is human by definition, frankly, is a question best left to the lawyers and the philosophers. Is she a free agent? Or something akin to a zoological specimen? I cannot judge. My immediate concern, call it professional interest, is to ask how the rest of the world will react to her. With alarm, undoubtedly. Probably with revulsion, and possibly with great hostility. As a society, we can barely tolerate even the smallest differences between ourselves, let alone between us and—other life. On the other hand, she surely can't continue to be locked away from sight, no matter what her status may be? Particularly in light of what this von Frakken character said about her longevity. The four of us cannot possibly hope to contain this problem. George, you've noted that she's unusually strong, for her height and weight?"

"That is so," said Hobson.

Inspector Barré refolded his handkerchief and placed it in his top pocket. "Which immediately raises a further question. Is she a danger to the public?"

"Absolutely not," said the professor, shaking his head.

"Not while it's warm and fed, no," said Jabez Pell. "What happens when it's let out of its cage, eh? Or else escapes! If the public won't take kindly to *it*, how will *it* take to the public? No, I agree with Charles, the thing's a significant threat to public safety."

"That's not what I'm saying," said Inspector Barré. "However, we must all admit the possibility that she *might*, for whatever reason, pose a potential threat. She knows herself to be—let's say 'unusual,' but she can hardly expect herself to be the result of such a grotesque story as we've heard this evening. There has never been another creature like her on this Earth. There is a chance she may come to see herself as outside the law, or beyond it."

"If she's subject to law, she is therefore human," said Dr Meers.

Pell snorted. Inspector Barré delicately replaced his monocle. "The overriding issue here is, as I see it, her long-term placement within human society, for good or ill."

At that moment, the door of the sitting room opened. All four of them turned, Professor Hobson expecting to see one of the servants.

Maria shut the door behind her and approached the fireplace. Its shimmering light threw moving shadows across her pale features, making her look—to the professor, at least—more unnervingly alien than she'd ever seemed before. He couldn't read the tightly held mix of emotions that played across her face.

Pell and Barré shifted in their seats, silenced by the sudden uncanny reality of what was standing in front of them. Dr Meers rose to his feet and extended his hand. "Delightful to see you again, Maria." She paid him no attention.

"I thought you were otherwise occupied?" said the professor.

"Millie went up to her room in the attic," said Maria, "and I can move about very quietly."

"How long have you been out there?" said the professor. "Did you hear everything?"

"I heard most of it," said Maria. "Enough to understand my situation."

The professor's hands pressed uncomfortably at his sides and he found he couldn't meet her gaze. "Believe me, I fervently wished the truth to be presented to you in a more—"

She interrupted him. "Nevertheless." She paused for a moment. "I too have no idea whatsoever where I might fit into society. I find myself agreeing with every opinion that's been expressed here, on all sides. I am human, yet inhuman, although I *am* certain I'm not some grunting farmyard swine, Mr Pell. No doubt, it would be better for Mankind if I simply removed myself from its vicinity, and found some remote spot in which to lead what may laughingly be called my life."

"Please, Maria," said the professor, "there's so—"

"What is the Promethean Society?" said Maria sharply. "Von Frakken mentioned them as fellow researchers in London."

"Never heard of them," said Pell. He scratched nervously at his chins.

"Fortunately," declared Dr Meers, "or, perhaps in the circumstances unfortunately, I'm in a position to answer that question. There are a couple of surgeons, who spend a few days each week at the hospital where I work, who are members. They run a highly successful clinic, a very expensive one I might add, which has produced some genuinely intriguing results. What George had told us throws an entirely new light on their activities. I've always assumed the Promethean Society was no more than a secretive club, something like the Masons for medics. Who else might be a member, or if indeed there are any other members at all, I truly don't know. I've never been asked to join and, since the pair of them are thoroughly unlikeable sorts, I've never enquired further." He looked from face to face. "Should we consider them a problem?"

"If they get to know of my existence," said Maria, "then Pell here will get his wish and I'll be sliced up on a slab."

Pell eyed her suspiciously. "Or, they—whoever they are—may be the perfect route by which to introduce von Frakken's work to the scientific community. If his research was a lot more advanced than theirs, surely it's more likely that they'll leave their scalpels at home and exhibit the same boyish fascination as our Dr Meers?"

"You've never met them," muttered Meers.

"I think," said Inspector Barré, getting to his feet, "we've arrived at a way forward. Since von Frakken is dead, this Promethean Society represents the most likely way to reach a fuller understanding of Maria's exact nature. They may have insights which are otherwise unavailable to us. Maria, what are your—your thoughts on the matter?"

"If these people are linked to von Frakken," she said in a low voice, "I'm not sure I want anything to do with them."

Professor Hobson nodded. "I can't believe that any group affiliated with the likes of von Frakken could be anything less than disreputable and untrustworthy."

"I don't like the idea either," said Dr Meers, "but I could make some initial enquiries? Ask some generalised questions?"

Silently, the others agreed. The meeting broke up as the clock above the fireplace chimed ten in high, fragile notes. Meers and Barré each politely took their leave of Maria, while Pell headed for the hallway, scowling. The professor watched all three of them leave the house without another word.

Jabez Pell returned directly to his factory in Whitechapel. As soon as he arrived, he sent his nightwatchman out with an urgent message.

CHAPTER X

An hour later, Professor Hobson was busy at the desk in his study. By flickering candlelight, he incorporated his account of his encounter with von Frakken into his personal journal. He rarely lit a fire in this room and there was a distinct chill in the air. There was a knock at his door and Maria entered.

"Still at work?"

"Yes, er, I seem to have a second wind. Too much in my head, I expect."

They regarded each other for a moment, words poised unsteadily on their lips. It was Maria who broke the silence. "I never thanked you, professor."

He was genuinely puzzled. "Whatever for?"

"You could have left me in that cellar, to meet the same fate as von Frakken. I wouldn't have known what was going on. I probably wouldn't have suffered."

Hobson put his pen down, gently laying it parallel to the lower edge of his writing paper. "No, er, I couldn't have done that." He cleared his throat, looking everywhere except at Maria. "Something my friend Charles Barré said this evening has been, um, preying on my mind. He said there has never been another creature like you on this Earth. It occurs to me that, unless the future holds strange secrets, there never will be again. That is my fault, and I am truly sorry for it."

"Why?" she said softly.

"Because you are utterly alone, in a way I can barely comprehend. And so you will remain, when I, and my friends, and every current inhabitant of the world has gone to their grave. It is not what I would wish for you, of that you can be assured."

"But do I even exist at all? I now know that my brain is nothing but a scattered pile of extracted experience, words and thoughts from other minds, fed into my skull. I recall reading, somewhere, that we are nothing but the sum total of our memories. But did I? Were those words seen by someone else's eyes?"

"Are you conscious of these other minds?"

She shook her head. "No, not at all. Knowledge, language, it all feels like my own, but it isn't and it can't be. My thoughts are ghosts, imprinted copies. I suppose it helps explain my nightmares."

"You dream?" muttered the professor. "I wasn't aware of that."

"The same suffocating fear comes over me every time I sleep," said Maria. "The sequence of events changes a little, but there is always an enormous Eye. Watching and judging me. It's a wraith I don't seem able to shake off."

"I hope what you've learned tonight won't make it worse. I very much regret that you heard us all talking about you in, um, such a cavalier fashion. Especially Pell. Try not to regard him too harshly. His business is a very busy and successful one, his factory exports to half the Empire. He's, er, used to seeing things a certain way."

Maria smiled vaguely. "There's no need for you to reproach yourself. Mr Pell's arguments were perfectly valid. Am I even alive in any real sense? Perhaps I am—undead."

"You're as alive as I am," said the professor.

Maria crossed the room and stood beside the half-open study door. As she looked back at the professor, she suddenly realised that over the last few days a great deal had changed, for both of them. He seemed to have almost overcome his fear of her.

"Goodnight, professor. At least, von Frakken is long gone, and that is a subject upon which we can all agree."

"It is," said Professor Hobson. "Goodnight."

She smiled at him tentatively. They were never to exchange another word.

CHAPTER XI

At the same moment as Maria was saying goodnight to Professor Hobson, Jabez Pell sat in the counting office at the Pell & Blight Ltd factory. Between the creaking, dusty floorboards and the low ceiling, a row of raised desks were arranged in front of the long, low internal window which overlooked the factory's enormous machine shop, dark and stilled for the night. The desks were occupied from 8am to 6pm by the ledger clerks, but now Pell was perched uncomfortably on one of their high stools.

Set out in front of him, on the desk's sloped top, were two weighty ledgers. A pair of half-melted candles, one to each side of the ledgers, threw a soft glow across the pages which were littered with columns of numbers. Most of the entries were written in the looping, neat hand of Pell's senior clerk, Mr Havelock, the rest were in Pell's own small, spidery scratch. One of the ledgers—the official accounts of the business—was kept in Mr Havelock's desk, the other—the more accurate version—was normally held in the safe in Pell's office, to which only Pell and Havelock had a key.

Pell took long breaths, his pen poised uncertainly here and there, writing nothing, occasionally refreshing the nib with ink from the pot. His breathing grew impatient, and the set of his mouth firmer, as he ran his attention up and down the pages, staring at the numbers as if a quick, elusive calculation was all that was needed to correct the widening discrepancy between one ledger and the other. The accurate one, with invoices and promissory notes tucked liberally between its sheets, foretold nothing less than impending ruin: losses, failed products, inevitable exposure, shame, disgrace, the workhouse. Even Havelock's numerical wizardry wouldn't be able to hold off the moment for much longer.

Pell searched the numbers with increasing desperation. The work of many years was draining away before his eyes. Too many poor decisions, too many risks—or possibly, too few. If the ledgers were opened up to scrutiny, other matters would also be dragged into the light, that much was certain. He rubbed at his forehead, feeling stuffy from his inflamed sinuses. Could he unload the factory onto some unsuspecting fool? Sell the lot, fast? There wasn't time. Grab whatever cash he could muster and run? There wasn't enough to keep him for a month.

A scraping noise out in the corridor made him suddenly sit upright. It sounded as if heavy boxes were being deposited at the top of the narrow stairs which led up from the ground floor.

"Who's there?" called Pell. Then he remembered the errand he'd given to the factory's nightwatchman, as soon as he'd returned from his friend Hobson's peculiar meeting. "Is that you, Barnes? Barnes? Answer me, man!"

A figure appeared silhouetted in the counting office doorway. Whoever it was wore a long overcoat and broad brimmed hat, and walked with a cane.

"Who are you?" demanded Pell, quietly shutting both the ledgers in front of him. "These offices are closed, sir, what do you want?"

The figure limped forward. It was the stranger who'd arrived at Charing Cross at twilight that evening, while Pell had been on his way to the professor's house. His face was still concealed behind spectacles and cotton scarf. He stepped painfully over to the low window and looked out into the darkness of the factory floor. His voice was hoarse and fractured. "You will forgive the intrusion. I was waiting in a cab for a while, for you to return, and the cold is rather biting."

"And when my nightwatchman returns, back onto the street you shall be thrown, if you don't state your business. Are you selling for one of the wholesalers? This is private property, you can't be here without an appointment! Most particularly not at this hour!"

"Would you be Pell, or Blight? My records of addresses were recently lost, but the name of this factory I recalled from correspondence with—with a colleague, so I came here. You know a Dr Clements, I believe? Your business has supported his research from time to time?"

Pell's face slowly slackened. "My name is Jabez Pell. Mr Blight is long dead. Yes, I know Clements, in fact something this very night has—who are you?"

The stranger lightly tapped his walking stick on the floor and the uniformed railway porter, Edward Smith, appeared in the doorway looking nervous and flustered. "All my belongings are unloaded?" said the stranger.

"Yes, Sir," said Smith, his eyes darting back and forth between the stranger and Pell. "If I might, Sir, ask when I may be free to return to my duties, Sir? Several hours have elapsed, and I am a little concerned as to the security of my position, Sir. You see—"

"Your reward will more than cover any inconvenience," said the stranger. "You may dismiss the cab and wait below." He turned to Pell. "This young man has proved to be an invaluable assistant."

With a final, uncertain glance around the counting office, Smith vanished into the darkness of the corridor. His footsteps retreated down the narrow wooden staircase.

"You will indulge my preference for privacy," said the stranger, bowing slightly. Slowly, he began to hobble along the line of desks towards Pell. His shimmering shadow was thrown across the ceiling by the candles on Pell's desk. "I have had a long and exhausting journey. I would have sent a proxy of some kind in my place, but the nature of my visit is both urgent and personal. There is property I must recover, at once."

"Property?" said Pell.

"Stolen, by a guest in my home." His voice wheezed and scratched. "If you are on intimate terms with Dr Clements, then you may have heard of me. My name is Wilhelm von Frakken."

Pell recoiled. "Good God!" Von Frakken emitted a rasping chuckle. The wooden stool creaked beneath Pell as he shifted his bulk, his hands gripping the edges of the desk. "Indeed I have heard of you, albeit mere hours ago! How the devil did you escape that conflagration?"

Von Frakken now stood directly in front of Pell. "Escape?" he whispered. He slowly picked the soft suede glove from his right hand, loosening each finger carefully. "I didn't." The glove slid free. Beneath it, his hand was a seeping mess of exposed muscle, held together with surgical thread.

With his undamaged hand, he reached up and delicately removed his hat and spectacles, then unwound the cotton scarf. The chemical fire in the laboratory had burnt away most of his scalp, leaving only thin, sparse wisps of hair. The flesh around the top half of his head, and down his neck, was eaten and weeping. Small sections of it were all but missing entirely, and the rest was fixed to his skull by many thick, metal surgical clips. Splashes of warped skin were scattered across his nose and cheeks. His right ear was gone, replaced with a hardened crust of tissue and gristle, and the right edge of his mouth had been pulled out of shape by the shrinking of scarred flesh.

As he spoke, the skin of his jaw flexed and twitched. "My right side is the worst. The leg is badly damaged, several ribs are smashed and the area around the scapula is in a poor state, but fortunately the spine is intact. Unfortunately, I breathed in a mix of toxic gasses and my lungs, as you can hear, have been rendered inefficient. In truth, I learned a great deal from the makeshift surgery I was forced to carry out upon myself. A few sharp knives, a few tools and thread. It is surprising what can be accomplished."

Pell could barely speak, his hand held involuntarily at his chest in an effort to control his stomach. "For heaven's sake, man, the pain must be unendurable!"

"Increasing infusions of laudanum keep agony at bay," said von Frakken. "However, the dosage is now at the point of killing me faster than my injuries. I suspect I have barely days left to live. Hence the urgency with which I must retrieve my property. Without it, I cannot—"

"This property," spluttered Pell. "Are you referring to that—" His hand fluttered in mid-air. "That ... thing you brewed up in a tank?"

Von Frakken glowered, taken aback. "Clements has been most indiscreet, I see," he muttered under his breath.

"That thing is a monster! A mockery of humanity!"

"You are disrespectful of my accomplishments?" said von Frakken, his dark eyes hardening. "Dear me, I have come all this way only to find another Londoner with violent opinions. And I was led to understand that the English are a courteous race."

"I was led to understand, sir, that the Promethean Society was one dedicated to advances in medical science! Not the bubbling up of homunculi! Oh, be under no illusion, Herr von Frakken, I am more than willing to aid you in recovering your property, since the sooner this city is rid of the peculiar-looking creature, the better!"

At that moment, there were quick, heavy footsteps on the stairs. Von Frakken shuffled to face the corridor, assuming that the porter had returned, but the man who appeared, blocking out most of the doorway, was Pell's nightwatchman Barnes. He was a lumpen, thick-set man, with heavily lined features and a thick mop of grizzled hair. He was about to speak when the sight of von Frakken shocked him into silence.

Pell's voice snapped his attention back to his employer. "Speak up, man! Did you get word to Dr Clements?"

"Yes, Mr Pell," nodded Barnes hurriedly, his face completely failing to disguise his shock at von Frakken's appearance. "He's come back with me. Insisted. He's brought his associate with him, Dr Polidori."

Von Frakken's lips twisted into their nearest approximation of a smile.

CHAPTER XII

One end of the Pell & Blight Ltd factory, which looked out onto a side street close to Whitechapel's Commercial Road East, had been rebuilt—after a fire five years earlier—to resemble the facade of a modern residential building that might have been found in the wealthiest parts of the city. This facade was no more than two bricks deep, since Pell's private apartments—constructed at the same time—occupied only a portion of the upper floor.

Pell's coterie of domestic servants, most of them ex-factory floor employees, were dragooned into preparing a bedchamber for the night for von Frakken, and moving his luggage into it. Smith the porter and Barnes the nightwatchman were ordered to remain on hand. It was close to midnight when Pell ushered von Frakken, Clements and Polidori into his meagrely appointed sitting room. Von Frakken, breathing in short rasps, lowered himself painfully into a high-backed chair, his good hand hanging on tightly to his walking stick.

Dr James Clements was a broad, athletically built man, with a heavy jawline and protruding brow. His mouth was wide, exposing short, flat teeth when he spoke, and his eyes were small and deeply recessed. He walked in a bow-legged, self-confident stride, arms exploring the space around him in a wide swing. His clothes were even more obviously expensive than von Frakken's and he carried a top hat which he handed silently to a manservant for brushing.

At the age of 38, he had made his mark on the medical profession, being credited with improvements in the treatment of Yellow Fever. This was the result of seven years spent in India, where his brother held a senior position in the Viceroy's office. James Clements's bag of tigers remained unrivalled among the imperial staff in Calcutta.

Dr Leonard Polidori was a decade older than his colleague. He was a narrow, sharply-featured man, with a semi-smile that permanently played about his thin lips. His eyes seemed slightly too large and round to suit his build, and his jet black hair was slicked back into a carapace that gave him a beetle-like appearance. Unlike Clements, Polidori came from a long line of doctors; his grandfather had, for a short time before his untimely death while on holiday at Lake Geneva, been personal physician to the notorious Lord Byron.

Clements and Polidori were the only members of the Promethean Society currently resident in London. Four more lived at Oxford and the remaining half dozen were scattered from Brighton to Birmingham. Jabez Pell's secret patronage of their research, undertaken on the promise that Pell & Blight Ltd would one day benefit from the production of exclusive medicines, had helped Clements and Polidori establish a reputation for their clinic at St Saviour's charitable hospital.

Dr Clements dragged his chair closer to von Frakken's. His voice boomed in the small room. "This is a signal day, an honour, to finally meet you in person, at last, von Frakken," he beamed. "Even if under such unfortunate, such distressing personal circumstances."

"Indeed," said Polidori, scuttling at Clements's shoulder, his fingers knitted.

"We were compelled to respond, in person," said Clements, "to Pell's note, it being scant of detail, simply due to the mere mention of your name, and so, imagine our delight in discovering your actual unexpected presence here, unannounced, even though the occasion is one upon which you require our professional assistance. This opportunity to collaborate, to confer, with the foremost practitioner in our field, is a chance we embrace with great anticipation. Our expertise is entirely at your disposal."

"Indeed," said Polidori.

"Too kind," said von Frakken flatly, visibly weary. His most recent dose of laudanum was beginning to lose its grip, but he dared not take another yet. He steadied himself for a moment. "From what I remember of past reports, you have successfully achieved the transference of internal organs in human subjects?"

"Assuredly so," declared Clements, "far beyond simple autografts, building extensively upon the work of your own esteemed ancestors and, of course, naturally, aided by such contributions, and suggestions, with which you yourself have been gracious enough to occasionally favour us. Our work, as you may appreciate, emphasises the purely surgical, rather than the galvanic aspects of your own endeavours. Polidori and I believe our experimental results to be decades beyond what might otherwise—"

Von Frakken tapped his cane against the floor. "You induce anaesthesia using chloroform?"

"We have extensively, not to say exhaustively, tested the usage of other chloromethanes, but have come to the inescapable conclusion that—"

"Intake is regulated?"

"Via the application of a Snow inhaler, to which Dr Polidori has added an additional safety valve which—"

"And in what context has this work been carried out?"

"Details of methods, of applications," barked Dr Clements, smiling, "and of the historical background thereto, have, of course, most assuredly, been firmly restricted to members of the Society alone. Our clinic is limited exclusively to those with discretion, who have the wherewithal to pay for such advanced, such progressive techniques."

Dr Polidori chipped in quietly, his voice like melting butter. "As said techniques are so radical, we present them to patients as simple surgical procedures upon the organs in question, rather than as the replacement of said organs. To spare the patient anxiety or embarrassment, you understand."

"To stop other surgeons stealing your thunder, you mean," said von Frakken in a rasping chuckle. "Yes, I understand." He waved his cane vaguely. "You will bring me the large brown trunk from among my belongings. Open it here."

Dr Clements snapped a look at Polidori, who bustled out. A few minutes later, the trunk was in front of von Frakken, leather straps undone, heavy lid swung back. Inside was a tightly packed assortment of papers, journals and other odds and ends. The damp, fetid odour of von Frakken's laboratory, mixed with the acrid smell of smoke, rose up into the sitting room. Clements and Polidori gazed into the trunk as if its contents were gold from a long-lost tomb of the ancients.

"I find I must open portions of my archive to your examination," breathed von Frakken. "What has survived of it, that is." He pulled out two bound volumes, singed at the edges, each of which had clearly been adapted and added to over the years. The papers they contained were of varying thicknesses and colour, and some had been carefully torn from earlier collections of notes. He handed them both to Clements. "This one contains the correct surgical descriptions, the other contains details of the enzymic fluids in which the body parts are to be stored before transference."

"Body parts?" asked Pell, alarmed.

Von Frakken's eyes fixed him. "Food would be welcome. I have eaten little today. I can manage cooled oats, mixed with honey or sugar, or finely chopped vegetables in a gazpacho. Nothing of a coarse texture."

Pell, his face set in a mask of indignity, left the sitting room to root out servants, as Von Frakken turned to Clements and Polidori. "Upon what range of organs have you operated? *Successfully* operated?"

Clements blinked and licked his thin lips. "Livers, von Frakken, would be the most numerous under our knife, some two dozen successes, to date, albeit exact numbers I could obtain only with reference to the relevant, securely held, paperwork. Also, following, it must be said, a series of disappointments, now a dozen or more hearts have been replaced without undue complications. Lungs, nine or ten, singly, and five or six pairs. Kidneys, six or seven. Replacements of the pancreas and spleen, five or six."

"Failures?"

Clements hesitated. "Many, in initial stages of research, those being some years past, but lately, I am gratified to inform you, a rarity."

"What about a brain?" said von Frakken. "Have you transferred a brain?"

The two surgeons glanced at each other. Polidori blenched and spoke in a slow, shaky whisper. "Indeed. Attempts have been made twice, on patients presenting with inoperable carcinoma. The first transference produced no result. The second produced partial consciousness in the recipient body, but the results were both inconclusive and short-lived. We cannot yet overcome the delicacy of the spinal nerve tissue."

Von Frakken tapped at the book in Clements's hands. "I can. As soon as the property I'm here to recover has been found. A cultured paste made from a sample of that flesh will force the nerve fibres into repair. You will remove my brain from this decaying shell you see before you, complete with optic tracts, chiasma, nerves and eyes. You will sever my spinal cord above the brachial plexus and thoraco-abdominal nerves. Familiarise yourselves with my written notes. If you cannot read German, I will translate."

"But, von Frakken—" protested Clements.

"You have another way to save my life?" said von Frakken. "I would be most intrigued to hear it."

"But what if we fail?"

"If you fail, gentlemen, then certain interests in my home country will track you down like dogs. However, you will not fail, provided you do exactly as you are instructed. For study, you have whatever time it takes to track down and secure what has been stolen from me. The thief is a biologist, Hobson, a professor attached to the British Museum. Is this a name familiar to either of you? No? So many vital records were lost but, in any case, I've no doubt he's in hiding by now, jealous to claim my living creation as his own."

"This creation, von Frakken," cried Clements, his face suddenly alive with excitement, "might I enquire, perchance, would you be referring to the humanoid form which you described as being prepared for assembly, as existing in component parts, at the time of our last correspondence, some time ago?"

Von Frakken nodded weakly. "Hobson took it. It's in this city, somewhere."

"Your design, then, I take it, is to transfer your brain into this constructed receptacle?"

Von Frakken glared at them. "What? No. Its brain is too valuable to discard."

"Then—?"

"The creature is to be farmed, for flesh," said von Frakken. "The artificial skin and bone of which it's made is the masterpiece of my career but, since the destruction of my laboratory, the creature is the only remaining source of it. Without its properties, the transference surgery upon me will fail."

"But, you could grow more?"

"To grow even a few simple ganglia, from scratch, would take more time than I suspect remains to me. To make muscular tissue would take many weeks, and complex organs much longer still. My work would be seriously delayed. This is time I am not prepared to lose. The creature's first job will be to give new life to *me*, her master."

Clements and Polidori were filled with barely-restrained astonishment and admiration. "But, this is most extraordinary, most encouraging. We had no idea, no inkling, that your illustrious experiment was reaching, has indeed reached, such a remarkable conclusion."

Von Frakken suddenly became motionless, then looked up at the two of them. "But—you told Pell about it."

"Indeed not," said Polidori, shaking his head. "No, truly."

"The man is a scientific ignoramus," cried Clements, "there would be no purpose in discussing such matters with him. We had no notion he was even aware of your name, still less your results. His note to me this evening was sketchy."

"So how—?" Slowly, von Frakken's twisted eyelids closed, as the truth dawned on him. "Of course. He knew about the fire. He referred to how my creature looks. He has *seen* her."

There was a moment of bewildered stillness in the little sitting room, then Clements jumped to his feet. He flung open the door and boomed through the building for Pell. Von Frakken reached down into the trunk at his feet and took out a small velvet pouch. He held out an arm and Polidori, taking his cue, helped him to his feet.

"Fetch my servant, the railway porter," wheezed von Frakken. Polidori nodded sharply and passed Clements, who was returning with Pell, just outside the door.

"Mr Pell," said von Frakken, his good hand gripping tightly to the top of his cane. "It's come to my attention that you must be acquainted with Professor George Hobson."

"I am, sir," snapped Pell, "and he is a gentleman, one you have grievously wronged! Kidnap is a crime in this country."

"Fortunately he was in France," said von Frakken icily. "Where is he now?"

"Tucked up in his bed, I've no doubt!" cried Pell. "And that monster of yours tucked up in his spare room, if you please! I told you I'm willing to help you retrieve the damnable creature, and so I am. I sent that note to my friend Clements here because Hobson, and a couple of others, were making plans. Naturally, Clements, I wanted to speak to you first, to forewarn you. However, now that you're in London yourself, von Frakken, none of that will be necessary. We can call at Wenham Gardens first thing in the morning, get this sorted out, then you can be on your way home at once. Get that vile thing out of the city before trouble is caused. Of course, I'm sympathetic to your dreadful condition, you are welcome to remain under my roof tonight and you have full use of whatever medicinal sundries my factory can provide."

Dr Clements began to speak but von Frakken silenced him with a raised hand. "Your clarity and decisiveness do you much credit, Mr Pell," said von Frakken. "In the meantime, your attention to the matter of a late supper would be equally appreciated."

As soon as Pell had gone again, von Frakken turned to Clements. "Can you gather a dozen men? Immediately. Tonight. Ones who do as they're told and don't ask questions?"

Clements's face betrayed an uneasy mix of exhilaration and nervousness. "Our researches, on occasion, have required, here and there, such services. Pell's watchman, Barnes, is connected with certain elements of society."

"Tell him he has an hour. I'll pay them whatever he likes, ten times the going rate, providing it buys silence. They're to bring rope and a large covered carriage. The necessary surgical implements, I have myself."

"But, cannot the—"

"I don't trust Pell," hissed von Frakken. "He's too much the fool. My life hangs on a thread. We act now."

He dismissed Clements as Polidori appeared, bringing Edward Smith. Ever since the porter had seen von Frakken's mutilated face, he'd grown increasingly nervous, finally sensing the depth of the trap into which he had unwittingly stepped. Von Frakken ushered him across the room, close to the window where there was more space on the carpeted floor.

"You asked to see me, Sir?" said Smith.

"It is time for your well-earned reward, Edward Smith," said von Frakken, reaching into the inner pocket of his overcoat. "You have been patience itself this evening. I promised you a sum in goldmarks equivalent to, what amount was it?"

"I believe, Sir, you said f-fifty?" He crushed his porter's cap back and forth in his hands.

"Fifty, exactly. For your service, however, I think no less than sixty is deserved."

Smith smiled despite himself. "Thank you, Sir, much obliged, Sir."

"In fact, I would like to offer you a change of career. A permanent job. You will be with me, always."

"That's most kind of you, Sir, and I wouldn't for a moment want to seem ungrateful, Sir, but portering is something I'm quite content with, Sir. I always say, Sir, if you'll pardon the pun, as it's my station in life, Sir."

Von Frakken cackled softly and pointed through the warped glass at the pitch black street outside. "This may change your mind, Edward Smith."

Puzzled, Smith peered out into the darkness, but could barely see the jagged outlines of the buildings opposite. He didn't see that what von Frakken removed from his inner pocket was the pouch he'd taken from his trunk. From inside the pouch he slipped a small, loaded syringe made of metal and glass, and quickly unscrewed its cap.

By the flickering candlelight reflected in the window, Smith caught sight of von Frakken's face behind him, then a momentary glimpse of something shiny. The needle was jabbed deep into his neck before he could react.

The fluid inside began its work instantly. Smith gasped as every muscle in his body tensed. He spun on his heels, his throat emitting a series of watery gurgles. Gradually, his limbs and neck slackened and he slid first to his knees, then back onto the threadbare carpet. Stark terror swam in his eyes, before they drooped and closed.

"A heavy sedative only," said von Frakken, "but there will be no need for further anaesthesia. When you cut into the parietal and temporal bones of the skull, be sure to also remove large enough sections of each supraorbital foramen to accommodate my eyes in their new sockets. It is all in the notes. Where is the hospital at which you work?"

Dr Polidori was steadying himself at the mantelpiece, drops of perspiration spotting his forehead. "Putney," he said in his softly mellifluous tone. "St Saviour's, near to the Wandsworth toll bridge."

"There is much to do," said von Frakken. "You have personal charge of preparing this patient. Meanwhile I, your other patient, will meet you in Putney as soon as is practical. You and Clements can aim to have the operation completed by sunrise. Now, I believe I hear Pell's servants bringing the supper tray."

CHAPTER XIII

Maria teetered unwillingly at the precipice of sleep. The slim Comtoise clock, out on the landing, gently chimed four. Her consciousness descended into shabby passageways, which twisted around in a constricting spiral as they moved deeper and deeper into the earth. She moved faster, walls becoming ever more narrow, floors ever more steep. Above, as always, the Eye. It became the sky itself, stark and unblinking, watching her, examining this hideous monster in every tiny detail. Weighing, evaluating …

Suddenly, a sound, a distant crack and tinkle of glass. Maria's eyes snapped open. Glass?

In the ghostly stillness of the house, she assumed at first that it had been part of the nightmare. It was only the dissonance between the sound and the contents of her dream that made her think again. The fact that she'd clicked back into wakefulness suggested to her that the distant splintering noise had been real.

She sat perfectly still for a moment, listening intently. She heard nothing unusual. There was a soft rustle of branches from the tall trees out on the far side of the road.

Feeling uncertain, she left her book where it had fallen from her fingers onto the counterpane and slid across the bed, breaking the silence of the room. She slipped her shoes back on and retied them, then noiselessly turned the doorknob and stepped onto the landing.

Darkness rendered everything around her as grey, featureless shapes. The clock ticked softly to itself. She placed her fingers on the polished handrail beyond which was the open stairwell. She glanced in the direction of the short corridor that led away to the back of the house and the professor's room. She listened at the chipped wooden steps which rose from the landing beside her, leading up to the attic and Millie's bedroom.

She took a couple of steps forward, taking care to avoid the creaky board that ran across the landing near the top of the stairwell. Slowly taking hold of the bannister with both hands, she leaned out slightly over the stairs, peering down into the grey that sunk to pitch black before it reached the hallway.

A thin, cool breeze drifted delicately past her cheek, as if air had been displaced somewhere below in the darkness, as if an outside door had been opened, down in the kitchen or scullery, and for a moment the chill of the night had flowed silently up into the house. Her fingers tightened on the bannister. She felt a cold sensation that had nothing to do with the temperature.

Maria could feel her chemically-grown heart beating. Crouching slightly, she steadied her breath and concentrated on listening.

There was something, down there. Something in the basement? It was a vague, indistinguishable shuffle that could easily have been nothing more than her own anxiety creating phantoms.

Carefully, she descended a single stair, then another. She listened again, but the sound had stopped and there was absolute stillness. She went down another three steps, silently placing her heel each time, gripping the handrail beside her.

A metallic clank. Pots and pans in the kitchen. A harsh "Shh!"

Maria froze, one foot suspended above the next stair. She pressed her teeth together to stop her jaw shaking and looked directly over the bannister, her eyes straining.

Footsteps on stone. Coming up from the kitchen, into the long hallway. Muffled sounds of movement. Breathing.

Maria glanced up and down the stairwell, uncertain what to do. There were no weapons in the house that she knew of, and there was no object within reach that might serve as one. She didn't know whether to retreat or to confront these intruders, the harsh "Shh!" indicating that there were at least two of them. She knew she wouldn't be able to rouse the rest of the household without the sound inviting an immediate attack. For want of a more considered plan, she decided that it was up to her to defend Millie and the professor. Pressing her lips together, she took one more step down and swung her head and shoulders out over the bannister rail, which in daylight would have given her a commanding view of the hall.

Directly below her, shadows slid within shadows, ghostly shifts in deep grey. There was a metallic creak as the shutter of a dark lantern was opened an inch.

A narrow beam of light spilled along the hall, suddenly illuminating a huge mass of movement—seven bulky, thick-set figures. All were armed, one with a crudely-fashioned club, one with a pick-axe, others with knives taken from the scullery, the lamp light glinting on their neatly-kept surfaces.

Maria couldn't help letting out a slight gasp of shock. Instantly, the intruders reacted.

"There! Tha's her!"

She turned to leap back up the stairs, but a hand was clamped onto her ankle within a heartbeat. She was jerked downwards violently, losing her grip on the bannister, her head bumping painfully against the steps.

Three of the intruders thundered past her, heading for the upper floor. The one at her ankle raised an iron bar in his free hand, aiming a blow to knock her senseless. With a yell, Maria landed a sharp blow on the man's jaw with her fist. He spun, collapsing back into the hallway and falling with a splintering crash onto the hall table. The others, who'd been behind him, surged forward. The light from the now fully-opened lantern swung wildly.

"The posh mobsman was right! All together!"

At that moment, a piercing scream came from the landing above. Maria saw a momentary flash of a white nightgown.

"Millie!" she yelled. "Run! Run!"

Intruders flowed up the stairs at Maria like an oncoming tidal wave. She twisted, kicking out at them to give herself time to regain her balance. Gripping the bannister with one hand, she pulled herself upright and bounded up the stairs. Loud cries and growls snapped at her shoulders. Panic and terror blew every thought from her mind.

She managed to reach the landing before they caught her. As she got to the top of the stairs, two of the intruders ploughed into her from behind, knocking her headlong. A third, the one wielding a pick-axe, leapt to pin her down.

Maria flipped onto her back as the pick-axe man's full weight dropped onto her. The flat head of the pick-axe smacked into her cheek and neck. The man gripped the upright handle with both hands, bearing down.

"Help me, lads! I can barely hold her!"

His yellowed teeth were inches from her nose. A sickening smell rolled from his greasy work-clothes. Maria grabbed hold of his side-whiskers and pulled hard. He cried out, the pain distracting him enough for her to heave him aside.

She was almost on her feet when the three of them hurled themselves at her once more. As they gripped at her arms and torso, she flung her weight as far forward as she could. They were each forced to take a step back. The axe-man's boot overlapped the top of the stairs and he slipped.

Maria pushed at them suddenly and they fell backwards, letting her go. Limbs flailing, grabbing at each other, they tumbled heavily down the stairs, yelping and yelling. Bannister rails were knocked out as they flew heels over head and hit the hall floor with a crunching thud.

Maria judged she had only moments before they'd recover. She spun around on the landing, hearing crashing sounds. The door to her room was open. Someone was inside, rooting through drawers and cupboards. Faint glimmers of moonlight filtered through the doorway from the street.

The soft glow shone on Millie's nightgown. The girl was lying near the foot of the attic stairs, tossed aside, her legs fallen at irregular angles, her mouth lolling open. The top half of her nightgown was soaked in blood and half her head was a pulp.

The breath caught in Maria's throat. Her eyes swimming, she retreated in horror. She turned and staggered along the corridor towards the professor's room.

His door was open too. A candle burned at his bedside and the sheets had been thrust back. He must have woken, lit the candle, got out of bed.

He was lying face-down on the rug, one arm outstretched towards the door. A thick trail of blood led back across the room to the bed. A large kitchen knife, one Mrs Sewell kept for special occasions, was buried deep between his shoulder blades.

Gasping, Maria knelt beside him. Her hand shaking, she reached out and gently touched the side of his neck, but felt no pulse. Turning his head a little, her eyes dripping, she bent and placed her cheek next to his.

She hadn't noticed that the professor's killer was still in the room. Jabez Pell's nightwatchman, Barnes, emerged slowly and silently from the shadow behind the bedroom door. He advanced towards her, carefully, a wooden club swinging gently from his meaty hand.

The floorboard next to the rug creaked as Barnes stepped on it. With a yell, Maria sprung up at him. Grabbing the lapels of his coat, she flung him back against the professor's night stand. She grabbed his wrist and squeezed until he dropped the club with a grunt of pain.

She was filled with a fury she'd never known could exist, a searing anger for revenge that set her brain alight. This vermin had to pay for his crime! This human vermin!

She hurled him out of the professor's room. He collided with the opposite side of the corridor and his legs gave way. Maria was upon him in a second. She gripped him by the throat and hauled him upright, pressing his head back against the wall.

He struggled and pulled at her arm, his face distorted into a defiant sneer. Her eyes blazed hatred at him. His struggles became wilder, fingers digging at the pale hand clamped around his neck, the muscles around his mouth twitching.

Maria's grip tightened. She felt flesh and sinews buckle beneath her fingers. She felt bones bend and snap. Barnes convulsed, a line of blood appearing on his lips, then his whole body went slack. She let go and his corpse slumped to the floor.

She stood motionless for a moment, a sudden, shrieking sensation of disgust instantly swamping the last traces of her anger. The man was dead, and she had killed him. Now, she was a murderer too.

Now, she really was a monster.

She barely noticed when the remaining intruders surrounded her. They carried her, in tightly closed arms, back down the stairs and into the hallway, dumping her on the patterned tiles close to the front door, looking down at her with a mixture of curiosity and contempt. She put up no resistance. Her mind was awash with grief, regret, self-loathing.

"Ugly-looking bunter, in' she."

"Call that swell up here, got to go before someone comes sticking their beak in."

A low, urgent whistle sounded along the passageway. Footsteps, alternately light and heavy, came up from the kitchen. Wilhelm von Frakken emerged, carrying a small oil lamp which threw a harsh glow across the intruders and their captive.

Maria, from where she lay, couldn't see him until he was standing over her. He was masked with his hat and scarf, and his breath came in pain-wracked rasps. As she looked up at him, a peculiar sense of dread wreathed her heart like a mist.

He pulled his scarf away. Deep shadows danced across his scarred face. "Well, well," he said. "Well now. Aren't you going to give Daddy a hug?"

BOOK THE SECOND

CHAPTER XIV

A tall butcher's wagon was parked in Wenham Gardens. The driver, with the horses' reins hooked over his knee, rubbed his hands together against the night-time chill and glanced nervously up and down the street. There were still several hours to go until dawn, and nobody was in sight.

He started as the front door of the nearest house swung open, and he turned to watch. Four of the intruders emerged first, faces pulled taut and arms locked as they grappled the writhing form of Maria between them. A thick rag had been tied around her mouth to keep her silent.

Behind them came two more, dragging the bulky dead body of Barnes. At the rear limped Wilhelm von Frakken, his whole frame trembling from pain and the cold air, his walking stick clicking against the pavement and his breath rasping hoarsely.

The driver hurried around and opened the back of the wagon. Maria and the dead body were bundled awkwardly inside.

"Three of you, hold her down," whispered von Frakken. "You other three are dismissed, I need space to work in there." He waved his cane at the driver. "You, get us to St Saviour's as quickly as possible, keep to flat roads as much as you can, no jolting. Slow down if you have to."

The driver gave a sharp nod. Von Frakken was helped up into the wagon and the back was closed up again. Three of the gang crossed the road and melted away into the night.

The interior of the meat wagon stunk coldly of offal. Dark stains overlapped across its floor and splash marks on the sides were brown with age. An oil lamp hung from a meat hook overhead.

Maria was pinned down, one of the gang laying with his full weight across her chest, the other two on her legs. The wagon moved off and the lamp above her started to swing. She smelled the blood that was soaked into the boards behind her head and the machine oil in the rag pulled tight across her mouth.

Von Frakken shuffled into view. He took off his hat and scarf and leaned over her, prodding with the fingers of his good hand at her chin and neck, lifting her eyelids, sweeping back her hair. His face was in shadow, his head haloed in the light from the lamp. Maria could glimpse enough of his damaged scalp and features to understand exactly what had happened to him.

Her mind was numb, from grief and shock at the attack on the house and from a flood of bitter self-loathing at what she had done to Barnes. She stared up at her creator, not knowing whether what she felt was fury or pity.

"You are my proudest moment," muttered von Frakken, running a finger along the line of her jaw. "A true triumph over Nature." He pulled the rag away from her lips. "You will have the privilege of being the wellspring from which all my future work will grow."

"You won't last long. What future can you have?" said Maria grimly.

He gave a wheezing cackle. "More than you might think, thanks to you."

"You should have died. I should never have lived."

He leaned closer, examining her. "Most interesting. Moral and emotional concepts are intact, as well as factual information. You wish your creator dead?"

"We belong dead, both of us."

"I, for daring to conquer the natural world, presumably? But you? All that you are, you are because of me. No matter, you're only what I made you." He tapped at the man pinning down her upper body. "Hold out her arm. Keep her still."

The man shifted his weight and pushed Maria's right hand out to the side, leaning against her forearm. Von Frakken reached into a Gladstone bag at his feet and took out a lidded glass jar, filled with a discoloured liquid. He placed it level with Maria's elbow and removed the lid. The liquid shook in time with the movement of the wagon.

He went back to the bag and fetched a short, curved surgical knife. He held it up to the lamp light. "I would have waited to do this until we arrived at the hospital, but every moment's delay is to be avoided."

Maria tensed and the men holding her down renewed their grip. "What are you going to do?" she said.

"Since you don't seem to value the life I have given you," said von Frakken, "then you will be equally unconcerned with the uses to which I shall put you."

"What do you mean?"

"The material of which you are made is extremely valuable, a vital resource for all my future accomplishments. Nothing will be wasted, I assure you. Every bone, every connective tissue, every membrane will be seeded. I think I'll keep your head intact for a while, I'll take the opportunity to study your mind before your skull is reused. Your brain will remain whole, preserved as a memento of my labours, like Harrison's clocks. I may put it to work. I have thoughts on designing a calculating engine, to improve upon the analytical machines of Mr Babbage."

"You'd cut me up, still living?" breathed Maria.

"You are property," said von Frakken. "Property that speaks, but nonetheless belonging entirely to me."

He leaned across her, and in one movement slit her sleeve from shoulder to cuff with the surgical knife. She strained to move beneath the weight of the three men holding her.

"If you struggle," said von Frakken flatly, "it will merely take longer." He replaced the tightened rag against her mouth.

Placing the sharp point of the knife against the skin of her upper arm, he paused for a few moments while the wagon bumped over a short section of cobbles. Then he made a swift, straight vertical incision into her flesh, about a third of an inch deep.

Maria gritted her teeth and screwed her eyes tight as the pain lanced through her. The oily gag reduced her screams to a low, gasping growl. Von Frakken cut down, then to the left, up and right, completing a roughly rectangular shape, six inches long and two in width. Blood spilled in jagged streams at its edges, thick and dark against the pallor of Maria's skin.

She bit into the rag as he lifted one end of the rectangle, inserted the knife and began to slice. Seconds later, he peeled away a thick strip of skin and subcutaneous tissue. Hooking it with the end of the knife, he lifted it free, slid it carefully into the glass jar and replaced the lid.

"There. You will heal quickly, in little more than ten days or so."

Maria glared at him, her eyes welling with fresh anger. From wherever, or whoever, it originated in her mind, she was discovering an instinct for self-preservation which suddenly overcame her feelings of helplessness and despair.

While von Frakken busied himself with replacing the jar in his Gladstone bag, she tried to move her uncut arm, which was pinned down across her stomach. The man holding her was distracted by the gruesome sight of her wound, visibly itching to get away from it. Maria's blood dripped onto the boards, like that of a thousand creatures before her. The man, his nose wrinkling, pulled back slightly.

Instantly, Maria pulled her arm free from beneath him and punched at the side of his head with all the strength she could muster. He yelped, his whole body flinching, a hand held over his ear. Maria grabbed at his collar and hauled him over. The two other men, at her legs, instinctively moved to spread their weight. One was knocked back with a kick, the other received a bloody nose. Von Frakken, too frail to intervene, sat with his bag held to his chest.

Maria looked back at him for a second, her expression grim. Then, clutching her still-bleeding arm, she flung herself against the back of the wagon. It flew open and without hesitating she jumped down into the road and ran.

The wagon's driver, hearing the noise, pulled the horses to a stop. By now the three men inside had recovered enough to chase after their prisoner, but von Frakken called them back.

"Leave her! It's more important that we get to the hospital. I have what I need, for now. She will have to remain unfinished business, for the time being."

CHAPTER XV

Maria ran until her lungs burnt. She paid little attention to whatever direction it was she was heading, but instinct sent her back along the route the butcher's wagon had taken.

Twice she stumbled in the darkness, once flying headlong into the dirt of the road and grazing her hands. She staggered to her feet and ran on, the pain in her arm throbbing madly. She ran blindly, her breath fogging in the cold, as if speed and movement would help her escape the thousand conflicting thoughts that buzzed in her head.

At last she slowed down, gasping rapidly and her limbs shaky with effort. She was on a road without street lamps, where the intense gloom of the early hours seemed bottomless and enveloping. Low, broiling clouds swamped all moonlight. Steadying her breath, she listened for signs of pursuit, but the silence was as thick and overpowering as the darkness.

Arm outstretched, she felt her way along a high, ragged brick wall to one side of the road, until she could take shelter beneath an overspilling canopy of leaves. She stood still, her throat raw from exertion and the cold air, feeling a helpless, lonely panic claw up through her.

She was utterly lost, directionless, and it would be light in a few hours. She had no idea what to do, or where to turn. There appeared to be not a living soul around. She was a creature of the night, her mind told her, the fanged monster lurking in the dark. She shut her eyes tightly for a moment, alone in her crowded head, fighting back the terror of what she was, what she contained, what she had done.

The searing pain in her arm bit at her attention. She couldn't see the wound clearly, but she could feel blood running in slow rivulets down her arm and hand. How much had she lost? With gritted teeth, and trying not to touch the areas around the exposed muscle, she tore away the remains of her sleeve and tied them around her arm in a makeshift bandage. She winced and hissed as stabs of pain lanced through her.

She shivered. Whether she was being pursued at that moment or not, they would be looking for her. If von Frakken had cheated death once, perhaps it was her duty—her, the monster—to see he didn't do so again. She thought of the thick, bloody strip of her flesh that was in that jar, and shuddered.

She carried on along the road, walking this time. The direction in which she'd run had brought her back into the area close to Wenham Gardens and as she reached a corner, where the brick wall ended and the street split into three, she suddenly recognised one of the forks. She had seen it from the carriage, when she and the professor had been to his room at the museum.

Mrs Sewell, the professor's housekeeper, lived near here. It would be to the left, then left again. She was sure of it, she recalled Millie describing the area.

Millie.

Pursing her lips tightly, Maria turned the corner and hurried on. Mrs Sewell would help her.

She trotted down a narrow road, the sound of her footsteps muted a little by the muddy pavement. Still there was no sign of life, until she passed a low wooden fence. A huge dog, pulling violently at its chain, suddenly leaped at her, emitting angry barks. She flinched and stepped out into the road. The dog's dark muzzle bobbed up over the top of the fence, which rattled and shook as the animal launched itself against the vertical slats. Maria quickened her pace and the dog subsided into a continuous snarl.

A few minutes later, she made her way along a haphazard row of dwellings that stood opposite a long patch of open scrubland. They were built in different styles, some from brick and some from timber, modest homes that opened onto the street and which had been added to and adapted over many years. Mrs Sewell lived in the seventh one along, a plain, whitewashed cottage that hardly looked tall enough to accommodate its two storeys.

Maria tapped at the door, shivering. Then again, slightly louder. She was about to knock for a third time when a curtain twitched in an upper window. Moments later, a latch clacked noisily and Mrs Sewell's mouse-like eyes peeped out.

"Good lord, you're out without the professor?" she piped. "What an hour to come calling."

She fussed and fretted, ushering Maria to sit down in the tiny parlour onto which the front door opened, while she set about lighting a fresh fire in the hearth, a thick woollen shawl pulled around her shoulders and her gnarled old feet wedged into thin slippers. By the time the fire was beginning to take the chill off the room, Maria had told her why she was there, leaving out the more gruesome details of the professor's and Millie's deaths, and any mention of von Frakken.

Mrs Sewell jabbed at the meagre fire with a poker. The greying logs sent bright embers dancing and popping as she tapped at the grate. Clasping her shawl, she plucked her handkerchief from the sleeve of her nightdress and plopped herself down onto the narrow monk's bench that stood against a wall beside a small table. She dabbed the handkerchief around her wrinkled face, pressing it to her wet eyes.

"The professor was such a kind and gentle soul," she said, her voice a squeak. "What he did, he did in all innocence, of that I'm sure. Oh, Millie, so young, so young. It's terrible. Attacked in his own home. What in the name of heaven is becoming of the world? Forgive him, Lord."

She blew her nose and noticed Maria's makeshift bandage. "You've been injured!" She fetched some clean rags for Maria to tie on her arm, then filled a kettle and swung it on a hook over the fire. "Do the police know what's happened?"

"Not yet," said Maria. "At least, I don't think so."

Mrs Sewell gave a sharp sniff. She scurried back and forth from the fireplace, fetching tea cups. She pulled her mouth into a rose of wrinkles and her eyes glittered in the light of the fire. "Not yet, no," she muttered to herself. "But they will, soon. What's to be done? No time to waste, no time at all."

"Will you help me?" said Maria. "Will you help me reach the professor's friend, Dr Meers? He'll understand, I think. There are things I must attend to."

Mrs Sewell nodded, then without another word made Maria a cup of tea and bustled upstairs. She returned fully dressed, tying the ribbon of a bonnet beneath her chin. She bent down slightly, to bring her face level with Maria's. "You sit here, by the fire, drink your tea and don't you worry. You poor, benighted little robin, I shall get help. I shall do what's right. Help is at hand."

A gush of cold air crossed the room as she left, the latch clicking shut behind her. Maria sat staring into the fire, her tea sitting untouched in her lap. A howling chaos wailed through her mind like the winged sirens of myth, luring her onto deadly rocks. Police would come, would see that the house had been broken into and ransacked. She'd tell Barré that von Frakken was still alive. A fresh wave of guilt surged over her when she remembered that the body of the man she'd killed had been removed. They'd never know what she'd done, unless she confessed.

Wind whistled softly through the ill-fitting window frame beside her. The fire in the hearth crackled and spat. Maria's face slowly crumpled and she wept bitterly.

CHAPTER XVI

St Saviour's charitable hospital was an austere, mid-Georgian building, not far from the southern bank of the Thames. Two high, symmetrical wings were joined by a smaller section where an angular portico jutted out above the entrance, lit with oil lamps. All but a couple of the tall windows were dark. To the right of the building was a scattering of rented canvas tents around the remains of the previous evening's fire, occupied by relatives of patients close to death.

The butcher's wagon rumbled past the gates. Dr Clements, bundled up against the cold, emerged from the shadows in which he'd been waiting and waved the wagon over to the left. He marched over to it as von Frakken was being helped down onto the stony forecourt.

"All is well, I trust, I hope?" he said.

Von Frakken handed him his bag. "Here is a section of the material. You understand how to prepare the substrate and the necessary catalysis?"

Clements nodded, leaning and craning to look into the back of the wagon. All he could see was a heaped section of old sacking, from which emerged a pair of heavily booted legs. "Your achievement, your creature, has it been retrieved, as planned?"

Von Frakken tapped the bag with his walking stick. "That's all we have for now, but it's more than enough for tonight's purposes and for setting up a number of new experiments."

One of the remaining members of the gang approached Clements, wiping his hands on the sides of his coat. "We want extra. Our mate Barnes is dead, we got to get rid of the body."

"Dead?" said Clements, shocked.

"Couldn't leave him, could we?" growled the man. "Police'd come sniffing round us."

Clements dug in his pockets for coins. "There has been violence? My impression, distinctly, was that the presence of a mob was for the guarantee of co-operation only! Hobson was armed?" He dropped a few shillings into the man's hand. His question wasn't answered.

As the wagon pulled away, Clements motioned for von Frakken to follow him. "It is arranged for you to avoid our Receiving room entirely, thus without official record, making use of the entrance towards which our private patients are directed."

Clements's marching gait kept him several steps ahead of von Frakken. Behind a polished blue door was a small, empty interior porch, which led into a voluminous corridor lit with hanging gas burners. The floor of the corridor was a chequered pattern of black and white tiles, the walls of stark, undecorated stone. Ornamental arches, reaching close to the high ceiling, punctuated the space every thirty feet or so. The air was cool and heavy, thick with the smell of carbolic and vomit. A distant series of screams, one voice crying out in the night, echoed somewhere up ahead through rooms, wards, passageways.

Clements's footsteps reverberated like a clash of metals. He halted and opened a side door, set deep into the wall, on which a brass plaque read DR J CLEMENTS ✦ DR L POLIDORI ✦ PRIVATE. He ushered von Frakken inside, as another shout and the sound of someone running ricocheted deep inside the building. The door closed behind them and a key turned in the lock.

"Our consulting rooms," said Clements, "are rented from the organising committee, in recognition of our charitable donations, totalling a sizeable sum, which we make, personally, at our own expense, to hospital funds each year." They passed through a comfortably furnished outer area into a large, oak-panelled office.

"You have a private operating room?" wheezed von Frakken.

"Through here," boomed Clements, holding out a hand. "The hospital is a progressive one and houses an operating room for regular patients, with viewing gallery, but ours is, naturally, reserved for our exclusive use. Polidori and I will be assisted by a thoroughly reliable, and discreet, member of the hospital staff, a nurse, Mrs Leath."

They went through a small antechamber and into the operating room. It was tall and rectangular, with high windows, as stark as the corridor outside. Gas burners hung low over a central wooden operating table, which had been overlaid with a white linen sheet. Racks of equipment were arranged around the edges of the room.

A second table had been moved in and placed parallel to the first. On it lay the railway porter, Edward Smith, still deeply unconscious. He had been stripped to the waist and his head had been shaved. His jaw and neck were held firmly in place, face up, by surgical clamps fixed to the wooden surface beneath him. Dr Polidori, his sleeves rolled up, was carefully dipping his hands into a bowl of cloudy liquid.

"We employ a solution of phenol for asepsis," said Clements, "and a steam process of the latest design is used for all instruments."

Nurse Leath rustled forward to help von Frakken out of his overcoat. She wore the standard dark dress, white pinafore and folded cap used by all the nurses at St Saviour's. She was a tall, middle-aged woman, her features set in a permanently hooded, blank expression. Across most of her face and neck, her skin was grotesquely puckered and pockmarked, the scars of childhood smallpox. She didn't react at all to the sight of von Frakken, as she took away his hat and scarf. She'd seen worse, over the years.

Clements took the glass jar, containing the section of Maria's flesh, and set about his work. Von Frakken watched, his good hand flexing around the top of his walking cane.

"Less than one ounce is required," he said in a low voice, while Clements tipped measured volumes of chemicals into a dish. "The rest should be stored in cooled conditions."

"I have, as requested, quickly familiarised myself with your notes, which are, I should say, most clear and concise," declared Clements. "I look forward, with eager anticipation, to reading all the remaining volumes of your papers, since those pertaining to tonight's procedures, in full, have been most illuminating, most educative."

Von Frakken eyed him, saying nothing. Then he started slightly, realising that Polidori was standing at his shoulder, hovering silently for attention.

"I'll begin," said Polidori, indicating the railway porter. Von Frakken nodded.

Polidori gave a ghost of a nod and crossed to where Nurse Leath held a wooden tray, lined with a crisply laundered cloth, holding an assortment of knives, bone saws and other cutting implements. He picked up a thin-bladed knife and, angling himself so that the light from the overhead burners fell across the porter's face, he began to remove the skin from the upper left side of Smith's head.

Peeling away the tissue to reveal the matted surface of the skull, he delicately replaced the knife and picked up a small saw, its serrated edge curved slightly upward to allow more accurate cutting into short sections of bone. By the time he had removed a large, wedge-shaped section spanning much of the parietal, frontal and temporal plates, Clements had finished preparing the enzyme wash that would be needed for von Frakken's eyes and brain.

"We will, of course," said Clements, "be opening the minimum apertures, those necessary to fully accommodate the replacement organs. However, owing to internal restructuring, some changes to the outward appearance, upon recovery, may be inevitable."

"If you think I care about that," muttered von Frakken, "you sadly underestimate me." He turned to the nurse. "You will help me onto the operating table. My new body should be ready to receive me in a matter of minutes."

Edward Smith was still alive, technically, when Dr Polidori pulled his eyeballs back through gaps made in their sockets. He died when his spinal cord was cut and the firm, bloody mass of his brain was inched out and dropped into a bucket at Polidori's feet.

CHAPTER XVII

Maria was jolted to attention by the sound of the latch. Mrs Sewell had returned. She batted at her nose with her handkerchief, her little eyes blinking rapidly.

"All arranged, come along now, off we go," she said, with mock formality, like a heavy-hearted mother encouraging a tearful child. "Cabbie's waiting outside."

"Are we going to Dr Meers?" said Maria.

"Off we go."

Maria, too wearied and too caught up in her own conflicting thoughts to feel suspicious, followed Mrs Sewell out to a waiting hansom. The horse was steaming in the damp, pre-dawn chill, its hooves pawing heavily at the ground.

The cab moved off without a word from Mrs Sewell, making a slow about-face before picking up speed. Inside, Mrs Sewell quickly tugged down the blinds at both windows. No light showed around their edges, and the first glimmers of daylight were still some way off.

Maria looked across at the housekeeper and, for a moment, thought she'd gone to sleep because her eyes were shut. Then she noticed that the old lady's hands were pressed tightly together and realised, with a flutter in her stomach, that Mrs Sewell was praying.

"Mrs Sewell?" she said quietly.

Her beady eyes popped open. "We'll be there soon."

"Where are we going?"

"For help. To find peace of mind and an end to troubles."

Peace of mind? Maria pulled one of the blinds aside, in time to see the glow of an oil lamp getting nearer. It had been hung up outside a—she looked up and made out the narrow point of a spire against the dark sky—outside a church.

The cab stopped beside a low, shabby wall, in which a broken gate was propped open. Mrs Sewell scurried out, holding the door open for Maria. They walked along a short, muddy path, between rows of dank, weather-worn graves, the leaning tombstones like an honour guard of the dead, greeting one of their own.

Peace of mind? Was such a thing possible? Maria's drowning thoughts clutched at a single straw. They were swamped by the terror of the night's events, leaving her with little in her head except an infant need for acceptance and comfort.

They approached the church. Mrs Sewell reached up and unhooked the lamp. Maria was encouraged to step inside, where dwelt redemption and understanding, where shone forgiveness and salvation. Step inside.

She emerged into a cavernous nave where candles flickered in sconces. Their light danced life into the carvings that swarmed around the walls and pillars, beatific hosts of angels, saints and cherubs which flew on solid wings and watched over her with sightless eyes. The stained glass in the immense, peaked windows was black, waiting for dawn to come. The air was cold and musty, the smell of stone and paper. Up ahead, above a covered altar, was a tall cross from which a sculptured man dangled and bled.

There were rows of pews to either side, ahead of the transept. Almost all were filled with people, over a hundred in all, showing signs of having been shaken early from their beds and dressed in a hurry. As one, they turned to look at Maria as she drew level with the nearest row. A low murmur rippled across them, gasps of surprise and curiosity. Many shrank back from her slowly, their faces draining as if retreating from a poisonous serpent in a zoo. Some muttered under their breath, or clasped their hands together and raised their faces to the angels. The sounds of their unease rose with each step Maria took.

Mrs Sewell scurried around the pews to take her place in the congregation. "Do you all see?" she squeaked, her voice magnified by the church's solidity. "Like us, but not like us."

A slim man dressed in black was standing at the head of the nave, his hands held open in a mirror of the supplicant gestures on the carved saints above him. His face was craggy, his mouth set in a smooth downward crescent, and his white hair was neatly smoothed back above his bushy, unkempt eyebrows.

He held up a hand, a gesture of benediction. The congregation subsided into silence, but their faces remained a cacophony of unrest. Maria stood still, her face set in questioning innocence, watching the man cautiously.

His voice was melodious and calm, polished to a shine by years of public speaking. He spoke directly to her. "I am the chaplain here, my name is Lemley. You are in the house of God, Maria, and thus embraced by His word and by the holy spirit."

"You know me?" said Maria softly.

At the sound of her voice, the congregation flushed anew. Mr Lemley waited for silence again. "Yes, we've known of you for some days, and your story has broken all our hearts. We thank our sister Mary Sewell for bringing us news of your arrival and your progress, and for bringing us all to our church this morning, so unexpectedly. All of God's creatures are welcome here."

"Here?" said Maria. She found her eyes were suddenly filling, and her lips trembled.

"Everything in His creation is cherished, all trespasses forgiven, all hates returned with love. This is revealed to us through the strength of our faith. We accept Him into our lives, and the truth sets us free."

Her shaky lips spread into a smile. "Then—perhaps I could accept that—I might have been wrong—about—?" Her voice tailed off.

"Do you claim to know right from wrong, Maria?"

Her eyes spilled and her lips twisted, her words fracturing as they emerged. "I want to find peace. I didn't mean to do it. He was dead so quickly. I didn't mean to do it."

The congregation gasped, louder than before. Mr Lemley's hands met delicately.

"All within His creation are blessed," he said, calmly and with measured sincerity, "but that which He did not create is damned. He did not create you, Maria."

She took a step back, her long fingers hovering in front of her. The cloth tied around her arm was patched with red and she felt a wave of dizziness.

"We had hoped your story was not true," said Mr Lemley. "We hoped that our sister Mary was mistaken, that our modern world of industry and commerce was no place for such crude sacrilege, such piteous misfortune, but we see with our own eyes that her fears were justified. She has prayed for an opportunity to bring this heathen blasphemy before us, and tonight the Lord answered her prayers. Her employer sinned, the wages of sin is death, now we ask Our Father to have mercy upon the soul of our departed brother."

The congregation murmured. Mr Lemley held Maria's unearthly gaze, the tone of his voice low, almost soothing. "You are not born of woman, or of any other natural thing. You are fashioned in the image of Mankind, but you are not His. Whether you are mechanical or corporeal is of little consequence. You are unholy, unreal, made in defiance of Him, without the divine spark and are—therefore, must be—a scion of evil, a lifeless puppet animated by demonic spirits. However, in this place, in the house of the Lord, you cannot call upon devilish powers. They will not operate here, and you cannot weave your magicks upon us. We do not fear you."

"Oh yes you do," said Maria, barely above a whisper. As Lemley spoke, she lost all traces of the grief and shock that had been keeping her mind suspended. In its place was a cold, grim resignation.

"We pray for you. We pity you."

"I don't need your sympathy."

A voice piped up in the congregation. "You listen to Mr Lemley, Hell-spawn!"

"God has seen fit to deliver you into *our* hands," said Lemley, "and there are no more rocks under which you can hide, as you have hidden thus far, no more dark corners in which to conceal yourself. From this moment, the full light of scrutiny is shone in your direction, exposing you to the world for what you are. We look upon this vile work and we are sorrowful. The demons possessing this body must be cast out utterly, by prayer and by trial."

"Thou shalt not suffer sorcery!" called a second voice. "Thou shalt not suffer a witch to live!"

Mr Lemley's attention remained fixed on Maria. "Are you prepared to renounce the devil and all his ways? Are you ready to cast out evil? It is our sad duty to punish that which is blasphemous and wicked."

Maria turned, to find that the end of the nave was blocked by half a dozen of the congregation. She was surrounded. "Punish?" she hissed, conscious that her voice sounded nowhere near as defiant as she wished. "Destroy me? Then you'd congratulate yourselves. You'd be every bit as bad as I am, you've no right to sit in judgement!"

"We do His bidding," said Mr Lemley. "We walk the path to salvation with the Lord at our side, and the casting down to Hell of your profanity will strike a blow for His earthly peace."

She let out a despairing half-laugh, half-sob. Peace of mind? Theirs. Not hers. How could she have thought otherwise?

"You will not submit?"

"I will not," she said through gritted teeth. The crowd rumbled their disgust.

Lemley smiled ruefully. "Sadly, we would expect no other answer from one possessed by darkness." He addressed the congregation. "The exorcism will begin immediately. The creature can be secured in the vestry for the duration, and I will begin with a period of prayer before the administration of rites. In the event that the demonic spirits inhabiting the creature do not depart when banished, only then will a fire be prepared. May we have some volunteers to hold her? There's no need to be afraid, we are on consecrated ground, her powers and influence cannot prevail."

By now, half the crowd were on their feet. Maria circled slowly, scowling at them, her eerie and unnerving otherness chilling their spines, plucking at their nerves. Husbands clutched protectively at wives and a woman close to the aisle, unable to retreat by the pressing of people behind her, raised a shaking hand to her mouth. A small boy began to cry in his mother's arms, sensing the rising atmosphere of hostility.

The half dozen at the back, blocking Maria's way, began to close in on her. Mr Lemley, his arms outstretched and his eyes raised to the carved angels high above, began to recite the Lord's prayer. All around, the stained glass windows began to glow with the vague first light of the day.

Maria tensed. For hours now, she'd been attacked, used, deceived, condemned. With a sudden lunge forward, she let out a howling scream, a bellow of pain and rage that she directed at everyone around her like a weapon. Terrified, the crowd shrank, voices bursting.

The half dozen advancing on her paused in shock. She sprang at them, shoving them aside, and ran for the door. The crowd spilled out of the pews, flooding the nave with bodies, shouts, raised fists, pursuing her like a tidal wave.

Lemley's voice cut above the noise. "In God's name, I command you wait!"

Maria shot through the arched entrance to the church only a few seconds ahead of the crowd. They flowed out down the path and over the graveyard, walking across the graves, catching their breath against the tombstones. Sluggish morning light crept beneath the low, yellow-grey clouds. The crowd spread out and searched for several hours, but could find no trace of their quarry.

CHAPTER XVIII

Inspector Charles Barré pursed his lips as he read through the report, printed in small type on the crowded front page of the *London Daily Examiner* dated Monday 20th October:

HORRIFIC EVENTS IN KENSINGTON

Murder of prominent scientist – Alarming and sinister creature discovered –
Local populace in fear for their lives

Few events in living memory have disturbed residents of the city like those recounted as having taken place in the early hours of Saturday, in the borough of Kensington. The effects of shock and terror visited upon witnesses recalls incidents such as those relating to the so-called 'Spring-heeled Jack' or the more recent supernatural hauntings reported in Berkeley Square, these being of a similar horrific and disturbing nature. Two occurrences, separated by less than a mile and by only a matter of hours, point to there being a highly dangerous person, or possibly animal, now at large in London.

The first occurrence was the brutal murder of Professor George Hobson, eminent scientist, a fellow of the Royal Society, associate of the British Museum and resident of Wenham Gardens. Police were called to this address in the early hours, having been summoned by concerned neighbours hearing a disturbance, and discovered the house in a state of disarray. Also discovered, in separate parts of the abode, were the dead bodies of Hobson and his housemaid, the former having been killed with a kitchen knife, the latter with an unidentified blunt instrument.

Initial conjecture indicated that a burglar had been disturbed during the process of robbing the house and had then committed these horrible murders to facilitate his escape, a supposition supported by the finding of a means of forced ingress in the lower portion of the building. However, other clues at the scene contradict this assumption, principally the fact that much damage was caused in the interior, suggesting a violent struggle between the deceased scientist and the culprit, a supposition which in itself is refuted by clear indications that Hobson met his end upon immediately arising from his bed.

An intimate acquaintance of Hobson, the noted industrialist Mr Jabez Pell (when asked by your correspondent for comment) put forward the notion that Hobson, being a student of Nature and the biological sciences, was keeping a dangerous specimen of the Great Apes, which escaped and accomplished the crimes as evidenced. In our opinion, such a fanciful explanation leaves as many questions unanswered as do all the others.

Of equal mystery is the second of the night's horrors, perpetrated by the same individual. As dawn broke, the congregation at a nearby church was terrorised by the sudden arrival of a bizarre creature in their midst, variously described by worshippers as being 'mis-shapen and brutish' and 'of spectral appearance,' possessing 'wild eyes' and 'emitting horrible screams like a banshee.' The consensus opinion, shared by the church's incumbent pastor, is that the monster was of supernatural origin, revealed through actions and questioning to be an example of demonic possession.

It is not known why this frightening apparition should have threatened the churchgoers in this fashion unless, in its flight from Wenham Gardens, it was simply in search of fresh victims. That the strange and deadly creature was responsible for the Hobson murders was made evident by its own confession to the killing, revealed while it spoke with the pastor in front of the worshippers. They courageously attempted to capture it, but the fiend escaped, fortunately before any of those present could meet with physical injury.

The identity of the church in question is withheld on the advice of the police investigating the incidents, led by Inspector Barré of Scotland Yard, whom readers may recall from the successful conclusions to the recent cases in Clerkenwell and the City. He is of the opinion that sensation seekers may be drawn to the site in numbers, should the location of such a bone-chilling and remarkable happening enter the public domain.

It remains evident that a murderous person, of some kind, is now at large either in the immediate area or in some other region of the city. Barré has insisted that a likeness of the villain will not be circulated, since the descriptions of the mysterious assailant given by witnesses at the church do not sufficiently tally to be of use in the ongoing investigation.

Barré pocketed his monocle and dropped the newspaper onto his desk with the others. Their headlines ran along similar lines: *Hunt for Freakish Killer; 'Demon' of Kensington Sought; More Fatal Attacks Feared.*

"Absolute bloody nonsense!" spat Dr Thomas Meers. He sat opposite Barré, on a creaking chair that was as well-worn and functional as the rest of the furniture in Barré's Whitehall Place office. The room was small but neatly ordered, with pinned maps and papers lining the walls, and files arranged on shelves and cupboards. The window looked west, towards St James's Park, and from outside the door came the constant scuff of feet moving up and down the nearby stairway.

"For heaven's sake, man," said Meers, "why not issue a proper description of Maria? Correct this press rubbish? At least that might help us to find her."

"For the simple reason," said Barré calmly, "that she's a distinctive type and would be spotted in five minutes."

"But surely that's the point?" Meers stood and started to pace the room.

"She'd almost certainly run, and keep running, until she was out of the reach of all of us." Barré brushed fluff off his sleeve. "Besides, I don't want chancers tackling her. My first concern, as you well know, is for public safety, something that's still an unknown quantity as far as that ... young woman is concerned."

Meers let out a sharp breath. "You surely don't believe that she killed George?"

"I'm not entirely sure what I believe just at the present," said Barré, arching an eyebrow. "The simple fact is, George and that poor girl are dead."

"The house was broken into, man! Even I can see that from the evidence."

"Break-ins can be faked, and they're a popular choice for covering up all kinds of things. It's a pretty peculiar coincidence, an unusually violent thief happening to turn up at that house just a few days after Maria, don't you think? I've got results on far more tenuous links. I've had constables go through the place and, as far as they can tell, very little was taken, just a few easily fenced trinkets. Not the actions of a burglar who'd be prepared to kill."

"Perhaps he panicked? Realised the noise would draw attention? For pity's sake, you've *met* Maria, you know she's not some sort of crazed monomaniac!"

"I assure you, Tom, the friendliest and most agreeable chap I ever met in my life poisoned seven members of his family and dropped them in a cesspit. I'd be wary enough if Maria was your average, tuppenny-ha'penny Londoner, but she isn't. She's not one of us, however you argue it, she's an artificial creature, grown in a tank and sewn together, and as sharp as a new pin, too. The very idea would give *anyone* the shudders, it's no wonder she frightened the life out of poor old George. And she's got a temper on her, we know that from the church witnesses."

"If anything they say can be trusted. Demonic spirits, I ask you, in this day and age!"

"She admitted to killing him, in front of them all."

"They've got it wrong," said Meers, running a hand through his grey-flecked hair, "they must have misunderstood."

"All of them?"

"All of them."

"I'm glad you're not a detective," said Barré dryly. "Her confession, in any case, clearly explains why she went to that church in the first place. She was seeking solace, she had a guilty conscience."

"So, you'll admit she has a conscience?"

"Regret makes her no less guilty. No, this'll be handled my way, I've got men working their way through the city, quietly, so as not to spook her. They know what they're looking for, minus the fact that she's not human, of course. We'll find her, make no mistake."

"I still don't believe she killed George," muttered Meers.

"Then why run away at all?"

Meers paused in mid-pace and flicked at the newspapers on Barré's desk. "What I also don't understand is what the devil Jabez is doing making ridiculous suggestions to the press? I think he's been reading too much Poe!"

"To put them off the scent of the truth, I presume, I've not had a chance to speak to him."

"But he's utterly opposed to Maria," said Meers, "you'd think he'd want the truth to come out. I suppose we'll see him at the funerals tomorrow."

Barré sat up and leaned forward. "In the meantime, I want an eye kept on these colleagues of yours, the ones you told us were members of this Promethean Society. I'd do it myself, but you're in an ideal position not to arouse their suspicion, and I can trust you to keep your mouth shut." He took a sheet of paper from a drawer, ready to make notes.

"I don't quite understand," frowned Meers. "Now that Maria's gone, why should I need to approach them?"

"Because," said Barré, "she might approach them. She knows of their existence, from what you said the other night. Apart from you, me and Jabez, nobody in London—nobody, anywhere—

knows who and what she really is. If she's on the run, she's hardly likely to contact the three of us. Should she find herself in need of help, and I'm guessing she most probably will at some point, then members of the Promethean Society are possibly the only persons around with whom she could be honest. They're aware of what that madman von Frakken was up to, at least in principle, so they might offer her a safe refuge if she was to reveal her presence."

"That seems logical, yes. What exactly do you want me to do? To be perfectly honest, I don't see a great deal of them."

"In the unlikely event that you happen to get the chance, ask them outright if a young woman has contacted them. Use whatever covering story you think sounds appropriate. She's an old patient of yours, confused in the head perhaps, or for whom you have a specific treatment? I'll leave that up to you."

"Unlikely indeed," muttered Meers.

"Failing that, keep whatever tabs on them you can. Anything out of the ordinary routine, anything you might not otherwise expect, that sort of thing."

"I'll do what I can, gladly," said Meers, "but opportunities may be limited. The only reason I'm aware of their membership at all is that it was mentioned in a meeting of the hospital medical staff, some time ago. I didn't even know their field of research, until George told us."

"Are there many members?"

Meers twisted his face, dragging information from his memory. "As far as I recall, I had the impression that they're the only ones in London. There are certainly others in the country and, as we now know, in other parts of the world. They are the only two to whom I can put a name."

"And what are those names?" said Barré, picking up a pencil.

"Clements and Polidori, that's p-o-l-i-d-o-r-i."

"A foreigner?"

"I don't believe so, no. My relations with them are perfectly cordial, and professional, but I can't say I like or admire either of them. James Clements is an arrogant snob, to be honest with you. He's all bluster and show and a bit of a social climber, but there's not much behind it, if you see what I mean. Polidori's his lapdog, he's a weaselly little tick."

"Good at their job?" said Barré.

Meers wrinkled his nose. "Depends who you ask. They run a private clinic from the hospital, which wouldn't normally be allowed since our charter states that our only income is charitable and philanthropic support, but the committee turns a blind eye. Clements and Polidori get their rooms for free because of the sizeable contributions they bring in. None of it from their own pockets, I hasten to add, all of it squeezed from their steady stream of wealthy patients. Their clinic charges frankly exorbitant sums, but it has to be admitted that its results are impressive. I know of at least one case of advanced liver disease which they cured completely, and several instances of heart and kidney failure. How they do it, they keep to themselves. Too early to publish experimental results, they claim, continuously. If you had asked me last week, my guess would have been the application of a poultice, either herbal or chemical, or else proprietary emetics of some kind to flush out the system. Of course, now I know what the Promethean Society actually researches, I shudder to imagine what kind of treatments they're carrying out."

"Do you think anything they're doing is illegal? I'm not too up on medical legalities."

"Unethical, probably. That would be an obvious reason for their secrecy. Although, so would simple monetary greed, keeping effective treatments exclusive for as long as possible."

"You say their competence depends on who is asked?"

Meers let out a sharp breath. "Well, from what I observe myself, you'd think they were a couple of third-rate butchers. A fair proportion of the patients we receive at St Saviour's present with physical injuries of one kind or another. Everyday industrial accidents, for example, that sort of thing. Clements and Polidori have a rate of success in these cases that borders on the embarrassing. Plenty die of infection, that's only to be expected, but you'd think their wards were never cleaned."

"Could that be down to the emphasis they place on their clinic? Divided attentions, and so forth?"

"Possibly," shrugged Meers. "More likely, a disinterest in those patients from whom they earn no profit. Not, it must be said, an uncommon attitude among my colleagues." He snorted to himself. "Although every time I express my distaste for it, Sophia gently upbraids me by mentioning the repairs needed to the roof of our house. She wants them done before the baby arrives."

"Do Clements and Polidori have any colleagues they're likely to take into their confidence? Any others we might need to keep an eye on?"

"They tend to run in their own furrow. Other personnel, that is to say the nurses and orderlies, work generally and aren't assigned to particular medics. If Clements and Polidori have one or two favoured members of the staff, I'm not aware of it."

"Well," said Barré, rising to his feet, his fingertips placed symmetrically on his desk, "I'm much obliged for your advice, Thomas. Do what you can."

Meers nodded. "On one point we both agree. Wherever Maria is, we need to find her before her notoriety takes on a more concrete and hostile form." With a sigh, he plucked the *London Daily Examiner* from the desk and re-read the headline.

CHAPTER XIX

HORRIFIC EVENTS IN KENSINGTON

*Murder of prominent scientist – Alarming and sinister creature discovered –
Local populace in fear for their lives*

Maria glanced at the stack of newspapers on the vendor's stand, paused for a moment, then walked on.

Why should it concern her? What did it matter, the lies and the accusations? She was done with humanity, its twisted morals and its hypocrisy. Done with it. She would trust no-one, not Meers, not Barré. She was nothing, to any of them, but a grotesque exhibit of one kind or another. They all belonged under the same slimy stone as von Frakken.

He was her driving force now, she told herself. Her only aim was to track him down and put an end to his activities.

And after that? What would become of her? What was to be her place in the world? Where was she to go? Questions for another day.

After she'd fled the church and had time to think, she slowly picked her way across the city, following the only clue she had at her disposal. When the intruders had attacked the professor's house, when she'd been pinned down at the top of the stairs by the man with the pick-axe, the stench that came from his clothes had echoed in her senses. Dredged up from the depths of her mind—from someone's mind—was the recognition of that smell. It was the pungent reek of a tannery, the noisome mix of quicklime and excreta that accompanied the production of leather. The city's few tanneries were located in the east, around Whitechapel and Spitalfields, so that was where the pick-axe man himself most probably lived. Since von Frakken, new to London, would likely have hired ruffians close at hand, then that same area was the most probable site of whatever lair or hideout he had established. It was a tenuous trail to follow, but the only one available.

Maria was sure that von Frakken was still in the city. He wanted her back, to fuel his hideous programme of experiments.

She briefly considered making some sort of public display, to announce her presence so that von Frakken's lackeys would snatch her and bring her to him. However, she quickly dismissed the idea. She needed the element of surprise, since she had no doubt that von Frakken would simply kill her if he suspected her of betrayal. Furthermore, any such display would only attract wider human attention, and of that she'd had more than enough. In any case, the police would almost certainly get to her before von Frakken. They were after her too. Or so the newspaper headlines trumpeted.

She moved away from the news vendor's stall, keeping her head down. Her clothes had been swapped with ones taken from washing lines, similar in style to her own but much more worn and ragged. Her hair was tied and her skin smeared with dust and grime to conceal its eerie lack of colour. She'd tried to find gloves, but none would fit her long fingers and so she'd dirtied her hands too. A pair of round, amber-tinted spectacles, stolen from a market stall, hid her eyes.

She blended into the people, an invisible, down-at-heel nobody. The anonymity it gave her was a welcome relief but the feeling which came with it, of being lost in the swarming millions, of becoming a single speck in the flow of humanity for the first time, gave her an unsettling sensation of vertigo. She fought against it.

She'd spent two days circling the tanneries, watching, and two nights wandering the city, crossing back and forth across the Thames, keeping to the darkest places, consumed in thought. She walked away the hours, keeping up a swiftly steady pace to stay warm, her route almost at random.

Here and there, from alleyways and shadows, she would peer into lit rooms. She watched people sitting quietly at their fireplaces, or cheerfully talking, or fighting and throwing crockery. One room, brightly furnished, was empty. For a while, she imagined herself its occupier, its owner, until she turned and hurried on. For the minutes she needed to sleep, she crept into the deep recess of a doorway, and the usual tortuous nightmares sunk their fingers into her mind—confusion, confinement, the Eye that watched and judged forever.

It was some time past eight in the morning when she crossed New London Bridge, heading north again, to continue her search for the pick-axe man. From a capacious pocket she pulled the small loaf she'd snatched ten minutes before from the basket outside a bakery. She tore a chunk out of it and filled her mouth. The taste was gritty and sweet, the flour loaded with alum to bulk it out, but hunger was gnawing at her belly and she ate it anyway.

A biting wind cut across the bridge, snapping at her ankles. Below, small boats slid under the tall arches, and the foul waters of the river stirred, the grey-brown colour of strong tea. Above, the thick miasma of cold smog seeped into the slowly swirling, yellowish clouds.

Carts and carriages trundled along beside her as she weaved her way around pedestrians. An omnibus, its horses straining, overtook her as she neared the north bank. She could see a line of faces and shoulders inside, behind the curtained windows. Along the side of the bus were elaborately painted signs listing stopping points and times and above the signs, on the roof, were two rows of men wearing near-identical hats and coats. They clung precariously to the knifeboard seats, fixing their attention on folded-back sections of news-sheet. How many were reading about her, wondered Maria. What would they say if they knew she was right beside them?

She wished she could board the bus and get out of the cold, but it was crowded and she had no money. The icy wind felt less sharp once she was off the bridge, and she hurried on through a busy street market, where vehicles made slow progress against the milling throng of people.

Along the outer edges of the pavements, in front of the rows of shops, stalls and barrows crowded to sell anything and everything. Vegetables, fish, household goods, musty secondhand garments, raw meat and fresh pies piled on fly-blown trays. Vendors vied with each other to shout loudest, or waved their produce at arm's length, or clanged pots and pans together to attract notice. Raucous shoppers amused themselves by sauntering up and down, sniffing out bargains, the firmest cabbage, the pinkest strips of cured bacon. Women hauled babies on their hips and men sold racing tips in sealed envelopes. Whelk stands filled the air with the zing of vinegar, competing with the acrid odour of the fried fish and potatoes that hissed in boiling grease. Steam from the stewing of eels fogged the windows of the shops and shreds of decaying vegetables were trodden into the mud of the road. A handful of children and gaunt-looking adults pulled canvas bags filled with odds and ends, rags and scavenged fruit, selling their whole bundles at a penny a time.

It all made Maria acutely aware that she hadn't a farthing to her name and wouldn't survive long on stolen bread. She kept walking, mulling over the situation. Most of the people around her were heading in the same direction, on their way to factories and warehouses. Almost without thinking, she turned off Bishopsgate and was soon at the corner of Flower and Dean Street.

Political agitators of assorted persuasions had gathered, handing out leaflets and manifestos to whoever would take one. They clamoured to be the voice of radical social change, declaring their affiliations over the top of each other in exactly the same way as the market traders had shouted their wares.

Police arrived suddenly, in a four-wheeler, scattering the few who had stopped to listen. The constables swiftly beat the agitators—*dangerous extremists!*—to the ground with sticks and dragged them away—*supporters of terror and insurrection!*—their faces running with blood.

Maria turned on her heels and ducked down a side street, her heart racing. She couldn't stay on the streets. Before she could continue her search, she needed shelter, food and money. She shuddered with cold, held her collar tightly closed against the invading chill, and hurried on.

CHAPTER XX

The factory floor at Pell & Blight Ltd was an inferno of heat and noise, one of the largest in Whitechapel at almost 5000 square feet. Along the length of one wall were gigantic, iron-framed Crittall windows, divided into a cross-hatch of small panes, reaching from shoulder height to the ceiling thirty feet above. All of them were opened up as far as they would go, to let in the outside air. Those who worked closest to the windows felt the least stifled.

Two small steam-driven engines, one at either end of the huge floor, pumped power to the mass of machines through pipes and pistons. Each engine had a huge, reinforced boiler from which sprouted clusters of gauges and regulators. The boilers were fuelled by glistening men who shovelled a continuous meal of coal through roaring apertures, like the feeding of some squat, insatiable fire-beast.

The manufacturing machines were a tightly packed forest of wheels, rods, benches and cutters, tall excrescences of hard, dark shapes which dipped and spun to their own individual rhythms. Workers stood or perched on stools, organic components slotted in among the iron and brass, pushing and pulling, turning and aligning, raising and dropping, hour upon hour upon hour.

Their lives were digested by the machines, which then pushed out a slow, steady progress of products.

Some machines produced headache pills and powders, mostly made of sugar, that were put into pocket sized tins and bottles. Some produced snuffs, made from camphor and salt, for the treatment of catarrh, or solid preparations of lobelia for asthmatics to burn and then inhale. Some boiled medicines for gout or influenza in wooden vats, or stitched trusses and cut bars of soap, or printed the metal and paper, all bearing the Pell & Blight Ltd name, into which everything was packaged.

Jabez Pell crossed the steaming factory floor as quickly as he could. The moist, sulphurous heat made his bulging waistcoat itch and the pounding, relentless hiss and clang left his ears ringing. He found the foreman he was looking for, shouted closely into the man's ear and retreated through a series of passages to the tightly compact stairwell which led down to the storage areas and up to the company offices.

Heading up to the accounting room, he paused halfway to catch his breath. The deafening noise of the factory, muted to a mere thump through the brick walls, throbbed in the air like the pulse of a giant. With trembling fingers, he reached for his hip flask and took a long swig, licking the brandy from his fleshy lips afterwards and fiddling awkwardly with the flask's stopper. He ran a hand around his bulky chin, wiping away sweat.

He glanced around, to make sure he wasn't observed, then plucked out his pocket watch. Eleven. George Hobson's funeral would be almost over by now. For half a minute or more, he stared at the seconds ticking away, unstoppable, taking him further into a future he could feel inexorably slipping away through his fingers, away from his control.

Sniffing, and tucking the pocket watch away with his thumb, he tramped up to the landing from which branched the company's administrative offices. He strode into the counting room, where the line of clerks instantly redoubled their attention on the scratching of numbers and the rubber-stamping of documents. The noise of the machines was louder in here, throbbing through the internal windows that overlooked the factory floor.

Pell approached the largest desk, the one occupied by Mr Havelock, his chief clerk and the only other person alive who knew the true financial state of Pell & Blight Ltd. Pell handed him a dozen slightly crumpled sheets of thin, onion skin paper, most of them invoices bearing a watermark or a notarised seal. Havelock took them without comment, peering at them momentarily over his half-moon spectacles. He stooped his lined, grey face to peruse their contents, slowly turning them over, one after another, before reforming them into a neat pile and gently pressing them flat against the surface of his blotter. Impassively, he looked up at Pell, his expression unchanging and neutral, the blankness of his rheumy eyes conveying everything he needed to say.

Pell's tongue peeked from between his lips for a moment, then he walked purposefully past the desks of the other clerks, scrutinising their rapidly moving pens, and left the office. Out on the landing, he was about to ascend to his private apartments when the factory foreman called up from below.

"Mr Pell, sir!"

"What is it?"

"Two gentlemen to see you, sir!"

Dr Clements and Dr Polidori appeared at his side. Pell paused for a second. His estimation of them had changed a great deal over the last two days, now that he'd been told what had happened and what they'd done, now that he'd accepted—with slack-jawed incredulity—that von Frakken was literally a new man. He let out a breath, then told them to come up and the foreman returned to his work.

"We've come to attend our patient," boomed Clements, marching ahead of Polidori. "I take it his presence is being kept confidential?"

Pell led them up to his rooms. "My workers know better than to gossip," he muttered.

The sitting room in which they had gathered, late on the previous Friday night, was now littered with personal and business papers which Pell had been rooting through the previous day and which he didn't want visitors to see. He quickly closed the door on them and led Clements and Polidori along the unlit passage that linked his apartment to the rest of the factory. Having knocked, he showed them into a large bedroom occupied by the recuperating von Frakken.

The room overlooked the same side road as the sitting room, with views across neighbouring roofs beneath the sullen, yellow-smutted clouds, and was warmed by a freshly banked fire. The décor and furnishings were functional, since Pell had neither the eye nor the inclination for ornament, with a wash stand in one corner and a narrow brass-framed bed in the other.

Von Frakken sat on the bed, wrapped in a red collared dressing gown, propped up against a hill of cushions. His new body, that of the railway porter, was more compact than the old one and his movements were still a little jerky and uncoordinated while he got used to different limbs. His shaved head now showed livid, bruised stitching in a straight line over the top and to one side, marking the area that had been opened up to fit in his original brain and connected eyes. One of those eyes moved normally, the other was fixed, looking ahead.

He was surrounded by books, spread across the bed and piled beside it. Next to them, occupying a dominant proportion of space on the floor, were a stack of fresh-looking wooden crates. Pell jabbed a finger at them.

"Are these what account for the expenditure that has just been brought to my attention? Expenditure totalling the astonishing sum of forty-seven pounds, nineteen and sixpence?"

Von Frakken's voice was hesitant and oddly formed, spoken with a new mouth, but its intonation had already regained its sibilance. "I could bring with me only a very limited range of equipment. I must rebuild my laboratory."

"At my expense, sir? I say no!"

"You will be repaid from whatever funds I currently possess," said von Frakken, his new eyelids drooping slightly. "Further amounts can be sent for, but that will take time. Until then, I'm sure Clements will oblige."

Dr Clements twitched sourly as he stepped forward. "With pleasure, that is, should Herr von Frakken's considerable purse prove, in the event, insufficient."

"By whose authority did you even arrange these purchases?" muttered Pell angrily.

"Yours. I instructed the girl who brings me food," said von Frakken. "My handwriting is a little eccentric at the present time, but she's able to read and write for herself. As soon as I'm more mobile and can recommence my work, I'll need a supply of human test subjects."

Pell glared at him. "Corpses? Brought here?"

"Dead tissue will be enough for some purposes," said von Frakken, "but for most I'll require living samples."

"From where, precisely?" cried Pell, his face flushing with indignation. "If you think you're going to start hacking limbs off my employees, you can think again! I won't let you touch a single hair on a single head! We operate at the minimal level of staffing required and could not afford to lose so much as one single worker!"

Von Frakken waved a shaky hand in the direction of the window. "The streets are lousy with the poor, the lost and the uneducated. An abundant source of material. In fact, one that is far more conveniently available than I could obtain back home."

"This, sir, is not the wild countryside of Bavaria! There are no indentured peasants to snatch from lonely forest tracks, nor fearful villagers who'll keep their mouths shut. This is London! You cannot simply take people without consequence!"

Von Frakken looked down at his new body with his old eyes. "I have already done so," he said.

"I am getting heartily sick of your cavalier attitude!" hissed Pell. "Already it has resulted in three deaths, to my knowledge. I considered George Hobson to be a decent man and a personal friend! If, as you claim, he fought like a tiger to prevent access to that walking horror of yours, then that is still no excuse for murder. Now I'm ashamed even to face others of his acquaintance."

"You are entirely free to go to the police," said von Frakken flatly.

"On the contrary, sir! You have involved me, and Clements too, in your skulduggery, and I dread to think what the implications may be."

"You said you were willing to help me," said von Frakken, spreading his hands.

"To get that monster dealt with, yes! To get people killed, or sliced up for your nefarious purposes, no! If any of us come to the attention of the police now, the result will be, at the very least, a public scandal! I am a respected and respectable businessman! I will not have questions, I will not have people poking their snouts into my affairs, into things that don't concern them. I have my reasons!" Exasperated, he turned and pointed an accusing finger at Dr Clements. "Why can't he convalesce at the hospital? Why does he have to be here? I can't see to his medical needs and I'll be damned if I'm hiring a nursemaid!"

Clements bowed slightly in deference. Polidori did likewise.

"These premises," said Clements, "are, in all manner of ways, the superior choice, you can be assured."

"Indeed," nodded Polidori.

"The noisy bustle of the hospital, at all times, would not be conducive to an atmosphere of recuperation and, as additionally, there would also be risk of infection. This is why we attend upon our own private patients in their homes, during such similar periods. Further, our apartments in the hospital, being limited, do not have sufficient space to accommodate a laboratory as envisioned by our esteemed colleague here. These rooms offer, in all respects, a more capacious tenancy."

Pell stared at them for a moment, his mood deflating. Then his attention snapped back to von Frakken and the crates. "You're not to order any more equipment without my personal authorisation. I will tell the girl who comes in here. Is that clear?"

"Entirely," smiled von Frakken. His smile gradually faded as Pell turned and slunk from the room. Footsteps echoed down the passage. Clements and Polidori approached the bed as if Pell had never been present.

"Our patient shows, so quickly, a remarkable degree of recovery," boomed Clements.

"Remarkable," agreed Polidori.

"You will notice, gentlemen," said von Frakken, "that my left eye is not yet properly functioning. My suspicion is that one or more rectus muscles have adhered to the upper surface of the maxilla, inside the socket."

"Temporarily?" said Clements.

"If the problem doesn't correct itself in a few days, a further procedure may be necessary."

"The heart rate remains constant?"

"Within acceptable limits, as is temperature regulation, which seems better than anticipated. There has been no fever."

"Processes of ingestion and excretion?"

"Some residual imbalance, but nothing about which I'm concerned. Interestingly, I find I now enjoy mutton, which before I could not abide."

"And are you able to walk yet?"

Von Frakken nodded. "With help." He reached out his arms, which wavered slightly in mid-air. The doctors grasped one each and assisted him to his feet. Gradually, they released their grip and von Frakken stood, his legs trembling. An expression of concentration crossed his face and his right foot shifted forward by a few inches. His left followed, and he moved almost a yard before indicating to the doctors that he wanted to sit back down on the bed.

"Quite exhilarating," he gasped. "I'd almost forgotten what it's like to breathe freely, to move without pain. How quickly the human body adjusts to changes in circumstance. I was so near to death, for so many days. Every heartbeat, every flexing of a muscle, was agony. Now all that is gone and I have survived." Leaning back against his bank of cushions, he raised his hands in front of his face and turned them back and forth, examining every line, bending his fingers into shapes and patterns. "Strong. Supple. Great things will be made with these hands. I have been practising my limb movement and coordination every hour or so, and I'm confident of achieving close to a normal range of motion within two days. I congratulate you, gentlemen, on a job well done. You followed my guidelines to the letter."

"The hair on the scalp," said Clements, "should soon regrow, and can be styled to conceal what will be, inevitably, unfortunately, some permanent evidence of fibrous cicatrices."

"Perhaps a wig, until then?" suggested Polidori.

"My appearance is of very little importance," shrugged von Frakken. "A human being is nothing more than a sensory housing for the brain, after all. Full mobility is the immediate goal."

"In the meantime," said Clements, "I see you've been reading?"

"Yes," said von Frakken. His new smile was still closer to a sneer. "I have an opportunity to widen the scope of my learning. So far, it's most enlightening, I realise there is much that I've missed, hidden away in my mountain retreat. On the subject of reading, you still have in your possession the two notebooks I handed to you. They should be returned immediately." His smile-sneer broadened. "You will appreciate, the records saved from the fire are particularly precious to me."

"Of course," nodded Clements vigorously. "Pure oversight, on our behalf, not to have brought them with us, on this occasion.

They are, you may be assured, safely locked away, as is the sample of flesh, from your creation, acquired by your good self."

"Which also should be returned immediately. Have your men made progress in tracking down my creature?"

"Considerable," said Clements, knitting his hands together. "Polidori and I were—"

"Are you using the same men who assisted me the other night?"

"Yes, and they have recruited others to the cause," said Clements. "Avenues are being pursued, trails followed. With the utmost discretion, naturally."

"Naturally. I want her found, soon. She could be anywhere. At least she has nowhere to go."

Clements cleared his throat. "With the flesh sample, under discussion, uppermost in our minds, Polidori and I were wondering if, perhaps for services rendered, we might be permitted to use a further small amount. The enzyme preparation, so vital a tool in the successful completion of your own treatment, would be of immense practical value, in our clinic, to selected patients."

"For services rendered?" said von Frakken. Their expressions were nervously eager. "I suppose it's a request I can't deny."

"It would allow us," added Polidori softly, "to carry out organ transferences which we hitherto deemed to have little or no chance of success."

Von Frakken's one mobile eye flicked back and forth between their faces. "You may have one ounce by weight. That should allow for three or four minor operations."

"Much obliged," bowed Clements.

"You are not to tell these patients about the enzyme preparation. My name and my work will not be mentioned."

"That is entirely agreeable," said Clements. "They will believe that their cures have been brought about by the surgical skills, alone, of myself and Polidori. We most gratefully thank you,

Herr von Frakken. Now, our business being concluded, we shall leave you to your recovery."

"I shall return the notebooks personally," said Polidori. "Tomorrow?" Von Frakken nodded and they took a last look at their patient from the doorway as they departed.

They made their way back to the staircase, Clements marching ahead and Polidori trotting along behind. Pell was waiting for them on the landing and escorted them, via a short corridor on the ground floor where the pounding throb of the factory was intense, out to the small cobbled courtyard at the front of the building. A hansom stood waiting.

Clements put the back of his fingers to his nose. Horrible smell of tanneries around these streets.

Pell spoke in hushed tones, out of earshot of the hansom's driver. "Von Frakken is a damned menace. I want him out of here as soon as can be arranged."

"Brilliant men, Pell, often have their peccadilloes," said Clement, "and von Frakken is by far the most brilliant man in his field. At the present time. Be glad that you have had an opportunity, an exceptionally rare one, to get to know him. Not all can be among the great and powerful, Pell, but a lucky few, such as yourself, can play a small part in their lives. When the history of our present age comes to be written, the likes of our friend up there will figure large."

Without another word, Pell sloped back into the factory while Clements and Polidori climbed into the cab. Clements tapped on the roof. "St Saviour's!"

The hansom rumbled out past the factory's tall wooden gates and was soon heading west along Whitechapel Road and Aldgate Street. The two doctors sat in silence for a few minutes.

"Extraordinary," said Dr Clements at last. "Beyond extraordinary."

"His recovery *is* unexpectedly rapid."

"I was referring, Polidori, to the feat of surgery we ourselves have performed upon him."

"Indeed," nodded Polidori.

"All we needed, additional to our personal skills, was the application of his specialised knowledge—which we, too, now possess."

"At least, in part."

Clements glanced disdainfully at him. "We have achieved what was, until three nights ago, the utterly impossible. Were I not able to see our handiwork, sitting there in bed large as life, I would scarce believe it myself. It is tantamount to miraculous. Should we, for our own part, be able to duplicate his results in the growing of artificial flesh, and thus aid our advancement in the transference of human organs, we would truly be among the titans of medical science—among Plato's elite, you might say." Polidori sniggered appreciatively. "Have you finished copying out those notebooks?"

"I will be finished by this evening," said Polidori. "Including those extensive portions which currently evade our understanding. There are many aspects of his work of which we are still ignorant."

Clements's voice dropped below its usual volume. "Of one thing, I am certain. We were right to lodge him with Pell at the factory, and not at St Saviour's. He is reckless. His actions could, with ease, lead to his own exposure and prosecution, and this will stain whomsoever is associated with him. No, far better that Pell have him, where we can keep him at a deniable distance. What we ourselves do, in pursuit of our aims, is judged unethical and illegal by the uninformed, but our actions are completely justified."

"Completely."

"However, von Frakken shows himself to be wilfully foolhardy. The taking of experimental specimens from the streets! With luck, the man's presence won't be needed for too much longer.

It is deeply regrettable that he failed to capture his wayward creation. I would dearly like to meet this peculiar experiment of his, and a proper supply of that flesh would allow us to continue our work at the hospital for some considerable period, giving us ample time to fully probe and comprehend von Frakken's secrets."

"Perhaps, then, we should be *genuinely* searching for the creature?" said Polidori timidly.

"Nonsense. The thing is dangerous. If it can kill a brute like Barnes, it can turn its murderous attentions to you and I, should it know we're on its trail. Let the police chase after it. It will have fled to the continent by now, in any case, it will be many miles away."

The cab slowly negotiated the heavily potholed road that led up to the Wandsworth bridge and arrived at St Saviour's Charitable Hospital a few minutes later. Clements and Polidori quickly retreated to their rooms and Polidori retrieved the notes he'd made on a patient who had consulted them at their clinic the previous Spring.

"Good," declared Clements, as he read through them. "For what o'clock have you made the appointment?"

"Half past eleven," said Polidori. "Ah! I see it is now nearly nineteen minutes past. I will go and wait by the side entrance."

"Now that von Frakken has given us permission, we have no fear of his suspecting the amount of flesh excised from the sample, so two or three ounces should be easily possible," boomed Clements with a grin.

Once Polidori had scuttled away, Clements marched into their ornate, oak-panelled consulting room and, after pleasurably surveying the photographs and testimonials that hung on the walls, he seated himself behind the solid, leather-topped desk. He sat with his arms straight, palms on the desk, chin at a haughty angle, listening to the steady tick of the clock out in the waiting room and contemplating the future.

He broke his reverie and stood up when he heard Polidori approaching. A gruff, well-built man in his sixties and an elegantly dressed woman a few years younger were shown in. The man's bearing was unmistakably military and he wore a patch over his left eye.

"Delightful to see you, Colonel Trevelyan, once again," said Clements.

"Brought my wife with me this time," said the Colonel.

"Enchanted, ma'am, please do be seated."

She bobbed her head with cool politeness. Polidori shut the door and stood at Clements's side, his expression fixed in a smile and his hands clasped behind his back. Clements arranged the patient's notes on the desk in front of him.

"What's this about?" said the Colonel, dropping heavily into a chair. "Back in April, you said you couldn't help me."

"The situation, I am pleased to inform you, has, in that respect, changed."

The Colonel and his wife exchanged glances. "It has?"

Clements leaned over the notes. "Your injury, let me remind myself, is a war wound?"

"It is. Afghanistan, I was with the 13th Light Infantry. Caught a bit of metal in the attack on Ghazni fortress in '39. Thought my career was over before it got started, but fortunately there were strings to pull."

"May I make a re-examination?" said Clements, walking around the desk.

"By all means," said the Colonel.

"I notice—if you would tip your head back?—thank you—I notice from reports, of late, in the newspapers, that conflict is again breaking out in that part of the world."

"Yes," said the Colonel in a mutter, keeping his damaged eye wide open and his head still, "since the Cavagnari massacre. Damn treachery. Sorry, m'dear."

The eye had been split, at an angle, across the centre of the iris. It had healed, but the cornea was milky and opaque. Clements returned to his seat and the Colonel swung his eye patch back into position.

"Yes," said Clements, "I am confident, fully, of effecting a repair."

The Colonel scoffed. "Good heavens, you're joking, the thing's a mess. I wasn't a bit surprised when you told me it was beyond help."

"That is no longer the case. Our surgical techniques, those developed by myself, and by Dr Polidori, in this hospital, have now advanced sufficiently to ensure a positive result."

"It's possible?" said Mrs Trevelyan. "An eye that's been sightless for forty years?"

"Well," said the Colonel, sitting back, "it's marvellous what medical science can do these days."

"Indeed," said Dr Polidori, leaning forward slightly to interject. "However, be aware that the surgery may result in a change of melanin in the iris."

"A different eye colour," declared Clements. "It may not happen, but, the procedure being a radically new one, you understand—"

"I see," said the Colonel. "Or rather, I *will* see!" They all chuckled politely. "Odd effect, but not one I can't live with, I'm sure."

"And, to reiterate earlier discussions," said Clements, "details of your treatment should be kept confidential, since it is available only through Dr Polidori and myself, and can only be offered to a very select, very distinguished clientele."

The Colonel nodded conspiratorially. "Goes without saying. You have the officers and the men on equal terms, you get chaos. Quite understand."

"Although," said Polidori. "we welcome any personal recommendations you may discreetly make to friends."

"I should think," said Mrs Trevelyan, "that when Henry enters his club with two working eyes for the first time in years, you'll be unable to halt the stampede to this hospital." They all chuckled politely again. "We only heard about your marvellous work because of the cure that was effected on Lady Hopkin's weak heart."

"We are always delighted to be of service to one such as her ladyship," said Clements, standing and extending a hand as a cue for his patient to leave. "If you would be so good, Colonel, as to return here at around three o'clock this afternoon—"

"You can do it *today*?" said Mrs Trevelyan.

"Our schedule is open from two, until early this evening, I believe," said Polidori, picking up a small diary from the desk and delicately riffling through it to check.

"With luck, we'll have you home in time for dinner," said Clements.

"Excellent," said the Colonel. "Until then, then—or—I say, would you gentlemen care to join us for luncheon, as our guests? We were on our way to Simpson's-in-the-Strand."

"Most kind," said Clements, "but, regretfully, we must make preparations for your treatment."

"Of course," said the Colonel. "Another time."

"We are free tomorrow," said Clements, "we have consultations only before noon and after three. May we say one o'clock?"

Polidori scratched in the diary with a pencil. "Simpson's."

"Ah. Yes. Tomorrow it is," said the Colonel.

As soon as the Colonel and his wife had been walked back to their carriage, Clements and Polidori locked up their rooms and headed along the echoing corridor towards the general wards. In both wings of St Saviour's, these were grouped along wide walkways on each floor.

Ward 7 was much like all the others, long and high, with bare floorboards and whitewashed stone. Grimy streaks rose up the walls, above the gas lights which jutted from the pipework snaking around the room at head height. The room was thick with the aroma of carbolic and human bodies.

There were twelve beds, six to each side, in which men of various ages stared, twisted or slept. This ward was used for those with serious physical injuries, and the time-greyed bedsheets showed a mottling of stains, both fresh and faded to a pale brown in the hospital laundry. Two patients at the far end of the room talked together in low voices, one displaying a heavily bandaged torso. Another, oblivious to his surroundings, grunted with pain on each spasmodic contraction of his limbs.

Close to the door was a small desk, at which the smallpox-scarred Nurse Leath filled out paperwork. She acknowledged Dr Clements and Dr Polidori with a brisk, blank inclination of the head.

The doctors toured the ward, asking questions of those who were awake, and receiving short, fumbled replies. In the bed opposite the pair talking, they found what they were looking for. A young man lay flat on his back, head pressed into his thin, flecked pillow, his left leg held tightly between a pair of wooden braces. The leg was swollen and covered in livid, purple-yellow bruises.

"Yes, shattered rather extensively," said Clements, his voice reverberating. "No breaking of the skin, however. Quite unusual. How did you do this?"

The young man was clearly trying to keep his mind off the pain. "I work at the Adelphi. I fell off the flaps. Last house, yesterday. I hit the stage on one foot." Polidori examined the leg more closely, before turning his attention to the young man's overall condition.

"Your age?" said Clements.

"Twenty-two."

"Do you have good eyesight?"

"Yes, sir."

Clements stepped back several yards. "How many fingers am I holding up?"

"Three." Polidori bent over the young man and pulled at his eyelids, rocking his head from side to side to get a better look. The young man caught a hint of cologne.

"Suitable?" said Clements. Polidori nodded. "Well, young man, your leg needs immediate attention, don't you agree?"

"Yes. Thank you. Yes."

Clements snapped his fingers to draw Nurse Leath away from her pen. "Would you be so kind as to enquire the availability of the operating room? If it is not currently vacant, we will deal with this leg down in our own rooms."

The operating room for general patients was available. Two orderlies carried the young man on a stretcher down the long walkway and deposited him on the stout wooden table. Polidori had a hushed word with Nurse Leath and she stood guard outside the closed door.

The young man kept his eyes firmly on the high, white ceiling, his heart hammering and his breath coming in short gasps. He heard the clatter of a metal bucket placed beneath the table.

"To begin with," said Clements, leaning into the young man's field of vision, "I'm going to insert this needle into the area to one side of your groin. It will feel sharp but please stay as still as possible. Do you understand?"

"Yes. Are you going to make me sleep? I was told they make you sleep, so it doesn't hurt?"

Clements bobbed out of sight and sniffed. "Yes, you will sleep."

Scissors cut at the young man's remaining trouser leg. Then he felt an intense stab at the top of his inner thigh and his face twisted for a moment. He kept telling himself to do as he'd been told and not move.

Attached to the thick metal needle which Clements had pushed into the young man's femoral artery was a long, red-brown rubber tube. The other end of the tube dangled in the bucket. Immediately, the bucket began to fill, blood pressure pumping a regular, pulsing flow.

"That's it—stay still, please—good."

The young man began to feel light-headed. This must be the sleeping part. He kept looking straight ahead as the seconds ticked by, Clements and Polidori standing silently beside him. He felt dizzy and sweat broke out all over his skin. Nausea churned in his stomach, his head ached and his face grew pale. He wanted to sleep, he'd never been so tired.

After a couple of minutes, Clements squeezed the rubber tube to halt the flow of blood. Polidori carried the full bucket to the drain in the floor on the other side of the operating room. The bucket was emptied carefully, to a swooshing, gurgling sound, then was put back under the table and the process continued.

The young man's skin became clammy and he felt himself drift away into the dark. His pulse gradually slowed and he was unconscious a full minute or more before he was dead. As Polidori emptied the bucket again, Clements fetched a surgical knife and began to cut away the young man's eyelids in preparation for the removal of the eyes themselves.

"Polidori," he said, not looking up from his work, "once you've finished there, go and ready the enzyme paste. Take a few ounces, as we discussed, but use a minimum, we may need it to last."

"Of course," said Polidori, rinsing out the bucket from a tap in the wall. "I will let Nurse Leath know that you'll be a few minutes, so she may arrange disposal."

Clements dropped a piece of skin onto the operating table and looked into the exposed eyes beneath him. "Hmm, green. We were right to warn the Colonel about the change of colour."

CHAPTER XXI

To the north of Whitechapel High Street, a spider's web of dim streets and alleyways crept out into Spitalfields and the Mile End New Town. Narrow passages met to form small backyard squares, overlooked by surrounding buildings and cloaked in perpetual shadow, like deep sinkholes in the forest of brick and slate. Chimney smoke from dwellings and factories oozed into the low clouds, congealing the air into a bilious-smelling, viscous mist that languished around street corners and upper floors, never lifting. The dulled thud and hiss of industry, of metal and steam, rose from hundreds of manufacturers large and small, an ever-present background rumble that tolled all day and long into the night.

Here, people walked with their heads down, minding their own business. The bright hubbub of the high street could have been a thousand miles away.

Devon Row, between Hanbury Street and Miller's Court, was a filthy, sorrowful place. Maria wrapped her arms around herself, mostly for warmth but also in an unconscious attitude of defence. The houses to either side of her were crooked shapes in the throat-burning smog, two rows of broken teeth, all of them a smeary dun colour from years of grime and weather. A couple of them had huge prop-posts wedged up against them, to fend off the slow collapse of a wall. Above her, the sky was a darkening, bruised ochre.

Thin, ragged children stood in little groups, in doorways and crevices, their bare feet caked in the mud and dirt that layered the street. Down the middle of the road ran a shallow drainage dip which trickled with a blackened liquid. Further up, straddling this gutter, was a metal trough with a rusted water pump. Several women were gathered around it, their sleeves rolled up, talking together and scrubbing at tired clothes. Here and there, along the length of the street, washing lines heavy with torn and greasy garments drooped from house to house.

Drab figures haggled on doorsteps over a bed for the night. Others clustered around shabby vendors selling sheep's trotters and cups of watery fish stew. A couple of hollow-faced toddlers played with a stray cat and somewhere out of sight a baby cried in pitiful, sickly gasps. In every corner, Maria could hear the pattering of rats.

Misery and death haunted Devon Row, and every street like it. A pale light came from the Five Beggars pub, located at the corner of a wedge-shape of buildings beside an alley which led deeper into the fog and darkness. It was marked only by a faded wooden sign nailed above a low window. Outside were nestled a couple of rickety benches on which a diminutive couple perched, clutching an even smaller bundle of possessions between them.

As Maria approached the pub, a burly man emerged unsteadily, followed closely by an unkempt woman wearing a dress that had once been brightly coloured, her lank hair rapidly escaping from a clumsily-tied bun on the top of her head. The two of them laughed loudly, braying into each other's faces, the man holding onto the woman for support. A few yards along, the man turned towards the nearest wall and a puddle began to collect around his boots.

The woman turned a hostile, territorial stare at Maria, and she realised that the woman was nowhere near as drunk as she was pretending to be. The man would be beaten and robbed by her husband as soon as she could lure him somewhere private.

Inside the Five Beggars, one wall was dominated by a mural, made from ceramic tiles, showing the local silk weavers of the eighteenth century. Next to it was a small, time-battered serving counter, beside a crackling fireplace. The place was busy but not as tightly-packed as most evenings, with knots of people crowded around tables or on refectory benches, some topping up their cups from broad-bottomed jugs, some swaying or leaning against a convenient surface. A group of men near the counter debated the contents of a newspaper. Half a dozen women, seated by the window, had the sunken, deformed jaws of those who'd spent years in a match factory being poisoned by phosphorus. A couple of girls in the corner giggled as they drank. The air was filled with voices and the stale aroma of beer.

Maria, alert to the possibility that members of the gang she sought might be regulars here, quickly scanned the faces but recognised no-one. She approached the counter, behind which stood the landlord.

He was immensely fat, with a bald head and a day's stubble. A spotted neckerchief was tied in a loose bow above a grease-dabbed, collarless shirt. He surveyed his customers with an offhand pout, leaning heavily across the counter in a way that made his neck and upper arms bulge. When he noticed Maria, he looked her up and down with an unconcealed unease. Weird-looking girl. *Is* this a girl? Moves weird.

"Yeh?" he said, his voice a hoarse growl.

"Do you have any work?" said Maria.

His pout shifted around his face. Weird ruddy voice, too. Them amber specs for weak eyes? Or for hiding? He vaguely wagged a pudgy finger in her direction. "S'you runnin' from the jacks, is yer?"

"No. I've got no money. I'm looking for work."

"Keeping out of the spike? Can't blame yer for that now, can we? What can yer do?"

Maria looked back towards the street. "I could help you sort out thieves who steal from drunks. I'm tougher than I look."

The landlord snorted. "What do I want that for? If some mug gets 'is pennies nicked on the way out, tha's his lookout, not mine. Having 'em nicked on the way *in*, that's what I don't want. Look, y'see them two dollymops over in the corner, there, see? Their madam can always use fresh tail, you ask 'em. Mind, you'd 'ave to stop dressing like a boy." He looked her up and down. "Although ... "

"I could cook, or clean. I can work hard."

"I s'pose we could use a slavey, collect the pots, mop up the puke."

"I need somewhere to stay, too. Do you have rooms?"

"Yeh, tha's different," said the landlord, heaving himself upright, "we got rents. Better than the flea-bitten flops you get over the road. We only does 'em by the week, mind, stops any old muck snipe turnin' up."

"How much?"

"Four shillings and a sprat. In advance. But tha's no good to you, is it?"

"Then for now I'll work for board and food."

The landlord scratched his stubble for a moment, his lips touring his face. "I'm Fred. You call me Mr Dobbs." He turned to shout up the twisting, rickety wooden steps behind him. "Polly! Poll! Oi!"

Dobbs served a customer, who slapped down a handful of coins and weaved his way back to his seat. Maria took another look across the noisy pub.

"There are tanneries near here," she said.

"You won't get work there," said Dobbs. He turned to the stairs. "*Oi! Poll! Where'ya?*"

"No, I'm trying to find a long-lost relative." She described the member of the gang who'd been armed with a pick-axe, the one with the reeking clothes. "I think he probably lives around here somewhere."

"Might be Harry Price, he's a tanner. He stinks like a burst gut. Hasn't been in for a while, though. Someone found out as he's a nose for the police. Narks ain't much welcome."

"Do you get trouble from the police here?"

He leaned against the counter again. "You takin' the piss? No peeler comes down these streets. Ever. *OI! POLL!*"

There was a clattering on the stairs and a woman appeared from the upper floor who was as thin as her brother Frank was fat. She galumphed on box-like heels, the stairs creaking and shifting slightly. Her arrival was greeted with a wave of calls from the customers, particularly the match-workers sitting by the window. The chatter in the room became a little brighter. One of the newspaper-debaters, a wiry man with a prickly, jutting beard, ruffled the pages of his paper and declared, "Here she comes!"

Polly Dobbs, enjoying her entrance, gave a general wave to all then thrust out her arm at the match-workers, her fingers waggling and her mouth set in an 'o.'

"Keep yer wig on, Fred," she piped, making a theatrical performance of it for the benefit of the regulars. "Where's the bloody fire, eh?" She laughed, her voice roughened with alcohol and her lined, ageing face garish with make-up. Maria was reminded of a horse.

"This is our new girl," said Dobbs, "an' she's for a rent n'all."

Polly grinned at Maria, showing darkened, peg-like teeth between bright red lips. "I'm Poll, dear. I see you've met ol' Grumpy-Fart." She cackled and the newspaper-debaters chimed in. She blinked at the new girl. Ooh, poor luvvie, fancy growing up with a face like that. "You not from round 'ere, m'little chuckaboo?" Without waiting for an answer, she turned to her brother. "Did I hear you mention Harry Price?"

"Oh, yer did 'ear me then, did yer?" said Dobbs. "Flap-ears."

Polly scrunched her face at Maria. "If yer find 'im, love, he owes my friend Mrs Mayberry three shillings. But careful, he's a nasty sod. He used to hang aroun' with them Baileys, and them Baileys is a bad lot. Am I right, Mr Crabtree?"

The bearded newspaper-debater agreed vigorously. "You are right, Poll."

"There. I'm right," said Polly. She whistled over to the match-workers. "Gert! You girls on for a fortifying glass or two before we go out?"

One of the women gave an unsteady nod, her eyes shining, and Maria suddenly realised that these workers had been poisoned in more than body. She felt a sharp tug of sympathy for them. These humans.

Polly raised a finger in reply and started to pour out glasses of gin.

"Go where?" said Dobbs, scratching his belly.

"Go where, he says," cried Polly, playing to her audience. "To Mrs Mayberry's! We promised 'er a visit, every night this week, didn't we Gert?" Gert nodded. "Yeh. 'Cos she's got all six of her brood with the croup, she's that vexed she can't tell her elbow from last Tuesday. She needs a fortifying glass like the rest of us." She carried a tray over to Gert and her friends.

"You and your little gang of haybags," muttered Dobbs. "You watch yourself."

"Listen to His Lordship!" cried Polly. The women giggled. "If there's any trouble, I'll give 'em me famous right 'ook. I'm a terror, me." She raised a comical fist and her audience laughed.

The bearded newspaper-debater tapped at a page. "No, you take care Poll. It's in the *Examiner*." He read the words carefully, a finger following the printed lines. "Subsequent to our previous reports, police continue to be engaged in the hunt for the mysterious apparition believed responsible for the deaths of two persons in Kensington. They seek what has been described as a horribly dangerous and maniacal individual."

"Bloody 'ell, the net's closin' in on yer, Frank!" cried Polly.

"I'm just tellin' yer to watch yourself," said Dobbs. "Walking the streets when yer full up to the knocker."

"Any maniac tries it on," declared Polly, "he'll get a smack on the chops. Ooh, I'm a right devil, I am. Me an' the girls an' Mrs Mayberry is entitled to a fortifying glass an' that's the end to it, Frank Dobbs. Dizzy his-self could pass the Polly Dobbs Ain't Going Out Act, in parliament, and I'd still be going." She downed her gin and turned her attention to Maria. "Right, love, I'll show yer the rents. Wha's yer name, darlin'?"

"Millie," said Maria.

"Right, you come with me, Millie."

She led Maria behind the counter and up the steep, creaking stairs. At the top were three rooms, one occupied by an elderly couple and another by a woman and her three widowed daughters. Maria's room was small, with a grimy, frame-rotted window and a straw mattress in the corner. Black mildew speckled the walls and a mass of wood lice seethed along a broken skirting board.

"Come back down in a minute," said Polly, "His Lordship will want to tell yer what's what before I go out."

Left to herself, Maria stood looking out through the smeared glass at Devon Row, filled with the intense loneliness that had rapidly become her constant companion. Somewhere along the street, a dog was barking furiously.

She pulled back the sleeve of her shirt and cautiously undid the dressing she'd made that morning from a stolen vest. It was stained with pus and needed to be replaced. Even so, the wound on her arm was already beginning to heal beneath its oozy surface. Tendrils of flesh were matting themselves together, bridging the gap, reforming living tissue. A few days more and it would be good as new.

CHAPTER XXII

A few days more, Pell, and I'll be good as new," said von Frakken. Delight beamed from him.

He'd commandeered a second room in Jabez Pell's private apartment at the Pell & Blight Ltd factory. A table made a sturdy laboratory workbench, while a bookcase served as storage for equipment.

Von Frakken's movements, in his new body, were becoming more stable and assured. He strode across the room with something close to the swagger that had been his habit back home. His wayward eye was still unresponsive, giving his face a disconcerting, almost lizard-like look, and the livid stitching that curled around his bald head seemed all the more grotesque in contrast to his general air of health. His clothes, taken from amongst the few he'd brought with him from Europe, and including a red velvet frock coat that had been specially tailored for him in Munich, fitted his new frame quite well.

"You'll be moving on soon, I take it?" said Pell.

"When my property has been recovered, it will be time to make more permanent arrangements. Until then, the work will continue."

Pell hooked his thumbs into his waistcoat. "You'll be returning to Bavaria as soon as possible, then, no doubt?"

Von Frakken smiled at him. He raised a finger, then pointed to the books he'd been reading during his convalescence, stacked haphazardly on top of the bookcase. "Perhaps not."

"What?" Pell was already feeling in need of a drink. Now one hand hovered involuntarily, halfway to his pocket. "You surely don't propose to continue your abominable programme of experiments in London? My co-operation was firmly based on the understanding that—!"

"I assure you, your co-operation will be given freely, in due course. I'm most grateful to you, Pell, while I've been recovering I have been able to expand my knowledge in entirely new and unexpected directions. I've been able to catch up with the modern world, and with modern thinking. As you know, I have been steadily pushing the boundaries of science for many years. However, I have come to realise that I have also shut myself away from other areas of progress. I left the Red College of Leipzig's university and immediately threw myself headlong into my research. Today, I can appreciate that my commitment, while necessary and exemplary, may have been a little too enclosed. There is so much that I have missed. I feel as if I have come up for air."

"What do you mean?" grumbled Pell.

"Economics! I have discovered the study of economics. I had no idea that the organisation of resources had become so systematised and so debated. I was aware of *The Wealth of Nations* but had, I confess, never read it. Now I find that the field has spiralled into all manner of philosophies and theories. Quite fascinating. I have been introduced to Burke and Bentham, to Ricardo and John Stuart Mill. The ideas of Jean-Baptiste Say are ones I find intriguing, the notion of the balances in demand and production. However, I can see that his reasoning is at fault when he imagines that money is no more than the representation of commodities. He forgets that the accumulation of wealth is something that human beings make a goal in itself, that money denotes power in the abstract as well as in the purchase of goods and services. Don't you agree?"

"Theories are all fine and dandy," muttered Pell, "but practical, hard-headed business is something else altogether."

"Exactly, Pell, exactly," said von Frakken. For a couple of seconds, the muscles in one side of his face gave a sudden, elongated pull and one arm twisted tightly. He ignored it. "An economy, either at the national scale or at the level of a single market, is a nebulous entity. It is unpredictable and inexact, no true science can ever capture its complexities. However, the very fact that economic forces can be subject to manipulation and deliberate change is nothing short of a revelation to me. It occurs to me that an economy is like a human body, self-sustaining unless diseased or injured, subject to the same periods of growth and stagnation. There's a theorist called Marx who would concur with that. An economy consumes human labour just as a body digests nourishment. He lives in London, I understand, I'd be most interested to meet him."

"I'm sure," growled Pell, "but where does it get you?"

"It has focussed me, and focussed my aims, it is as simple as that! My creature, the one still roaming the streets, is the culmination of many years of work but may also be, I now appreciate, the starting point of something entirely unexpected. I had anticipated that my research would continue along similar lines, that I would create original forms for the artificial flesh that I have designed, that I would continue to develop it and refine it. Not so! My recent studies have shown me a fresh horizon. The underlying motive of my work, that is to say the conquest of Nature, remains steadfast and whole. However, I have formulated a radically different approach to its ultimate fulfilment."

Pell's hand played around the hip flask in his pocket. "How? In what way?"

"You'll see, Pell, all in good time. You yourself will directly benefit, that I can promise."

"Pah!" spluttered Pell. "I've had empty promises before. Is Clements in your self-same line of business? He is. Have any commercial applications resulted? They have not."

"Unless we count his private practice."

"And does that accrue any profit for *me*? No. All I have to show for my investment is vague assurances."

Von Frakken smiled thinly to himself. His voice became low. "That will no longer be the case. Clements is a capable physician but—as I think you may lately suspect?—not a man of my calibre. I was wise not to remain at the hospital, and to keep him at arm's length. Circumstances forced me to trust him, and Polidori, but circumstances change. I've no doubt they are racing to understand the knowledge that has come into their possession. Circumstances may need to change once more, before that happens. Clements is a fumbler. I, on the other hand, expect results. Given the proper resources, I achieve those results."

"The proper resources," growled Pell. "What can you possibly hope to achieve from—*this!*" He waved a hand towards the workbench, then pulled the flask from his pocket and drank.

The workbench was piled with chemicals, mechanisms and instruments, including a pair of old lead-acid power cells, salvaged from von Frakken's original laboratory, from which coiled a nest of wires. Embedded in the organised chaos were two experiments in progress, two live rats. The first stood, untethered and apparently untouched, on a raised metal plate. It was free to scurry away at any time, but instead it remained almost motionless, its head swaying gently back and forth, its tail curled around its rear legs.

The second was held in a small clamp normally used for flasks and test tubes. Its limbs had all been removed, along with its tail and the area around its lumbar vertebrae. Delicate rubber tubes ran from several of the sections that had been cut away and electrodes inserted into the top of its head sent a needle juddering on a nearby gauge. The animal didn't appear to be in any distress, and its nose explored its surroundings as if it was running in the street outside.

"Repulsive," muttered Pell.

"I'm not interested in your arcane morality, Pell. I am at the forefront of a more progressive and far-sighted ethic."

"Where the devil did you get those damn things?"

"I am something of a night owl," said von Frakken. "Your nightwatchman, the new one, is an accommodating fellow. He trapped them for me."

"I have asked you *not* to speak to my employees beyond what is strictly necessary."

"I told him I was your long-lost relative, from the continent. These are my pets."

Pell took another gulp from his flask. "I repeat, what possible value can there be in dissecting vermin?"

"It is clear, Mr Pell, that you would gain from a study of my field of expertise, just as I have gained from my study of yours. This is methodology which goes back to the ancients, to Galen and Avenzoar. I am establishing the efficacy of certain chemical mixtures of my own formulation, which are designed to induce specific emotional and mental states in the subjects. These can include lethargy, as you see here, complete neurological disassociation, or even violent hostility. I will require these findings as I apply tests to human specimens. These specimens I will now need immediately."

Pell snorted with exasperation and all but spun on his heels. He struggled for a moment to find words. "I am feeling as if I am a music hall turn, sir, that runs through the same act five times a day! I say again, you cannot abduct people from the streets of London and not expect the severest consequences! This is a modern, civilised city in a modern, civilised society! There is the rule of law! I will not have further crimes committed under my own roof! Risk scandal and ruin on your own time, I will not have the police at my door!"

"Despite the enormous financial benefit for you?"

Pell's fists shook uselessly in mid-air. He screwed up his face for a moment in an effort to control his temper, pulling his spectacles from his face and letting out several long breaths. "I fully realise," he said at last, with subdued fury, "that events have somewhat—overtaken my ability to object. You know I have little choice but to accept your presence, but I would ask you not to take advantage of that fact. I would appeal to your common sense. You are still very much a stranger to this part of the world, and I don't think you understand the—"

Von Frakken loomed over him. "Do you think me a fool? Do you think a fool could have done what I have done?"

" … No."

"Do you think I am incapable of acting with care and diligence?"

"Of course not, I merely—"

"I will attend to the gathering of specimens myself, have no fear. I will not involve you, or your staff, or anyone else." One side of his face gave another spasmodic twitch. "All specimens will be contained within these rooms. Unless you'd care to make other areas of the building available to me?"

"You can't go out there so soon after your—operation."

"I am perfectly fit," said von Frakken. He leaned against the workbench on outstretched arms, examining the two rats.

"Don't think I'll supply you with arms! A gun or a knife."

"Nothing like that will be necessary."

"You'll overcome the assorted footpads and dragsmen of London, will you? In the dead of night? Without attracting attention of any kind?"

"Violence will not be needed. Those I select will come here willingly. It's simply that they will not leave. Persuasion and promises are quite powerful enough, thank you."

"I think you underestimate the potential pitfalls."

Von Frakken faced him blankly. "I think you overestimate the worthless guttersnipes who teem the streets."

Pell held von Frakken's gaze for a moment, then snorted and left him to his own devices. He shuffled back downstairs, into the thrum and hiss of the factory. While he was still alone, he took out his hip flask and shook it. It was empty again.

CHAPTER XXIII

"I fear the turbot was not the freshest," declared Dr Clements.

"I thought mine very enjoyable," said Dr Polidori apologetically.

They alighted from the cab which had collected them from their lunch appointment with Colonel and Mrs Trevelyan and headed back into St Saviour's, Polidori scampering to keep up with Clements's strides. They passed through the Receiving Room inside the central section of the hospital, where a pinch-faced clerk logged patients' comings and goings at a broad, elevated desk, and plunged into the labyrinth of dim, echoing corridors.

At lunch, Colonel Trevelyan had expressed delight at his new eye. He had made an amusing pantomime of perusing the menu and he'd flagged down an old army friend specifically to introduce him to his miracle-working surgeons. Now that Clements and Polidori had marvelled at the Colonel's swift recovery, and were growing more confident in the use of von Frakken's enzyme, they were preparing to spend the afternoon repairing a patient's severed spine and replacing several of her branching blood vessels.

"Lady Bitterlea is due shortly, is she not?" said Clements, his voice bouncing off the stone walls.

Polidori quickly checked the diary and his pocket watch. "Twenty minutes."

Clements tutted. "We should not have stayed for the lemon syllabub. You will, of unfortunate necessity, have to receive her yourself, keeping her in good spirits, while I secure the required material." Half a dozen yards further along the corridor, he changed his mind. "You attend to finding a suitable source, I shall meet Lady Bitterlea. The fee must be paid in advance. We want no repeat of the delay which followed her son's liver."

"Indeed not," agreed Polidori.

Without another word, Clements turned and marched off into the hospital's east wing, while Polidori continued on to the wards. Briefly, he stood aside while orderlies wrestled and removed a naked male who'd just run screaming and weeping from one of the upper floors. After a short search, he found a patient in the required condition and approached the ward nurse in charge.

"The man there, in Five," he enquired. "Is he a recent admittance?"

"A printing press pulled his arm off an hour ago," said the nurse in a subdued tone. "They managed to staunch the bleeding at his workplace, but you can see he's very agitated."

Polidori crossed the aisle between beds and stood over number five. The man was shaking violently, his face a mask of shock fixed on the remains of his right shoulder, heavily wrapped in blood-soaked cloth. He sweated profusely, muttering over and over to himself that his livelihood was gone, was gone, was gone.

Polidori asked the nurse to turn him over. He yelled out as she rolled him to one side. Polidori pressed his fingers to various sections of the injured man's spine and, satisfied that there was no damage to that part of his body, stepped away and indicated for the nurse to roll him back. The patient in the neighbouring bed watched all this from beneath a sheet.

"I will operate immediately. The wound must be closed."

The nurse nodded, impressed and grateful that Dr Polidori was being so decisive and compassionate. "Yes, doctor, I'll call the orderlies."

"And Nurse Leath, if you'd be so kind."

"I can assist you."

"Nevertheless."

She nodded again and hurried away. As Polidori left the ward, a passing colleague noticed him and trotted over. "Dr Polidori, may I have a word?"

"Indeed, Dr Meers, although I am a little short of time."

Meers smiled amiably. "It will only take a moment. Is Dr Clements not with you?"

"In consultation," said Polidori.

"Ah! I was wondering if you or Clements have lately come across an adult female patient who presents with very unusual or fantastical claims about her own nature?"

Polidori frowned gently. "No. In what respect fantastical?"

"I have a friend at the Middlesex in Hanwell. This young woman was admitted there a short while ago suffering from hysterical delusions. She believes herself to be something other than a human being."

"An animal?"

"Ah, no, I'm not sure of the exact diagnosis. She was receiving treatment from this friend of mine when she absconded. She is believed to have come into the city and may well be seeking medical help."

"Then, why abscond?" enquired Polidori mildly.

Dr Meers's eyes stretched a little. "She, ah, took a personal dislike to my friend. Part of the hysteria, no doubt. My friend has asked me to spread word of her, since it's extremely important that she's located and returned to Hanwell as soon as possible. She is a significant danger to public safety."

"She is violent? Raving?"

"She is normally as calm as a millpond, but will become murderously aggressive if her mood turns. Hence the importance of finding and detaining her."

Polidori's expression suddenly blanked. Suspicious thoughts spun behind it. "A unique case," he said with intense calm. "Disturbing."

"Very much so," agreed Meers. "She is educated, I should add, knowledgeable in areas of science related to galvanism and the electrochemistry of the body. This may possibly even be the source of the hysteria. I know you and Clements to be interested in this line of research yourselves and, as she is aware of those currently engaged in this field, she might be likely to approach you."

Polidori's face remained a mask. "Indeed. Is there a description of this unfortunate person?"

"She is slimly built, a little over average height and very pale of skin. Her features are distinctive, somewhat coarse, her eyes a sharp blue. She has long fingers with no nails. Torn out in her own fury, I understand."

"Most precise. Thank you, Dr Meers. I will alert Dr Clements and you can be sure we will keep a close eye out for her."

"I must emphasise, she should not be engaged in much conversation. She is easily riled."

"Duly noted. If you will excuse me?"

Dr Meers smiled and went on his way. At that moment, orderlies carried the injured man out of the ward on a stretcher. He jostled and swayed with each plodding step the orderlies took, his mouth pulled tight and his hair matted. Polidori stood for a few seconds, indecision washing over him like a high tide, blinking nervously and glancing back at Meers as he disappeared along the corridor. At last, he followed the stretcher to the operating room.

Once the relevant tissue had been collected and the patient was dead—officially logged as cardiogenic shock, unavoidable, most unfortunate—Polidori scurried to find Clements. He was in their consulting room, in conversation with an elderly woman in mourning dress who was tucked neatly into a high-backed wooden wheelchair.

"—was told that my condition was permanent by surgeons in both London and Paris, supposedly the leading men of their profession. You now claim otherwise?"

"You will, Lady Bitterlea, if I may be so bold, see proof of this claim, unequivocal, before the day is out," declared Clements with a grin.

Lady Bitterlea's eyebrows danced in search of an objection but found none. "Well. Should this be the case, you will have earned your usurious fee. For which I require a receipt, if you please, my secretary is reliably efficient and will want the expenditure accounted for."

"Immediately," bowed Clements. He snapped his fingers at Polidori.

"Oh!" said Lady Bitterlea, who hadn't noticed Polidori glide into the room. "I thought we were alone. Dr Pollock, isn't it?"

"Polidori, ma'am." Flustered, he turned to Clements. "Dr Clements, a matter has just come to my—"

"The receipt, first and foremost, thank you," said Clements, his grin broadening. Polidori bustled to the bureau. "Lady Bitterlea's secretary is waiting out in her brougham. Inform him that he may station himself, for as long as necessary, in our waiting room, until such time as Lady Bitterlea, following her surgery, is ready for the journey home."

"Also, ask him to let our housekeeper know that we shall return later than anticipated," said Lady Bitterlea. "We expected another wild goose chase."

Polidori wrote out the receipt. It was a further ten minutes or more before he could take Clements aside, clicking the consulting room door shut, to tell him about his encounter with Dr Meers.

"A nonsensical story," whispered Polidori, "for which I can arrive at only one sensible explanation. Meers knows of the existence of von Frakken's inhuman creature."

Clements's eyes narrowed in thought. "If so—he may have discovered the nature of our work here."

"I think that's unlikely," said Polidori quietly. "Would he not simply say so? Report to the committee? I believe he is unaware of our connection to von Frakken, otherwise he would not feel obliged to spin such a yarn. He does not know where the creature is, or he would hardly bother to trouble us at all."

"Then how and why does he search for it?"

Polidori dabbed at his cheeks with a handkerchief. "The waters of this entire affair grow deeper by the hour. What if von Frakken has allies of whom we have no knowledge? And if this is the case, then why?"

"He's treacherous, that's why," snarled Clements. "We must devise some way to expose him without endangering our own activities, a plan in case we find ourselves in an awkward position."

Polidori's lower lip shuddered. "You think that likely?"

Clements huffed. "I don't know. I do not know."

"There is so much of von Frakken's work we cannot yet duplicate. Even rapid progress will still require quite some time. Surely, until then, we should make every effort to convince him of our loyalty?"

"We must watch our every step. That much is certain. For now, we have work to do. Prepare our operating room."

At shortly after 8 o'clock that evening, Lady Bitterlea was wheeled out to her waiting carriage in her chair. Clements assured her that the feeling she had already regained in her toes was merely the beginning, that after a night's rest she would be able to move her legs, that a day or two would find her walking for the first time in ten years. It would be as if her fall had never happened. Her secretary lifted her into the faded, much-repaired brougham and wrapped a warming blanket around her.

The carriage set off down the hospital's short drive, the breath of the horses clouding in the cold air. It passed a small handcart that was being pushed by a woman and her brother-in-law. On the cart, tightly wrapped in bloodstained cloth and collected for a shilling from the mortuary, was the body of the printer who'd lost an arm. Behind walked a small boy of seven or eight, carrying a small bundle of clothes which he squeezed against his chest.

CHAPTER XXIV

The evening shift change was due at the tannery. The wrought iron gates to its back yard were generally left open to allow a steady drizzle of carts to come and go, and most workers came and went the same way. From across the yard came the noise of scraping, beating and pressing, over a low roar of boiling liquid. The air stank, filled with a greasy fog of gushing steam, sickly lime and the thick, faecal soup in which the hides were washed.

Maria kept as far as possible to unlit areas of the street. She was now on her third round of the city's tanneries, watching and waiting, and this one was the closest to Devon Row. She loitered among the pure-gatherers, who roamed the area collecting up turds from the streets to sell to the tanneries at tenpence a basket. Most of them were little girls or hard-up grandmothers, bulking out whatever they found by mixing in mortar scratched from old walls. The more alkaline the mash, the better it was for scrubbing the leather.

Maria crossed the street and stood in a shadowy alcove from where she could see the workers going in and out without being directly observed herself. A steady parade of human faces, young and old, men and women, coming to work or leaving it, back and forth, one set of labourers swapping for the next.

For a second, she didn't spot the pick-axe man. As he came out of the gate, his head turned while he spoke to a woman beside him, but Maria quickly recognised his lined, heavy-brow features and his unwashed work clothes.

Her heart skipped and she pressed herself deeper into shadow. She fixed on him as he sloughed across the street with a dozen others. They dispersed, disappearing down alleys or into the soot-laden evening mist.

Maria followed him, keeping twenty yards or more behind, stepping as lightly as she could. After two corners, he was alone, trudging down a narrow side street and across a yard where low windows intruded on candle-lit domestic scenes and children made pictures in the damp dust. Without breaking stride, he hocked up a spit-ball of phlegm and headed down a long slope towards a road lined with creaking tenements.

Grab him now, thought Maria, or wait until he's at home? She had no way of knowing how many friends he might have in the building he inhabited. Better to collar him while he was off guard and away from help.

The pick-axe man heard a couple of swift footsteps behind him, but before he could turn he was shoved violently in the back and tumbled forward into the dirt of the pavement. With a grunt of surprise and anger, he flipped over and Maria landed heavily on his chest, pinning one of his arms with her knee. She grabbed the other and twisted it sharply.

"I *got* y'money!" he spat through gritted teeth. Then he looked up at the face above him, its highlights picked out by the dampened light from nearby buildings. "Ha! S'you! Yeah, I heard you'd bolted."

Maria tightened the twist of his arm and he winced. "The man who hired you. The one with half a face. Where is he?"

"How much?"

"What? I haven't got money, and if you don't answer me you won't have an arm!" She gave it an even fiercer turn and he cried out. "Where is he?"

"He didn't hire me," groaned the pick-axe man. "I don't even know 'is name! It's my mate who got me the job and you killed him!"

He saw her expression darken. Guilt.

"Where did your mate contact him?" she snarled. "*Where? I'm warning you!*" Her other hand suddenly gripped his throat.

"I'm no snitch," he growled. "I don't grass, no matter what people think."

Two workmen sauntered out of the darkness, talking together. They saw what was going on, silently turned around and vanished again.

She tightened her hold on his neck. "You will tell me!" she hissed. "Now!"

His mouth spread in a grimace. "Or what? *Eh?* Or what?"

"Or I'll kill you too."

"Will yer?" He glared up at her. "Will yer? Go on, then. I don't know nothing, I ain't saying nothing. Go on."

Her hand squeezed against his throat, but her face slackened. "Tell me."

"I don't care what you want, and you ain't goin' to make me care, girlie. Who are you? Eh? *Who are you?*"

Her face folded into a sneer of rage but her grip loosened. "Tell me."

"You haven't the guts. Y'see, that's why the likes o'me beat the likes o'you. Whoever you think you are. Now piss off before I put your lights out, you ugly bitch."

For a second, Maria's grip tightened again, then she let go and sprang to her feet. She stumbled away up the slope, back towards the tannery.

The pick-axe man, coughing, hauled himself upright and stared after her, mulling things over. He'd read the papers. He reckoned it would do him some good, to tell the coppers he'd sighted the Kensington Demon.

Maria hurried in the direction of Devon Row, a boiling stew swirling in her head. Several times she took a wrong turn, too preoccupied with her thoughts, and found herself in unfamiliar streets.

Navigating her way back, she walked along a wide thoroughfare where huge factories rose up all around, brick giants which dwarfed the people who scurried around them. Here the clotting night was punctuated by street lamps on both pavements, casting a weird, illusionary light where women—and a few men dressed as women—stood in groups of two or three, eyeing potential customers as they passed close by.

In the largest of the factories a light burned way up on the top floor, high above the street, a faint rectangle against the black sky. Maria glanced up at the elaborate lettering over the factory's entrance: PELL & BLIGHT LTD – PURVEYORS OF TONICS & HEALING CURATIVES – EST. 1862. The memory of Professor Hobson's friend scratched momentarily at her heart and she walked on. There'd be no welcome in that place for her. Even less, she was certain, for someone like Wilhelm von Frakken.

She arrived at the Five Beggars in Devon Row a few minutes later. The nightly crowd of regulars were all in their usual places. Polly was raising a sing-song by the fireplace, arms windmilling in time to the stamping of her foot. Her brother Frank, leaning over the counter, jabbed a pudgy finger at Maria.

"You're late," he grumbled. "Where yer bin? *Oi Poll!* Shut yer bloody noise!"

Polly stopped in mid-flow. "We're only being cheerful 'ere, Majesty!"

"Well, yer not makin' me bloody cheerful! Shut up!"

"You shut up! We're goin' out in a minute, anyway."

Mr Dobbs twitched his head at Maria, indicating for her to start refilling the beer jugs. "What, again?"

"Yes, again!" squeaked Polly, putting on a music hall cross-talk voice which drew a hearty laugh from her audience. "You know where and you know why. It's just Gert and me tonight, in't it, Gert?"

Gert nodded. "Right," nodded Polly.

The bearded Mr Crabtree piped up from among the newspaper-debaters. "He's still worried about maniacs stalkin' the streets, Poll!"

Dobbs tapped a forefinger on the counter. "Listen! That bloke with the flophouse on the corner, that bung, him and one of his lodgers never came home last night. Between here and that corner, not fifty yards, gone, both of 'em."

"Must have fallen in love and buggered off!" declared Polly. Her crowd laughed appreciatively.

"I spoke to his Mrs," said Mr Crabtree. He paused to down his beer. "She said he'd never leave home like that." Maria refilled his cup. "Thankin' you, love."

"Well," said Polly, going into her prize-fighter act, "any murderin' maniacs will have me to deal with, and they won't like it! Come on, Gert, we got to be off, poor Mrs Mayberry will be gasping."

Polly Dobbs never arrived at Mrs Mayberry's for a fortifying glass, and nobody at the Five Beggars ever saw her again. Gert was found several hours later, crouched tearfully in a doorway. She said a nicely dressed gentleman had taken Polly away.

CHAPTER XXV

Mr Havelock, the chief clerk at Pell & Blight Ltd, gently closed the door of the office behind him and eased his meagre frame onto the chair in front of Pell's paper-strewn desk. Pell sat with his hands on the desk's edge, his fingers silently drumming. Havelock cleared his throat and adjusted his spectacles, then reached into his frock coat for a neatly folded letter, written on expensive notepaper that was exclusive to the Albion & Imperial Bank of Threadneedle Street. He held it out and his employer snatched it from his hand.

Pell read and re-read the letter, flexing the paper in his hands as if the ink would shake loose and rearrange itself into a message that was more to his liking. He pursed his lips and set the paper down, and his fingers returned to their tapping.

"One week," he said at last. He looked up at Havelock, who didn't respond. The old clerk's sallow, wrinkled face was unchanging, neither judgemental nor emotional. The way he removed his half-moon spectacles and tucked them into his top pocket was all the comment he needed to make.

"One week," repeated Pell. "And then the veil is torn away." He flicked at the notepaper. "They still believe the official books? They think we'll cover the debt?"

Havelock dipped his head slightly. Pell sat back and was silent for a few moments, looking down at himself, plucking idly at the chain of his pocket watch.

He shut his eyes and spoke slowly. "Hmm. Perhaps there's yet hope for a financial miracle. Such things happen, from time to time, I am reliably informed. One of the banks may not discover—our accounts with the other banks. Naturally, should the worst occur, I will—face up … naturally, I shall remain at the wheel, a captain on board ship. However, there is still time for you, Havelock—escape abroad—desert your post—betray my trust, should that be what you desire."

Havelock quickly and quietly got to his feet. He gave Pell a shallow bow and left the room. Without acknowledging the other clerks in the counting office, he took the five pounds and eight shillings that were in the petty cash drawer and left the building, never to return.

Pell, alone with an aching sensation in the pit of his stomach, searched his desk for brandy in vain. He'd have to go upstairs. He had some upstairs. His face thunderous, he tramped up to his private apartment.

Von Frakken had now taken over a third room, the floral wallpapered parlour beside Pell's sleeping quarters. As Pell headed for his sitting room, von Frakken was leading a stocky, scruffily dressed stranger out of the parlour and along the corridor. Pell hurried to the parlour door and saw a second stranger in there, standing still and silent. Flustered, he followed von Frakken into his laboratory.

"Who are these men?" he demanded. A moment's thought gave him the answer to his own question. He knew the answer to his next question too, a second after it had passed his lips. "Have you got them in some sort of mesmeric trance?"

"Tests on rats were successful," said von Frakken. "Now I apply the same principle to human subjects. They are completely docile."

"I hope to God you got them from some distance away," muttered Pell.

Von Frakken stared at him condescendingly. "The greater the distance, the greater the chance of being observed. I thought you wanted me to be discreet?"

"I want you to be gone."

Von Frakken tutted. "Is your stubborn ignorance deliberate, Pell?" Suddenly, he had an idea and his old eyes lit up in his new skull. "Here! Observe!" He pushed the man gently and he walked compliantly into the centre of the room. Von Frakken fetched a pair of filled syringes and, standing behind the man, attached them both to a catheter that had been inserted into the man's neck, close to the top of his spinal column.

"Docility and aggression," said von Frakken with a grin, taking up a syringe in each hand. "Demand one or the other, you shall have it. Just a very small dose, I think."

He pressed the plunger beneath his right thumb, injecting a tiny amount of liquid. Almost immediately, the man's breathing increased. His face distorted with rage. Von Frakken whispered into the man's ear. "That chubby fellow, standing over there, he's your enemy."

Immediately, the man turned towards Pell and walked forward, his hands held out, grasping for Pell's throat, his expression blazing with hatred. Pell staggered back, terrified. Von Frakken laughed and quickly pressed down the left plunger. The man rapidly calmed, and within seconds was completely docile again. Von Frakken moved him to one side of the laboratory, where he stood in a blank-faced, lethargic stupor.

"What the devil—?" gasped Pell, wiping at his forehead with the back of his hand.

"You see?" laughed von Frakken, thoroughly enjoying himself. "As I explained to you, I am thinking *commercially*, for the very first time. My study of business has opened my eyes to a bold and tantalising future."

"What commercial use is turning someone into a raving nightmare?" cried Pell.

"You don't see it? You really don't? A simple chemical mixture, easily manufactured and sold to the military. An instantaneous warrior caste, to make the hordes of Genghis Khan seem like a collection of spinsters!"

Pell put a hand to his chest, feeling his heart gallop. He gulped, looking back and forth between von Frakken and his test subject with a mixture of stark horror and reluctant admiration.

"And this," said von Frakken, removing the two syringes and brandishing them with a flourish, "is nothing. An amusing parlour trick. Yet it could become as essential an item of equipment to the modern soldier as a gun and a stout pair of boots. You *must* see that?"

Pell's lips quivered. "I—yes, I suppose I do."

Von Frakken leaned across his workbench and tapped at the lid of the glass jar that Dr Polidori had returned to him shortly after their last meeting. Inside, pale and bloody, the section of flesh taken from Maria's arm. "These chemical mixtures are derived from *this*. The important work. *This* is where profits can be generated. You want products to sell? I will give you *Mankind* to sell."

Pell glanced at the slack-faced test subject. "It is immoral," he breathed unsteadily.

"Yes, Pell. But what is morality, compared to *money*? Money keeps you safe. Money is freedom. With enough money, you can break any barrier, take any action, evade any law. Money opens the ears of the masses and closes their eyes. Does it not?"

"It does," muttered Pell to himself.

"We are in a perfect position, you and I, to create freedom and power on a staggering scale. We are in London, in the living, beating heart of the British Empire. More than three quarters of the entire wealth of this Earth flows through its veins. What powers the Earth? Not governments or leaders, but the Colonial

Office and the legacy of the East India Company. It's a power we can grasp. I can refashion the world in my own image. Nature will be defeated forever."

"I think … " muttered Pell, " … you are mad."

"But you still want the money," smiled von Frakken. "You are to call a full meeting of the Promethean Society. Get the names from Clements and Polidori, tell them to arrange it immediately. It is time to share my vision of the future, and the members of the Society will be an important part of its realisation."

CHAPTER XXVI

The atmosphere in the Five Beggars was nervous and subdued. Some of the regulars, the minority of booze-ridden patrons, talked and revelled as usual but most whispered in huddles, either drinking more than usual or less, depending on their personal inclinations. A handful kept away from the pub altogether, but they were few and far between. Better to have fearful company than none at all and, in any case, what was spent on drink here would mostly be saved on fuel at home. The fireplace was banked up and roaring but the chill couldn't be dispelled.

The landlord surveyed his customers, his weight pressing hard against the counter. His eyes were hooded, his lips greased and his uncharacteristically pallid demeanour suppressed an anger that was kept in check on a hair-trigger. Beside him on the counter was a tin plate, scattered with the remains of that morning's bread and cheese. Once he'd examined his customers for the hundredth time, he glanced down at it and scowled.

"Oi, Millie," he grunted, holding the plate out to the new girl as she passed by. "Take this away."

"Yes, Mr Dobbs," muttered Maria. She retreated to the tiny scullery behind the counter.

The door to the street swung open, showing a patch of swirling darkness beyond, and the bearded Mr Crabtree arrived, accompanied by the rest of the regular newspaper-debaters. Dobbs's expression asked Crabtree for news; Crabtree's expression said there was none.

The newspaper-debaters took up their usual seats beside the counter. Mr Crabtree hesitated, not sure if he should give Dobbs a full report or not. "We went to the King's Head and the Waterside," he said at last, his voice moving carefully from word to word. "And the one up by the match factory, that little thin one."

Dobbs suddenly noticed that none of the match factory girls were in tonight except Gert, who was wrapped up beside the fire, sipping noisily from a tankard and watching the flames. Did the rest of them know something? Maybe Gert had—no. No, they'd have said. He grunted to himself and his thoughts flicked uselessly up and down the surrounding streets, searching for some forgotten corner—of course! that's it!—in which his sister might be hiding.

Stupid cow. *Who the hell had she gone off with?*

"We asked at all the shops on Commercial Street," said Mr Crabtree. "Y'know, places she went." He noticed that Dobbs was eyeing the copy of the *London Daily Examiner* that was folded up and sticking out of his pocket. He slid it free and put it on the table in front of him, leaving it folded and shuffling it uneasily.

"There's, umm—there's nothing in it, Frank."

"Y'sure?" growled Dobbs. "That the evenin' one?"

"Yeh, yeh," said Mr Crabtree quickly. He pointed to the whiskered, red-cheeked man sitting next to him. "Me and Jack went, both of us, di'n we Jack? But—well, the reporter bloke we spoke to was sympathetic ... "

"He said i's not really news," said Jack. Mr Crabtree shut him up with a withering look.

Dobbs shifted his weight around to face them, one arm leaning against the counter. "People gone missin'? Not news? What kind o' nit-buggering gibface did you talk to?"

"He was very sympathetic, Frank, he was," assured Mr Crabtree.

"Yer told 'im right?" said Dobbs. "Including them up the street? That's three! Same place, two nights!" He held up the relevant number of fingers.

"We told 'im," said Mr Crabtree, shaking his head, "but—he says if there's not no actual crime been done … "

"Wha?" cried Dobbs.

"There's not been a robbery or someone hurt, as we know of," said Mr Crabtree. "He said if there's not—y'know, evidence—like, bodies or somethin' … "

"Wha' about wha' Gert said? This toff Poll talked to?" At the sound of her name, Gert looked up from the fireplace, her eyes awash with alarm.

Mr Crabtree's tone was apologetic. "He just asked if the police are involved."

"Is'e bloody joking? Has'e ever bin down 'ere? *Eh?*" Dobbs's temper was spilling over and he slapped the counter a couple of times with the flat of his hand to make it subside. He stared at the counter, the grain of the wood, the stains and chips and worn edges, a thousand nights of noise and drinking. His mouth sunk into a downward curve and his voice dropped to a low rumble. "If it was this toff 'ad vanished, that'd be different. That'd be bloody news."

"If Gert was right," piped up Jack. "Her and Poll was both tight as a boiled owl."

Dobbs glared daggers at him. "Get yer bloody neck oil down yer and shut up. Millie! Fetch the wet!"

Maria busied herself with jugs of beer and gin. Above the background noise of the customers, she didn't notice the arrival of a new one. Inspector Charles Barré had self-consciously put away his monocle and tucked his pocket square out of sight, but he was so obviously out of place and ill at ease that he drew suspicious and hostile looks right across the pub. His awkwardly un-police-like air was all that prevented him being instantly identified as a detective. Maria only failed to spot him because she was facing away, pouring a cupful for Mr Crabtree, then weaving between tables to serve a sullen-looking set of workmen in the corner.

Dobbs pulled himself up to his full height as Barré approached the counter. Neither of them liked the look of each other. "Yer a new face," growled Dobbs. "Around 'ere last night, were yer?"

"No," blinked Barré.

"Not up the end of the street? Talking to passers-by? Passin' the time o'day?"

"I'm afraid not, I've never set foot around here."

"Is 'at right? Hey, Gert!" The factory girl looked up again. Dobbs pointed to Barré. "You seen 'im before?" Gert's deformed jaw shuddered for a moment, then she shook her head in a definite no.

Dobbs switched his attention back. "What, then?"

"I'm looking for a young woman," said Barré.

"If yer want tail, yer go over to Mrs Lewis, across the street."

"I mean a personal acquaintance. I've been informed she's in this area and I'm checking places she may be living or working."

Dobbs looked him up and down with quiet contempt, chewing at his lip. "She runnin' away? You sound like a bluebottle."

"That's not very likely, is it?" Barré smiled. "I'm just a citizen, searching on behalf of a friend." He caught Dobbs's momentary glance across the room and resisted the urge to follow it. By now, he was convinced he was on the right track.

"There's nobody 'round 'ere like that," sniffed Dobbs. "Only stranger is you."

Barré juggled a few coins in his hand. "I'll have a beer and a chat with your regulars. If you wouldn't object?" Dobbs slapped a smeary glass down on the counter.

Maria appeared at Barré's side. "It's all right, Mr Dobbs. I know this gentleman." She filled the glass from her beer jug. Surprised that she should be so bold, Barré raised his eyebrows for a moment, looking around the pub in case Maria had some kind of heavy-handed back-up. She led him to a broad bench near the window, the one normally occupied by the match factory girls, and sat opposite him. Dobbs returned to Mr Crabtree and his friends, but kept a suspicious watch over both Barré and Maria.

"You've blended in well," said Barré, his voice low enough not to be overheard above the ambient hum of conversation. "You look like a street urchin."

"I am a street urchin. How did you find me?"

"You accosted a police informant the other evening. He told us exactly where you were, once he'd asked a couple of friends and one of them happened to have seen that there was a new skivvy at the Five Beggars." He took a drink from his glass, examined it at arm's length with his lips pulling his neat moustaches to one side, then put it down. "You saw me before I saw you. I'm surprised you didn't make a run for it."

Maria pointed towards the street. "You're not exactly subtle. There's a cart out there that isn't loading or unloading. Not very common in Devon Row, so I assume it's full of your coppers. Everyone out in the street knows."

"What makes you think that?"

"They've all gone inside."

"So the next customer in here will spread the word, no doubt," muttered Barré with mild irritation. "Since you know the game's up, I'd appreciate your coming quietly."

"I'm not going anywhere," said Maria.

"You're under suspicion of murder."

"That informant was one of a gang that attacked the professor's house. Why else would I have tracked him down?"

"He says you robbed him, jumped him like a common mutcher."

"He lied. Why go to the trouble of informing on me if I'm nobody? I was taken from the house by force."

"If it's any consolation, I freely admit that you don't seem the killing type, but then few killers do. Barely half a dozen people even knew of your existence, so the problem with this story about a gang is one of motive. You need to be in custody. You've attracted attention and could easily start a panic if your … nature became public knowledge."

"Those attackers had a motive. They were led by Wilhelm von Frakken. He's alive and in London."

Barré sat up straight, frowning. "Alive? You seriously expect me to believe that?"

"He was extremely damaged."

"And the first thing he did was to chase you across half a continent?"

"I'm sure he has some sort of long-term plan," said Maria. "It involves me."

"Well," said Barré archly, "it's hardly going to succeed if you're sitting here, free as a bird."

Maria rolled up her sleeve. Taking care not to let anyone nearby overlook her arm, she showed Barré her livid, rectangular wound. The edges had continued to blur, as tendrils of growth knitted together. "Before I escaped from him, he did this."

"Which could be self-inflicted," said Barré with distaste, "but I'll grant you the benefit of the doubt. Was it punishment?"

"No, he's kept the flesh he took. He needs it for something. To grow more, presumably, first to repair himself I'd imagine. I have no idea what his ultimate aims may be, but I think we both know they will be appalling. I'm going to find him, and stop him, somehow."

"On the contrary, if what you claim is true you'll leave his fate in the hands of the law and the official constabulary. We have far more resources with which to find him."

"But fewer reasons. Why can't you let me go? Why won't you humans leave me alone?"

"Precisely because you can address us as 'you humans'—"

"I'm not going to allow you to lock me up, cut me apart or put me on show. By what right do humans have a monopoly on being in charge?"

"I'm not here to engage you in debate," said Barré. "You're to come with me. If you won't be cooperative then I have enough manpower to compel you."

"To subdue the monster," muttered Maria. "The ability of your species to hate is breathtaking."

"You consider yourself above humans like me, do you?"

"No, I most certainly do not, but I'm beginning to understand this world a little better. You think yourself superior to the people in this pub and on these streets. The only time the warm and well-fed look at us is when they can't look away. When we're their entertainment. Murders. Riots. The degenerate poor." She poked at the glass of beer on the table. "It's no wonder people poison themselves with this filthy stuff. Humans can't tolerate outsiders, they want everyone around them to be the same. Standardised. You've come here, in force, to deal with an outsider. Which I am, in every way. Instead, why not help the landlord over there? His sister has gone missing. And others. The last thing they'd consider is asking for help, because they know they'll never get it."

"Unfortunately, that sort of thing is nothing out of the ordinary, around here," said Barré.

"Ask yourself why. Humans. You're all just crawling around in the slime, biting and reproducing."

"Is that self-pity?" said Barré. "Or are you being hypocritical and thinking yourself superior?"

"I will not cooperate with you, Inspector. I'm going after von Frakken, and nothing is going to interfere with that." She stood up. "Is that clear?"

"Clear as day," said Barré. He leaned back, reached out, and tapped loudly on the window.

Heads swung in his direction. Maria turned and hurried for the staircase behind the counter.

"Wha's goin' on?" said Dobbs.

Barré was on his feet. "Stop that woman!"

Voices erupted across the room. A number of regulars jumped to their feet and blocked Barré's way, assuming this posh-looking stranger was up to something they wouldn't like.

"Out of my way!" he shouted above the din.

Dobbs's gaze wavered between Barré and the stairs, up which Maria was rapidly disappearing. The pub door was flung open with a crash and half a dozen uniformed constables entered. Gert, by the fire, shrank up into a ball and began to scream. Dobbs took a step back from the counter. There was a noisy surge of movement among the customers, tables and chairs pushed aside, fists raised.

Barré realised he needed to adopt a more underhand tactic. "That woman," he yelled, "is wanted on suspicion of murder! Let my officers through!"

Dobbs's head spun, the rolls of fat around his neck shaking. "*She* knows what 'appened to Poll?" he barked.

"She only turned up the other day," piped Mr Crabtree. "Bloody 'ell, what if that toff Gert saw wasn't a toff at all? What if it was her, in disguise?"

The constables, shouting commands, pushed their way past the tight crush of drinkers with Barré leading the way, Gert screeching and Mr Crabtree's newspaper-debaters looking bemused. Dobbs, his anger exploding with the possibility that he'd been harbouring a killer all along, was the first on the stairs.

Barré and two constables piled up behind him. Customers flowed over and around the counter and joined them. A flood of people rose up the steps, their weight making the whole stairway creak and sway alarmingly. Dobbs grunted, his cheeks flushing as he shifted his bulk with surprising speed, the others pressing at his back.

They burst onto the upper floor, an unstoppable wave of righteous resolve. Dobbs, who never bothered with the rents and left all such arrangements to Polly, kicked open every door he came to, unsure where Maria might be lurking. From behind one of them came an indignant male yell.

More and more surged up the stairs, filling the dark, seeping rooms with thudding feet and grasping hands. Dobbs slapped his fist on the last door and it shuddered aside.

Maria stood in the dark, silhouetted against the window, a sickly moonlight picking out her slightly irregular shape. For the first time, Dobbs could see past the grime on her face, to the unnervingly odd creature beneath. Her otherness, the living-doll quality of her form and movement, suddenly chilled him exactly as it had first chilled Barré and everyone else. There was something unnatural in the room, looking at him.

Barré was at Dobbs's shoulder and pulled him to one side. The inspector took a step towards Maria, hands outstretched, eyes locked on her. She retreated a little, and without turning pushed at the window behind her, which opened with a squeak.

Two constables forced their way through the noisy mob and flanked the inspector. The three of them spread out, inching ahead slowly. Maria crouched, her fingers curling into fists. For a moment, their stand-off was motionless.

With a sudden flick of Barré's head as a signal to the constables, the three policemen leaped to grab Maria, to a chorus of cries from the people crowding behind them. Silently, Maria dived through the open window. Barré's hands missed her by a hair's breadth.

"Back!" yelled Barré. "Back downstairs! Out of the way! Out of the way!" He began to heave through the mob. One of the constables stuck his head out of the window, blowing his whistle repeatedly to alert the officers who'd remained posted outside the pub.

Barré shouted and squeezed his way down the creaking staircase. Mr Crabtree, and the handful of other regulars who hadn't thundered after the dangerous fugitive, were milling about helping themselves to gin, while Gert sat wailing and stamping her feet with terror.

"Somebody shut that girl up!" cried Barré furiously, dashing across the room and into the street. Outside, there was a confusion of barked orders and blue uniforms, which quickly resolved itself into a haphazard line of constables looking upwards.

"Where the devil did she go?" demanded Barré. "She can't possibly have got past all of you!"

"She's on the roof, sir," said the nearest officer.

Barré spun on his heels and stepped back to get a clear view. A narrow shape was clambering up to the apex, hands gripping the upper ridge. She slipped and a slate tile tumbled away, twirling off the guttering and smashing at the inspector's feet.

Barré, always conscious that his background and his dapper precision made him the butt of mockery in the ranks, was bitterly aware that Maria's escape would see him the subject of gossip for some time to come. He abandoned the cautious, even-tempered habits of a lifetime and began to harangue his men like a drill sergeant major. "Don't let her get away! You four! That way up the street and circle around! You one, two, three, the other way! The rest of you keep up with her, go through houses, over walls, whatever it takes. Any man who loses sight of her will be *out on his ruddy ear!*"

Shocked into instant action by their inspector's unprecedented forcefulness, the constables scattered. They spread up and down Devon Row, co-ordinating their positions with yells and whistles, all of them continuously glancing up to keep track of the moving shadow high above them. Some disappeared down alleyways and across connecting yards, barging through crowded back rooms if they met a dead end, while others went further afield, trying to anticipate where the suspect would end up. Wherever they went, they stirred up a cacophony of shouts, screeches, howling children, barking dogs.

While the police covered the ground, Maria went from chimney stack to chimney stack as rapidly as she dared. The agile strength which had allowed her to amuse Millie by bounding up the stairs at Wenham Gardens now enabled her to jump from roof to roof. Several times she stumbled, her heart lurching with the sudden fear of falling, but her progress was more straight-line than the police could manage in the labyrinth of little streets below.

The constables lost track of her after fifteen minutes or so. They went on searching for another half hour.

CHAPTER XXVII

"Must we do this here?" grumbled Jabez Pell.

Von Frakken laughed and held his arms wide. "What better place could there be? Tonight is a special occasion and it demands a suitably dramatic and appropriate setting."

Although the workers had now gone, the factory floor at Pell & Blight Ltd was still warm from the long day's work. Machines ticked and clicked as they cooled. The air was liquid with human sweat and mechanical exhalations. The vats wheezed softly and the throb of the steam engines subsided minute by minute, like the failing of a heart.

An open space, close to the stairs and beneath the high internal window of the counting office, had been cleared of the stacked boxes of finished goods it usually contained. A series of oil lamps were placed on the floor. They half-surrounded von Frakken's makeshift workbench, brought from upstairs, and the dozen chairs arranged in front of it which had been taken from various parts of the building.

Pell's voice echoed around the forest of machines. "I normally have a man stoke the generators at night, saves starting from cold every morning. We'll lose production tomorrow." Von

Frakken didn't appear to be taking any notice. He was busy putting a bottle of whiskey and some glasses on a side table.

Pell muttered to himself. "Good thing we haven't had a night shift in months." He looked up, as if he was trying to breathe above the fug of labour that hung around, but he couldn't see the ceiling. It was pitch black outside and the light from the lamps barely extended twenty feet. From the darkness, the machines watched like a zoo of ogres carved in metal, stilled and mutant.

Pell looked at the sheet which covered a collection of objects on the workbench. "That thing under there is disgusting," he said.

"That thing," said von Frakken, unconcerned, "is the last stepping stone on our way to victory." He surveyed the scene, pleased with himself. He tapped lightly at the cap on the whiskey bottle and smiled.

Voices could suddenly be heard. "They're here," said Pell, trotting awkwardly to greet their guests. Dr Clements and Dr Polidori led a group of nine other members of the Promethean Society, their words and footsteps suddenly reverberating around the factory floor.

There were eight men and one woman, their ages ranging from late-thirties to late-sixties. Five were academics—four of them university lecturers, one a professor of philosophy—and the rest were either medics or independent researchers. Several had gained notable success in their careers, despite the controversy of their views and the dubious ethics of their methods or, as they would prefer, the progressive originality of their views and the unsentimental utility of their methods. None of them, hampered as most of them were by the need for an income and for maintaining some semblance of standing in society, had been able to dedicate their lives to galvanic and Hallerian studies in the same way as von Frakken. They revered his work almost as much as did Clements and Polidori.

Nevertheless, between them they had achieved some impressive results and the information they chose to pool had been of great benefit to other members of the Society. Dr Joseph Stokes of Birmingham, for example, had kept a dying child alive for almost six months through the application of electrical stimulation to the brain. Dr Anne Patchkey of Liverpool had developed two devices, one for insertion into the chest cavity to maintain the regular beating of damaged heart muscle, and one to restart a temporarily interrupted heart. No less than five of them had successfully transferred at least one organ between human patients, although none had achieved this on the scale of the St Saviour's surgeons.

Von Frakken greeted them all warmly and, after a few minutes of pleasant and admiring small-talk, ushered them to the chairs in front of the workbench.

"Gentlemen, and lady," boomed Clements, his unctuous bombast in full bloom, "it is, without doubt, undoubtedly, indeed a pleasure, to welcome you all to the first full assembly of the Society in more than twelve months. Full, that is, with one exception, most unfortunate, this being Dr Pinkloe of Penzance, unable to attend owing to the unexpected result of an experiment involving an item procured from a travelling circus. However, that being the case, we are most indebted to our guest of honour, a colleague whom, I may say, with all due modesty, I have been myself able to help in no insignificant way, only a matter of days since." He beamed at von Frakken, who beamed back. "It is at his request that we are here gathered in order, so I understand, to hear of his latest progress. Thus, gentlemen, and lady, our esteemed associate, Wilhelm von Frakken."

There was a ripple of applause as Clements took his seat between Pell and Polidori. Von Frakken stood squarely in front of his sheet-draped workbench, his one mobile eye scanning across them genially until there was silence.

"Seventy-seven years ago," he said, his voice clear and authoritative, "Signore Giovanni Aldini, the nephew of the great Luigi Galvani himself, toured Europe. On his visit to London, he gave a scientific demonstration so intriguing, so dramatic and unusual, that it inspired the founding of this very Society."

There was another ripple of appreciation. "I am standing here before you," said von Frakken, "as living proof that the lines of enquiry he, and others, set in motion continue to be every bit as intriguing and dramatic. I understand that Dr Clements has given you a brief outline of my—let's say, recent history."

He gestured to the stitching over his head and the Society murmured in amusement and respectful awe. His facial muscles and right arm contracted sharply for a couple of seconds.

"Tonight, I intend to honour the memory of Signore Aldini by conducting a demonstration of my own, one that will be a tribute to the outstanding progress, and to the many sacrifices, that we have all made. That we are here is thanks to men who stand tall in the history of science. Men such as Thomas Willis, two hundred and fifty years ago, who postulated the delivery of messages along the nervous system. Or Newton, studying the transmission of force, Von Haller's *vis nervosa*, Benjamin Franklin's therapeutic use of static, Alessandro Volta's work on electrical storage, and of course my own grandfather, Victor von Frakken, the pioneer of reanimation. The list is both long and inspiring, and we have made great strides in their wake. I see with us Dr Fish, whose discovery of the four-part categorisation of blood, and subsequent methods of counteracting their incompatibilities, have proved invaluable to us all. I see Mr William Bell, whose recent production of living insects from electrically charged crystals *proved* that Andrew Crosse was right in 1836."

Von Frakken paused while the Society bathed in self-congratulation for a moment. "I will now demonstrate the most recent results of my own efforts. They point the way to nothing less than a vision of the future. It is a vision inspired by *this*!" He flung his arms out in the direction of the factory's machines. "By commerce! By the power of the profit motive!"

He walked behind the workbench and drew the sheet away. The Society leaned forward, fascinated by the collection of objects that were revealed.

To one end was a human arm, severed just below the elbow. It was held horizontally, off the surface of the workbench, in a metal laboratory stand. From the hefty fingers and dark forearm hair, it had obviously been taken from a man. At the other end, encased in a large glass jar, was a brain which nearly-floated on the surface of a yellow-green liquid. Between them was a head, a woman's, fixed upright on a steel container. The top section had been removed entirely, cut neatly along a line just above her heavily painted eyebrows. The head was angled so that the Society members could see that the skull was hollow inside, and that the face was bloodless and slack, with closed eyelids and drooping lips.

Between the arm and the brain, and between the head and the brain, ran filaments grown from the artificial flesh von Frakken had cut from Maria. They were narrow and pale, and quivered slightly. The only other connections were from the brain to a small battery and a control box that sat beside the jar.

"You will observe," continued von Frakken, "that the brain has been extracted in full, and that the only link between brain and skull is composed of tissue that does *not originate* from the subject's body. The nature of this link, I will explain shortly. There is a similar link to the arm. The apparatus is powered by a simple, high-yield voltaic pile, but of course this would be unnecessary if using a complete or living specimen. I will apply the correct voltage."

He bent over, resting his elbows on the workbench, and slowly turned a fat dial on the control box. A hum of power pulsed through the air. As he increased the current, the artificial connections began to vibrate and turn, as if drinking in the electrical energy. The liquid around the brain began to bubble and pop.

Von Frakken held the voltage steady for a few seconds, then took a small surgical knife from his pocket and, holding it by the blade, rapped the handle a couple of times on the workbench, in front of the severed head.

The eyes snapped open. They swerved left and right, dulled but alive. The cheeks, rouged with make-up, started to shake and puff. The mouth shivered. Von Frakken loomed over the workbench.

"Can you hear me?" he said.

The eyes continued to swivel and jerk as if they couldn't stop. The lips wriggled haphazardly. Von Frakken adjusted the voltage and tried again.

"Can you hear me?—Can you hear me?"

The lips shook and the tongue poked in and out. The mouth and throat struggled to form sounds. It managed a half-syllable and repeated it a number of times before the right muscles would respond. "Y ... Y ... Ye ... Y ... Y ... es."

"Good," smiled von Frakken. "What can you see?"

The face wrinkled and stretched, its upper lip pulling into a lacrimal pose. "P ... P ... Peep ... ple."

"People, that's good." He turned and addressed the Society. "You will note that the brain activity is communicated by this single link alone." He went back to the head. "What is your name?— Tell me your name."

The eyes fluttered and skipped, the mouth shuddered. "P ... Pol ... P ... P ... Polly ... P ... W ... Where ... Wh ... Wh ... Pol ..."

"Move your fingers for me," said von Frakken. "Move your fingers."

Almost at once, the fingers on the severed arm began to twitch. In a few seconds, they were flexing wildly. Von Frakken walked around to the end of the workbench and grasped them.

"Pleased to meet you."

The Society laughed heartily. Von Frakken ran a pointing finger over the connections between head, arm and brain. "As I have stated, this connective tissue is not taken from either of the original human bodies you see before you. Here is the essence of my demonstration! *This* is what shows the progress achieved since Aldini's arrival in London all those years ago and my purpose in honouring him this evening! For this tissue has not been taken from a human being at all. In fact, it is taken from no living being of any kind. It is artificial, manufactured from galvanised chemicals and minerals in a process of my own design."

He jabbed at the hand with the point of his surgical knife. Polly Dobbs's face reacted to the pain.

The Society hummed with amazement. Pell sat, pale and drawn, feeling lost and that everything was overtaking him, that he would never understand where he found himself.

A cultured voice came from somewhere behind Clements. "Mr Von Frakken, do you mean that these connections are akin to the Post Office telegraphic system? They are wires?"

"On the contrary, Dr Fish," said von Frakken, "they are biological. They are nerve tissue exactly as is found inside every one of us, except that they were grown outside of any womb, or any human developmental conditions."

The hum of interest rose in pitch. Meanwhile, von Frakken switched off the apparatus and the panicked, screaming thoughts in Polly Dobbs's brain faded away into nothingness.

"Absolutely extraordinary—"

"—can hardly believe it."

"Years ahead, *years* ahead—"

Von Frakken soaked up their astonishment as he crossed to the side table he'd set up. He uncapped the whiskey and began to pour out twelve measures.

"Von Frakken," called out Dr Joseph Stokes of Birmingham, "can this process of yours be adapted? To create more than neurones? If so, the possibilities must be enormous."

"A very intelligent and far-sighted question," said von Frakken, continuing to pour. "And indeed it can. Using different formulations of chemicals and specially prepared enzymes, using varied electrical fields, I can create any organ of the human body, from a simple sheet of skin, to a femur, to a brain."

"Great Scott!" declared Dr Joseph Stokes of Birmingham with a laugh. "The potential applications are legion! Sir, I have little doubt that history will record you as the greatest benefactor of our time!" He looked around his fellow Society members. "I'm sure I speak for all of us here, if I extend to you our congratulations and our sincerest enthusiasm for all our future endeavours alongside you!"

There was a rousing wave of approval. Von Frakken carried a large serving tray over to them, laden with whiskey-charged glasses.

"This'll be one in the eye for all the doubters!" piped up Dr Fish. "All the gossips, all the moaners and ethics committees. Progress relies on fearless, unemotional enquiry."

Applause. Von Frakken toured the guests, each taking a glass. He took the last one himself, leaving no glass for Pell, and returned to his spot in front of the workbench. Pell's eyes darted from glass to glass, huffing to himself. He craned his neck to see the bottle on the side table, but it was empty. He quietly slipped his freshly refilled hip flask from his pocket.

"I would like to share with you now, my vision of the future," said von Frakken, his voice low and calm, swirling his whiskey. "The human body is weak. It is a bag of flesh and bone. It ages rapidly, it breaks easily and it is prone to destruction even by the tiniest creatures that crawl upon the Earth. How much of human history, I wonder, has been conditioned by that weakness? We fight to survive through enough years to give ourselves a life, we struggle to preserve our youth and our families, we call upon our gods to protect us from harm. Mankind, clinging to this rock in space, is forced to battle every plague, every famine, every flood and fire that an uncaring Nature flings in our path. Because we are human, and we are soon damaged. However, what if Nature could be beaten, defeated forever? What if we could overcome our weakness? What if we could master ourselves as we have mastered the ploughed field and the steam engine? By replacing weak flesh with strong, this is something we *can* achieve. I believe Mankind has a glorious future that will dwarf the past! To the future!"

"The future!" The Society raised their glasses and drank. Von Frakken emptied his in one swift gulp. Pell quietly suckled at his flask.

"I foresee that this golden future will be underpinned by, indeed yes, by gold! By the driving, unrelenting, unstoppable might of commerce. Once that is realised, once that is known, then my vision becomes inevitable. Not simply possible, but inevitable. I foresee three phases to the transformation of the human race.

"The first is the one that begins here, in this very factory. Around you are the instruments of change, the machines that will make the first products based upon my unique and ground-breaking work, products that are possible through the development of my artificial flesh. What are they, you ask? Mr Pell will introduce the first to the market, very soon. You'll see. Its profits will pave the way for others, which in their turn will create more profit and more products, and so on.

"Before long, we will live in a world where a lost limb can be replaced with ease, not by using the limb of another human, something I and my predecessors have accomplished in the past, but with a limb grown from scratch. Where diseased lungs, filled with soot, can be replaced with new ones. Where burns, deformities and defects of birth can be remedied with new skin, new muscle, new cartilage. People will want these things, so very, very badly. They will cry out for freedom from disease and pain. Imagine it! That demand will be colossal! Spectacular! And the ensuing profits, equally immense.

"This first phase need not be limited to organs. My process of growing artificial flesh can also grow organic substances with which to bathe the brain. Thus can be induced almost any sensation or state of mind you care to name. This *alone* has a hundred practical applications. The worker can be spurred on to dig, the sportsman to win, the scholar to think, or the madman to find rest.

"All these things, these products, directly alter the human body and thus alter the very foundation of Nature's glacial, evolutionary grind. Spencer's 'survival of the fittest' will be superseded by the survival of the altered. Or, to the economist, the survival of the consumer, the survival of those who buy. Thomas Huxley himself, here in London, states that the progress of humanity may not only entail a break with the forces of evolution, but *require* one.

"Thus, phase two, when such alteration becomes normal. After a few years of my products being avidly desired, then they will become unavoidable. They will become the routine solutions to a thousand problems. Once economies of scale are in operation, as so many economic theorists argue, then commodities become cheaper and as they become cheaper, so they become more commonplace. The replacement of a stopped heart or a ruined kidney will no longer be merely possible, it will be expected.

"Thus, phase three. From unavoidable to indispensable. From medication and repair to the abandonment of the evolved body entirely. There will be complete human forms created from my artificial flesh, at prices determined by the market, via which the sick and dying can find a renewed life, superior to any that was possible before. Initially, of course, such transitions will require the storage and re-insertion of complete human minds. My research had made significant advancement in this respect, but thus far has been able to extract from living brains only facts, skills, specific memories, not individuality. An entirely new mind can currently be constructed—and I have done this with great success—but containing the totality of an existing one is, for the present, elusive. However, I am fully confident that this difficulty will be overcome soon, aided by the profits generated over the coming months.

"The wider picture remains intact. Weak human beings will demand strong new bodies, and I will supply that demand, with artificial flesh that is easily changed, that is resistant to disease, that will last for hundreds of years. The choice for all will be an easy one, between a frail and limited human existence or one made better in every way. In the open market of everyday society, there will arise competition to attain this better existence. No mother would deny her child health, or strength, or long life, the very idea is absurd.

"And then, biological reproduction itself can be consigned to history! The growing of one human being inside another will come to be seen as archaic and disgusting! Better the clean and controllable environment of the Erlenmeyer flask. The fresh minds of our infant sons and daughters will be produced in the same way as their physical forms—by design, and to order.

"I would estimate that the completion of these three phases may occupy the space of fifty years or so. By 1930, there may be no more human flesh at all. Evolved humans, as they are now, will have *chosen* their own extinction, willingly, through the simple mechanism of profit. Mankind will become a commodity! Mankind will become a manufactured item, like any other, assembled from skin and bone. People made in factories, like this one, to exact specifications and only when required. No more surplus population. An exact match of supply and demand.

"People may even be manufactured in a dozen different shapes and sizes, depending upon market conditions. Brawny miners, leaders with enlarged brains, simplified workers for manual labour. An eternity of structure and certainty, thanks to free enterprise!

"It is a vision I might never have seen, had I not found myself in London! How different the world might be, but for life's little caprices!

"Economics is the everlasting common denominator. Pounds and pennies, buying and selling, fulfilling wants and needs, accumulating in masses to power the production of more wants and needs. Profit is a beautiful, cyclical thing. Don't you think, Pell?"

Pell shifted awkwardly in his seat, his bulbous face sweating. He put his empty hip flask back into his pocket. "P-Profit, yes," he muttered. "Fair reward for useful endeavour."

"Quite," agreed von Frakken, grinning.

Pell pointed at the members of the Promethean Society. "But how in God's name does *this* profit us, may I ask? Why didn't you tell me—?"

One of the eleven, a surgeon from Dorset, was dead. A fatal embolism, caused by an adverse reaction to the enzyme he'd swallowed in his whiskey. The others, including Dr Clements and Dr Polidori, were silent and staring, their minds exiled into a nightmarish fog of confusion from which they struggled in vain to escape.

"You wanted me to avoid sourcing specimens from the local streets," said von Frakken with impatience. "I have done so. I'll store them upstairs and keep them quiet. One or two may die before I get around to using them, there's no point in their being fed. Don't fret, Pell, all unwanted material will be shovelled into the boiler of one of your generators over there." He grasped the dead man's hair and turned his head back and forth. "A nuisance," he sighed. "The dosage couldn't be precise. I suppose I can use some of the organs. Although! I had an idea recently, of adapting an abandoned revivification technique. I may try that."

"But you drank the whiskey too," mumbled Pell.

"One medicine can easily be made to counteract another," smiled von Frakken.

"They must have families? Friends? These two will be missed at St. Saviour's! Where the hell are they supposed to have gone?"

"Their destination was communicated in advance only to Clements. He's hardly likely to have broadcast this address. Nobody will come here."

"Enquiries will be made."

Von Frakken's voice dropped to a conspiratorial whisper. "If so—dear me, the temptations of the city—scandalous and shameful indulgences—last seen entering a Limehouse rookery."

The mention of scandals snapped Pell's thoughts back to larger concerns. He swallowed hard, then wiped his forehead and around his collar. The contents of his flask, and the closeness of the air in here, were making him feel unwell. "Why, for pity's sake?" he said weakly. "I thought these were your peers, your allies? I thought you wanted their help with these new products? Products, I remind you, I have yet to see! The situation—"

"In entering either a new or existing market, the most advantageous position is that of a monopoly. All those who may have understood the workings of our forthcoming products and approached competing manufacturers have now been removed as potential business rivals." He turned to the Society and clapped his hands loudly. "Stand up! Stand up!"

Unsteadily, they did as they were told. Their expressions wavered between fear and dumb lassitude and their arms hung heavily, any attempts to reach out ending in slow, feeble grasps at the air. They were conscious only of a blank, featureless half-dream of elusive thought, of waiting, waiting. Clements's jaw worked idly, drooling a little as if chewing treacle. Polidori's head lolled in small, uncertain motions.

"The products!" demanded Pell. "I need them *now*! I need the money *now*! You may swan about as if you're Sir Stafford Northcote, but you don't appear to understand that credit has a limit! Credit, both monetary and in the turning of a blind eye! Good God, it's like I'm living in some feverish phantasm from which I can't escape!"

"Tomorrow," said von Frakken calmly. "Now that I have my sample of artificial flesh back, now that specific tests have subsequently been carried out, now that competing interests are overcome. Tomorrow."

"What? I can have something? To sell?"

"Yes. All is now ready. We begin. Tonight, I have paid tribute to Signore Aldini by staging a demonstration along similar lines. You, in turn, can stage a demonstration of your own. Not scientific, but commercial. One which requires your salesmanship, your business acumen."

Pell was taken aback for a moment. He wiped his sweating palms against his waistcoat. "Yes—good. I should damn well think so—what is it, precisely? What will I have to sell?"

Von Frakken's smile was broken for a second by a spasmodic twist of his right side. "You will have it, in a small, round tin."

BOOK THE THIRD

CHAPTER XXVIII

"Madam, there's a peculiar woman at the back gate."

Sophia Meers frowned at her maidservant. "Peculiar, Edith? In what way?"

Edith, dumpy and sour-faced, shrugged her shoulders in a way that shifted her ill-fitting dress up her broad neck. "Peculiar. Dirty, she is. Scruffy and funny-looking. Bit creepy, I reckon."

Sophia immediately wondered if … "Who is she? What does she want?"

"I was going to tell her to sling her hook. She says she knows you. And Dr Meers."

Sophia's tongue glanced across her lips as she thought. "She didn't give her name?"

Shrug. "Says she knows you. Knows *your* names."

"Where's my husband? Is he still upstairs?"

"Far as I know."

She came to a decision. "Ask her to wait for a minute or two. I'll send Thomas out to her."

Edith trudged casually back down the corridor while Sophia, lifting her skirts a little, hurried up to a room on the second floor that was part of the way to being converted into a nursery. Dr

Meers was in the middle of a jumbled assortment of boxes and bric-a-brac, rooting through papers in an old tea chest.

He flashed her a smile as she entered. "Tell me, my dear, how on earth have we accumulated all this detritus?"

"Tom, that horrible synthetic creation, the one George showed us, Maria. I think she's here."

"What?" Meers dropped the papers back into the chest. "Where?"

"Quickly, we can see from the back bedroom."

They sped into a neatly cosy room, set aside for visitors, which overlooked the narrow garden at the rear of the house. Half the garden was lawn and flowers, the other a flourishing vegetable patch. At the end of the slabbed path that ran from the back door was a low wooden gate. Edith was sauntering her way towards a figure who stood in the alley beyond, used for deliveries.

"That's her," breathed Meers. "What's she doing here?"

"She's wanted by the police," said Sophia. "Suppose she wants us to hide her?"

"Then, until we hear her out, we will keep her hidden."

"Tom, we can't! She could be dangerous. She might have murdered George and that poor servant girl!"

Meers glared at her. "You know I don't believe that, not for a moment! I'm surprised at you. Where's your compassion gone?"

"In here," said Sophia, a hand on her domed belly. "I told Edith you'd go out to her."

"Good. I'll find out what's been happening."

"Tell her to go away."

"Go down to the sitting room. I'll bring her inside, I need to talk to her."

"Tom!"

Meers held her shoulders. "There is no danger. I am certain. Please."

Sophia looked down at the garden, at the back of Edith's head, at Maria's long hands holding the top of the gate. A deep, uneasy fear stirred in her veins. Without another word, she went back downstairs.

In the sitting room, she paused for a moment then went to the bureau. She spent a minute hastily writing a note and sealed it into an envelope. She listened at the sitting room door and, hearing nothing, stepped out into the hall.

"Edith!" she hissed. Nothing stirred. "Edith!"

She was about to call again when Edith appeared at the end of the hallway. "Edith, when are you going to the shops?"

"About half an hour. Same as always."

"Take this with you," she said in a hushed tone. "I'd ask you to go at once, but my husband will notice you've gone if he's bringing that—that visitor into the house, and I don't want a break of routine to make him suspect anything. Here, take it! You'll see it's addressed to a man Thomas knows at Scotland Yard. Please deliver it, in person, direct into his hand."

"Just post it," said Edith, pulling a face.

"It needs to get there straight away. Take a cab. It's a journey of five minutes, then come back and go to the shops as you normally would. Is that understood?"

"Can't I send a boy?"

"No. Please do it yourself. It's extremely important. And equally important *not* to tell my husband about it. Please. Understood?"

Edith shrugged. "Yes."

Sophia darted back into the sitting room. Edith, the letter stuffed into the front pocket of her pinafore, passed Dr Meers as she reached the way down to the kitchen. The doctor's peculiar visitor looked to Edith like some lush dragged from the gutter. What a state. Smelled to make you sick, too.

Meers noticed Edith's sneer. "This is a patient, Edith. Would you bring us some tea, please, in the sitting room?"

"Yes."

"And something to eat."

"You just had breakfast."

"For our guest."

"Oh."

Maria was already finding the house very warm. She'd become acclimatised to the cold of the streets and the single fireplace of the Five Beggars.

Walking into the Meers's sitting room, she felt a strange, heart-pulling rush of emotion. The room's comforting homeliness, its soft and enveloping domesticity, almost moved her to tears after the unrelenting hardship of Whitechapel and Spitalfields.

The bureau was tucked into one corner, and in the corner opposite was a narrow dresser dotted with small objects, souvenirs of seaside holidays, arranged around a leafy pot plant. Above the hearth was a large, antique mirror, enhancing the cloud-dulled daylight into a bluish glow, its ornate wooden frame filled with niches and protrusions on which stood porcelain figurines. Over the delicately green wallpaper hung painted scenes, mostly of beaches and rugged coastal landscapes. Thickly upholstered chairs were arranged on a brown-and-gold patterned rug that almost spanned the room, with a footstool and a small book stand beside them.

Sophia sat furthest from the door, her hands held tightly entwined in her lap. Dr Meers sat down next to her. Maria, self-conscious of the layered grime that covered her clothes and shoes, perched on the edge of a high-backed armchair.

She looked around herself. "This is a lovely house," she said. "You have nice things."

"Thank you," said Sophia quietly.

Dr Meers sat forward. "Maria, we're eager to know where you've been, and what has happened to you. You may speak freely. You can trust us both."

"I can trust no-one."

"I can assure you that we place no credence whatsoever in the wild stories that have been circulating in the press. Do we, Sophia?"

"Really?" said Maria. "Perhaps you should."

Sophia felt the hairs on the back of her neck bristle. At that moment, Edith brought in tea and a plate of hot buttered toast, eyeing Maria with distaste.

"I'll be off to the shops soon."

"Thank you, Edith," said Sophia.

Dr Meers continued to talk while Sophia poured cups of tea and Maria devoured her toast. "I'm aware that the police have been making extensive enquiries as to your whereabouts, but I've spoken to Inspector Barré myself and he's entirely open to my point of view, but naturally he wishes to err on the side of caution. Which reminds me. Have you, by any chance, been in contact with anyone at St. Saviour's? I have a particular reason for asking."

Maria finished a mouthful. "At the hospital itself? No."

"Not with either Dr James Clements or Dr Leonard Polidori?"

"I've never heard those names before. Why? Do they know about me?"

"I think that's very unlikely," said Meers, scratching at his smooth chin. "However, since you're here, I'll need to speak to them later today. I did attempt to find Clements yesterday, as I hadn't had an opportunity to see him in person earlier, but I was told that neither of them have been in attendance on the wards or in their consulting rooms since the previous afternoon."

Maria finished her toast. "Has Barré told you that Wilhelm von Frakken is alive and in London?"

"What?" cried Meers.

"Your—?" murmured Sophia.

"*Alive?* You've seen him?" said Meers.

Maria sipped her tea and, speaking as calmly and dispassionately as she could, gave the Meers an account of everything that had happened to her since their last meeting in Professor Hobson's office at the museum: the attack on the house; the murders and the man she'd killed; her encounter with Von Frakken; her betrayal by Hobson's housekeeper Mrs Sewell; her wanderings around the city; Devon Row and the pick-axe man; her flight from the police at the Five Beggars.

As she spoke, she appeared to diminish, as if the words had been holding her in place and were now draining her body of energy. Dr Meers glanced at his wife and she seemed deep in thought, listening intently.

Maria puffed her cheeks and looked up from her empty tea cup. "Before I came to your back gate, I walked all the way to the professor's house in Wenham Gardens. I really don't know why. I suppose I was muddle-headed enough to be looking for—what?—a past? A simpler time? I imagined, for some reason, I'd be able to walk back inside, but the place is boarded up."

"Yes," said Dr Meers. He paused, looking down at the pattern of the rug, not sure how much to reveal. "George had a brother, near Bristol. They hadn't spoken for some years, I understand. George was regarded as the black sheep of the family, something related to an argument with his parents, apparently, whose side the brother took. Anyway, he's taken charge of the estate and it seems he's to sell the house. I have his address in Somerset, if there's any item of George's belongings, or anything he gave you, that you … ?"

Maria shook her head. "All he gave me, I carry inside my head," she said. "I'm fearful about where I'll end up, and what will happen once Barré catches up with me, as he or some other representative of the law will eventually do. I really can't spend a few hundred years as a wanted fugitive, now, can I?"

"It was self-defence. That thug had it coming," said Meers.

"It was anger. I did an evil thing."

"With sound reason."

"I am no different to whatever benighted monster Victor von Frakken stitched together from the dead all those years ago."

"That's nonsense," said Meers.

"A human being wouldn't be let off, why should I?"

Meers ran a hand through his grey-flecked hair. "Or, as our friend Jabez Pell would say, you can't put a talking horse on trial."

"Thomas!" snapped Sophia.

"Whatever may happen afterwards," said Maria, "my goal has been to find von Frakken. I've tried and I've failed. I need your help, despite my stubborn assumptions to the contrary. I have to admit that, at the very least."

"First," said Meers, "you need rest. You look absolutely done-in. That's my medical diagnosis."

"I sleep very little, but I do feel very tired," said Maria. With her elbows on her knees, her head dipped to rest on her hands. Her long fingers were spread across her cheeks like the legs of a large spider. "When I sleep," she said wearily, "it's as if my mind starts to feed off me. Everything that's crammed into my brain starts to shout. And always, there is a huge Eye, judging me. Always this Eye, always judging. I try to escape, but I can't. I wake up in terror. It must *mean* something, I suppose."

"No doubt an alienist would be most interested," grinned Meers gently.

"Will you help me? I was wrong to think I could succeed alone."

"Of course. That maniac von Frakken must be brought to justice. You say he's going to *repair* himself?"

"He'll have to, in some way. If he's not already done so. Nobody could exist in that state for long. What he took from my arm must be sufficient for *something*, at least for his immediate needs but, as soon as he can, he wants to anatomise me for raw materials."

"That's horrible," muttered Sophia, one hand shaky in front of her lips, the other guarding her stomach. Maria seemed to notice Sophia's bump for the first time.

"Are you going to have a baby?"

"Yes," said Sophia, with a crinkled, uncertain smile. In listening to their visitor, her heart had begun to thaw. "In February. I've felt him moving again this morning, Tom."

Maria stared at Sophia's bump for a moment, half fascinated, half repelled. One human, forming inside another. Was her own birth really any more strange?

"Before we can decide on a plan of action, Maria," said Meers, getting to his feet, "we must give you a chance to gather your strength and get yourself cleaned up. I'll show you to our guest room." He shot a look at Sophia. "My dear?"

Sophia smiled at him and nodded. "I'll have a word with Edith."

"Thank you," said Maria. "These doctors, Clements was it? Polidori? We don't need a plan of action, if you think they may have some sort of connection to me, then we should go to them directly."

"Very well," said Meers.

He led Maria out into the hall and upstairs. As soon as they were out of sight, Sophia hurried along the corridor and called down. "Edith! ... Edith?"

With a look of alarm on her face, she descended into the kitchen, her skirts rustling. No Edith in the kitchen. No Edith in the back garden. Flustered, Sophia went up to the dining room. No Edith. What time was it? Where was there a clock?

"Edith!"

No Edith anywhere. Sophia dashed to the front door and stood on the step, looking up and down the cold, grey street. Cabs and carts trotted back and forth, blocking her view of the people walking on the far side of the road. Was that—? She caught a glimpse of the housemaid outside the greengrocer's on the corner.

She waved with both hands. "*Edith!*"

Edith peered at her sullenly for a moment, then slowly made her way across the road, paying little attention to the carts jostling around her.

"Edith," gasped Sophia, "did you leave early? Are you on your way back?"

"No. I'm just going now."

"Did you deliver that letter? Have you still got it?"

"Urgent, you said."

"I did. Have you still got it?"

Edith sniffed and reached into her pinafore. She handed over the slightly crumpled letter.

"Thank you," sighed Sophia. "Well, I'll let you get on."

She closed the door with Edith still standing on the step, and ripped the letter in two. She went back into the sitting room and dropped the pieces onto the fire.

CHAPTER XXIX

The ballroom of the Clanborough Hotel on Bond Street was the third largest in London, built to comfortably accommodate three hundred. Tall columns were recessed into the walls, to give the impression of a grand colonnade. On the ceiling, thirty feet above the polished floor, were six circular mouldings from which hung enormous, lead crystal chandeliers, designed in the Adam neoclassicist style. They spun the daylight into something that glittered and shone.

The floor was filled with perfectly aligned circular tables. Each was covered in a crisp, white cotton tablecloth, and each had a floral centrepiece of red and white roses.

One hundred and seven people were in attendance at an invitation-only event, an Afternoon Tea organised by Mr Jabez Pell, noted industrialist, sole proprietor of Pell & Blight Ltd. One hundred and sixty had been invited, but some were unable to attend owing to the short notice given for the event. Others had turned down the invitation for exactly the same reason.

Most of the attendees were seated around the tables, sipping Darjeeling and Earl Grey or selecting glazed pastries from tiered silver racks, while others congregated in social groups. A coterie of liveried waiters danced smooth attendance, gliding around tables delicately inclining their heads in answer to requests.

The guests were almost exclusively from among the city's most respected, most influential, most unobtrusively powerful. Here were bankers and brokers, landowners and captains of industry, two Viscounts, two newspaper proprietors, three Members of Parliament and a Duke, along with a number of Dr Clements's and Dr Polidori's ex-patients, including Colonel and Mrs Trevelyan and the elderly Lady Bitterlea. Several fashionably dressed women were gathered at Lady Bitterlea's table, eager to share her delight at the success of her recent surgery and the address of her doctors. Lady Bitterlea gleefully remarked on the rediscovered pleasure of buying shoes, while Colonel Trevelyan, a few tables away, caused further hilarity with his here's-me-using-my-new-eye routine.

The tinkling of a little glass bell cut across the hubbub of voices. For some seconds it seemed that nobody had heard it, but then the standing guests took their seats and one hundred and seven faces, all of them registering an indulgent tolerance, were turned in the direction of Jabez Pell.

He stood next to a table which had been separated out from the rest and placed to one side of the ballroom, so that he was clearly visible by everyone present. His evening dress, complete with wing collar and tailcoat, neatly cased his rotund figure. He could feel copious amounts of sweat trickling down the small of his back. He stood very formally, with legs together and hands clasped, so that nobody could see how much he was shaking with nerves. The only thing on the table was a small, round metal tin.

Despite Pell's anxiousness, he was exultant at the sight in front of him. A demonstration of his own, von Frakken had said. Salesmanship, he had said.

Pell cleared his throat and he spoke at an authoritative volume. "Good afternoon, ladies and gentlemen. I am honoured to be among such august company, and I thank you most sincerely for your kind attendance. I do hope you have had a pleasant time thus far. They do an excellent bun here." Smiling broadly, he waited for the amusement to subside. "I am aware that this gathering is an unusual one, arranged at some haste and being essentially commercial in nature, but I am sure that your attention will be amply rewarded. You will have noticed a bold claim set out on the invitation you received, namely that this afternoon will present you with an *Experience of Unparalleled Interest, introducing to you a Miracle of Science*. I must advise you, ladies and gentlemen, that this claim is no exaggeration."

He paused, pretending to gather his thoughts. "We live in an age of marvels. Our cities grow taller and larger every day, we travel at unprecedented speeds by road and by locomotive, we communicate across thousands of miles by telegraph. Industrial processes give us manufactured goods which improve our lives in a hundred ways. Progress, in industry and business, continues to accelerate and has made this nation, and the Empire, the dominant power of the modern world."

The applause was accompanied by a few calls of approval. "Ladies and gentlemen, all of us here in this magnificent ballroom play our part in that triumphant progress. We are familiar with all that is new and radical. However, I promise you that you will leave this room with a fresh understanding of what is possible in our rapidly developing society. This will be thanks to one thing alone."

He took the small tin from the table beside him and held it up high between two fingers. Printed on its lid, inside a twirling circular decoration, were the company name and a few accompanying lines. "Ladies and gentlemen, I give you Pell & Blight Restorative."

Sceptical bemusement filled the ballroom. There were whispers of anti-climax and snake-oil charlatans.

Pell raised his other hand as well. "Ladies and gentlemen, your doubts are both understandable and expected." He nodded to one of the waiters, who nodded to someone outside the room. A moment later, two waiters appeared wheeling a tall mirror which had been borrowed from one of the hotel's suites. Behind them was a woman Pell had chosen from among his employees. She had been bathed and her short hair washed specially for the occasion. Pell had bought her a lilac dress, since she possessed nothing suitable herself. She wore it with embarrassment and discomfort, walking with her head down, awkwardly nerve-wracked by the suddenly watching crowd of toffs.

The mirror was placed behind Pell. The woman was placed at his side. "Stand up straight," he whispered to her. "I've told you, there's nothing to worry about. These people will think you're marvellous."

She stood with her fingers knitting rapidly behind her back, no idea what was about to happen to her. She was of average height, but thin and undernourished. Her face looked considerably older than her thirty-two years, sallow and blemished, a lifetime of scraped existence etched deep into every line.

Pell addressed his guests again. "This is Annie, ladies and gentlemen, an employee at my factory in the east end of the city. An excellent employee, punctual and hard-working. You may notice that she bears a scar, here to one side of her forehead, the result of an altercation in her youth. You may notice also that her complexion is dulled and somewhat mottled, and that her skin is aged, with much wrinkling to her mouth and neck. Annie is to be the very first recipient of the benefits of Pell & Blight Restorative."

Here he flourished the round tin. A demonstration of his own. Annie silently stared at the assembled guests, her heart thumping, and the guests stared with intrigued puzzlement at Annie.

Pell unscrewed the lid of the tin and carefully set it down on the table. He angled the tin to show that inside was a thin layer of white, waxy-looking paste. "Produced exclusively by Pell & Blight Ltd, and the result of many years of experimentation."

Using two fingers, he scooped out the contents of the tin, a blob roughly the size of a pebble. With the other hand, he raised Annie's face with a push beneath her chin, then held her steady by her shoulder.

He smeared the paste across her chin, cheeks and forehead, rubbing it in circular motions to cover the whole of her face in a pale, even sheen. "Pell & Blight Restorative is—no, don't touch your face, my dear—is absorbed into the skin within approximately thirty seconds. A single application, as shown here, will last for around one week and a half. Pell & Blight Restorative will be on—don't touch your face—will be on sale to the public from the end of next week."

Annie could feel the paste as hot and cold at the same time. It was a peculiar, creeping sensation, a tingling like a thousand needle points held against her face. She pressed her fists to her hips, to stop her hands straying upwards. She could feel her skin warming.

Every eye in the room was fixed on her. She trembled, trying not to move, one hundred and seven guests watching intently. The waiters watched too, poised in mid-glide.

Her face began to give off a faint glow. It seemed to blur at the edges, almost to ripple, like the beating of a fish's fin.

A murmur flashed across the room. After a few seconds, there was no denying that her entire face was bathed in a shiny haze. Gasps and mutterings broke out among the guests. Several at the back stood up for a clearer view.

Gradually, the lines that had covered Annie's cheeks and brow smoothed out, then disappeared. The scar on her temple faded like a twisted twig sinking into calm, still water. Her skin flushed and plumped, mellowing into an even tone. The shine seemed to throb before it faded and as it did so, all trace of the paste now gone, her face was softened and young. Years had melted from it. She had the face of a girl barely out of her teens.

Her fingers fluttered hesitantly at her cheeks, afraid of what they might find. Untouched by the paste, her hands remained gnarled and worn, her neck wrinkled.

The guests burst into flustered astonishment, eyes widened and tongues loosened. Utterly unnerved by their reaction, and not knowing what had happened to her face, Annie staggered back, fingers pressing searchingly at her cheeks. She looked at Pell, then turned to the tall dressing mirror behind him. She was only inches from it before she could spin it on its wheels and see herself.

The sight struck her mind like a hammer blow. Instantly, her reflection became a mask of shock and she found herself unable to breathe. Trembling, she pawed at her skin, neither understanding nor trusting what she saw. Dear God in heaven! Her face! As she was, long ago! Her face! The change, so unexpected and extreme, drew an uncontrollable surge of awe and terror from the depths of her soul.

She screamed, a faltering, high-pitched shriek. Then she dropped to her knees, her hands gripping the sides of the mirror, unable to look away.

The sudden sound raised the guests into action. There was a commotion of voices, cries of amazement and joy, shouts of disbelief, pointed fingers, waved hands. Some guests at the nearest tables jumped to their feet, chairs squeaking on the polished floor, and walked purposefully towards Pell and Annie. This set off similar movement right across the ballroom. One hundred and seven elegantly dressed bodies moved closer, their exclamations rising, chattering, demanding.

Pell felt a jolt of nervous fear as several dozen guests came towards him. The small of his back bumped against the table and he realised he was retreating. He stumbled slightly, the table shifting under his weight. Suddenly he was surrounded by an orderly but insistent crowd of men and women, their wagging lips, their proffered hands, the smell of soap and pastries, the faces of industrialists and financiers.

"—absolutely astonishing—"

"—will offer any sum you name for the manufacturing—"

"—buy up your entire stock—"

"—how much—?"

"—not exaggerating when—"

"—prepared to offer you double the amount he just stated—"

"—for a tin, how much—?"

Annie was oblivious to the excitement until half a dozen female hands grasped her by the arms and hauled her upright. She was finally forced away from her reflection, with fingers jabbing at her nose and forehead, eyes coming close enough to examine every pore. She was frightened and wanted to go home.

Pell's mind raced. They kept asking him the price, the price, the price. An hour ago, he'd settled on a figure which he'd considered breathtaking in its audacity. Now he doubled it, and added more.

With a smile and a nod he said, "Nine guineas a tin."

The only reaction was a flurry of orders. Five—a dozen—two dozen—a monthly delivery—will it be available in Whiteleys?— offer you an exclusive contract—are you writing this down, Mr Pell?

He looked down at his hand. The two fingers he'd used to scoop the paste were smooth and rosy, noticeably different to the others.

And suddenly, he understood von Frakken's vision of the future completely. Here, before his very eyes, von Frakken's Trojan Horse was being dragged eagerly into Troy, inside a little tin of Pell & Blight Restorative. Products would, indeed, be first demanded, then expected, then required. The human race would, indeed, willingly *buy* its own conversion, slowly, limb by limb. It would clamour for new flesh, new brains, more life, perfected offspring.

The inevitability of it all was mind-shattering. And he, Jabez Pell, would make millions. Billions. Safety, and respect, and power. All he'd ever wanted. Von Frakken wasn't mad, he was a genius, a prophet of profit!

Pell's wealthy guests pressed in around him. For the first time in years, he was truly happy.

CHAPTER XXX

It was late afternoon when Maria and Dr Thomas Meers made the journey to St Saviour's. Drizzle was beginning to patter and splash in the puddles along the road and the last of the daylight was thinly strung in shades of purple across a heavy, swollen sky.

At the Meers's house, Maria had borrowed fresh clothes from Thomas, but beneath one of Thomas's old high-buttoned jackets was a white, embroidered blouse of Sophia's, frilled at the cuffs, which Maria favoured for the distracting effect of its tall, elaborate collar.

She had tied her long hair up into a compact chignon. How she'd gained such a skill—whose it had once been?—she had no notion. So much of her jigsaw mind was still a mystery to her. She had looked into the oval mirror, above the night stand in the Meers's guest room, and adjusted her neckline. The peculiar horror she'd found in her reflection was less acute than it had been, but she could only bear to look at herself for a second or two.

Meers had applied a fresh dressing to the wound on her arm. He'd learned his lesson and had asked permission before peering at it through a magnifying glass with undisguised fascination.

Street lamps were being lit as they drew up at the gates of St Saviour's. A spattering of raindrops plopped heavily on Maria's shoulders.

A short distance outside the hospital's grounds, a few dilapidated caravans were gathered tightly together, taking shelter under a canopy of trees. A scurrying handful of children searched around for fallen scraps and branches with which to make a fire.

Maria suddenly recognised the freak show that she'd passed with the professor in Hyde Park. Between the caravans, a dozen or more people sat quietly in a circle of unfolded canvas chairs, all of them reduced by shadows and the gathering gloom to little more than grey outlines. Some of the outlines seemed to be shaped in a different way to the others, and some seemed oddly incomplete.

Dr Meers followed Maria's gaze. "They'll be spending the winter being moved on from place to place around the city," he said, "looking for whatever work is available. We quite often employ them as porters or orderlies, when we're short of help. The able-bodied ones, I mean."

She kept glancing back as they crunched down the gravel driveway to the main entrance. The grey outlines were piling up whatever odds and ends the children had found.

Meers led her past the hawkish clerks in the Receiving Room and down the first of the ward corridors. "I don't see very much of Clements or Polidori, but on those occasions we meet it's most often a case of paths crossing amongst the patients. I'll ask."

Moving from room to room, Meers spoke to any of the nurses and orderlies he knew by name, but none of them had seen the surgeons today, nor yesterday either, no, I'm sorry Dr Meers. They arrived at a ward where a heavy pooling of fresh blood lay scattered across the floor. An orderly appeared with a bucket of carbolic and a dirt-soaked mop.

Maria was feeling increasingly uncomfortable. The harsh, omnipresent echo; the shouts and cries; the acidic smell of the place; Meers's untroubled demeanour at it all. She told herself not to be so feeble.

So weak.

So human.

The sudden harshness of this last thought chilled her more than the blood close to her feet. The orderly sloshed steaming water around it, spreading it into a rectangular patch.

Meers was talking to a young nurse with a bundle of bedsheets in her arms. "Are you sure about that?"

The nurse heaved the bedsheets to stop them falling. "That's as I heard. Two of their posh patients turned up for appointments yesterday, and they were nowhere to be found. The posh patients made a fuss and marched off."

"Do you know if anyone from here has tried to contact them at their lodgings?"

"I don't know. I shouldn't think so. They come and go as they please, don't they, just like all the doctors."

Maria stepped back a little to allow space for the orderly's mop. She felt a touch at the leg of her trousers and turned to find an old man lying in the nearest bed, a blanket pulled up to his chest, his arm outstretched to her. He wore a smeary work shirt, from which his head emerged like a turtle's from its shell, on a thin and ropey neck. His eyes were sunken and filmy, and his skin was so fleshless and tight that the shape of his skull was evident. He breathed in shallow steps, his voice crawling frail and sickly from deep in his throat.

"Meg? … S'you Meg?" His swaying hand returned to his side, exhausted. His arm was no more than wrapped bones.

"No, I'm—" said Maria.

"So glad y'here … so glad … oh Meg—" His eyes filled slowly before they overflowed.

Maria bent over him. Meers noticed what she was doing but continued talking to the nurse.

"M'eyes—" said the old man, his lips attempting a smile. "N'good n'more … Fit for n'thing … I'm nearly a deadlurk altog'ther, eh?" His smile dissolved into the shadow of a sob. "I'm scared, Meg … I'm scared t' die … I know … I can feel it coming—"

His fingers wavered, searching for her. With great reluctance, Maria took his hand. It felt fluttering and delicate, a tiny bird.

"I've—tried to be good," he whispered. "Tried … to be a good man … But I've not—al'ays … But I love you, Meg … I love you … all m'heart … Tell her … I'm sorry, for—what … I'm sorry—that I hurt her—"

He tried another smile. "Eyes packin' up … y'r … beautiful as ever, Meg … all packin' up, eh? … Buggered … No good, man nor beast, eh? … Will y'tell her? Will you—?"

The words formed awkwardly in Maria's mouth. "I'll tell her."

"Y'r good girl, Meg."

Maria gave the old man's hand a gentle squeeze. She stood upright and walked briskly out of the ward, stepping over the pink, damp stain left by the orderly's mop. Meers left the nurse to her work and caught up with Maria in the corridor outside.

"There's only so much we can do," he said. "When the heart fails or the lungs clog, that's the end of the matter. We get one life, kings and peasants alike. Medicine has its limits."

"People die. There's no need to explain."

"It comes to us all." He suddenly checked himself. They walked in silence for a few moments. "The geriatric cases shouldn't really be here, but the committee doesn't object provided the families have paid for us to take them. Ah, if we go along here, we'll get to Clements's and Polidori's consulting rooms. It seems neither have attended their clinic the last two days, and unexpectedly at that. Which of itself seems suspicious, don't you think?"

A couple of minutes later, Meers knocked at the consulting room door. "Dr Clements? Are you there? Dr Polidori?" He listened at the keyhole. "I can't hear anything." As soon as his head was out of the way, Maria aimed a sharp kick at the lock. The door frame cracked.

"For heaven's sake, woman!" hissed Meers, looking up and down the corridor in alarm. Nobody was in sight.

A second kick broke the handle and the door opened. "Your colleagues are missing, you were worried about them, we broke in to ascertain their whereabouts," said Maria. With a final look to make sure that they hadn't been seen, Meers pushed the splintered area around the lock back together as best he could, and followed Maria inside.

They quickly checked the office and the private operating room. There was no sign that anyone had been there in the past few days. Meers opened the notebook diary on Clements's desk.

"There are many entries in here, including one for an appointment this morning. They go on for weeks." He turned pages back and forth. "There are references I don't understand. It says—this handwriting is atrocious—it says 'transference of liver' and on the preceding page 'transference of heart.'"

"Is there any mention of von Frakken?"

"Not that I can find. The only names are those of patients. This is purely a record of consultations." He tried the desk's drawers, to find all of them locked. "I suppose we've no alternative. In for a penny, in for a pound." He fetched a pair of gleaming bone saws from the operating room and, handing one to Maria, he used the other to jemmy open the locks.

Maria forced a pair of cupboards and removed handfuls of papers, some of them tied in bundles with strips of red ribbon. "These are invoices and those are medical notes. You'll need to look at the notes, I can't follow a word of them."

Meers quickly sifted through the papers, slowing down as he did so, his face growing steadily darker. Maria crossed the office and ran a finger along a narrow gap that ran at chest height along a short section of panelled wall.

"I can feel air movement," she said. "I think this is a hatch." She put an ear to the gap. "There's machinery behind it."

"I'm sorry, what did you say?" said Meers, looking up. The colour had drained from his face. "If I'm interpreting this correctly," he said, tapping at the stack of notes in front of him, "these two fairground quacks have been falsifying records of deaths. This is monstrous! No wonder they seemed like ham-fisted butchers! What in the name of God have they been doing?"

Maria wedged a bone saw into the gap she'd found and levered it. A thin covering sprang open, revealing a deep recess in the wall. Occupying most of it was a hefty-looking wooden box which gave off a low, intermittent hum. In front of it, connected by electrical wires, were a pair of chemical power cells of an advanced design.

"It's a refrigeration box, I think," said Meers, "one of those gas compression types, I've read about them. Expensive. I had no idea they possessed such a thing. What would they want it for?"

Maria lifted the weighty, brick-insulated lid. Inside the internal compartment were half a dozen cold objects wrapped in thickly bloodstained cotton. Two were human livers, two were pairs of kidneys, one was a lung and one was a set of five human eyes.

"Good God" breathed Meers, staring into the box. "What the devil would they be doing with these? They don't teach anatomy."

"Should we be surprised? We know the Promethean Society is dedicated to the creation of extended life, through surgery, galvanism, whatever yields results."

Meers pulled his fingers through his hair, aghast. "There is no possible medical reason for this—this human abattoir! My God, how long has this been going on, right under our noses?"

Maria reached into the box again. Tucked in between the organs was a small glass jar, containing a few ounces of von Frakken's artificial flesh. She held it out to Dr Meers. "This came from my arm. They do know von Frakken."

"That does it!" cried Meers, his emotions boiling over. "We must alert the authorities. No argument! If Clements and Polidori are in league with von Frakken, then we have to round up the lot of 'em! Oh my God, this will close the hospital!"

He paced the floor with nervous agitation. Maria closed the refrigeration box and started to sort hurriedly through the jumble of papers on the desk. "There must be something here to tell us where von Frakken is. Dr Meers—listen to me!—is it possible that he's in this building?"

"What? No, there's nowhere you could remain undisturbed. All the main floors are occupied, the basement is used daily and the attic has been set up as accommodation for auxiliaries."

"There must be an address, or a name," said Maria. "I think there's one simple link we're missing."

"I'm going to fetch help," declared Meers, tugging the front of his jacket straight. "Stay here. You won't—run off, will you?"

She didn't answer him, but instead began rooting through the desk drawers again. Meers hesitated momentarily, then hurried through the waiting room and back out into the echoing hallway. Ahead, he could see a porter and two or three nurses crossing the wide gap between stone pillars.

"Nurse! Any one of you! Quickly, please!"

The eldest of the nurses broke away and came over to him at a sedate pace. She was tall and her face was heavily marked with smallpox scars.

"Can I help you, Dr Meers?"

"Do you know where either Dr Clements or Dr Polidori are at this moment?"

"No. But I'm aware they haven't been seen in the hospital for two days or more. I was getting worried. Are they quite alright?"

"I don't know, but I'm afraid I have a very serious task for you to perform," said Meers. "A few minutes ago I—and a friend—discovered evidence that Dr Clements and Dr Polidori have been involved in unethical procedures and have links to a known criminal."

"Procedures?" The nurse's eyes hooded slightly.

"I hesitate even to describe them," said Meers. "What I want you to do is fetch the police, immediately."

"The police?" She took a step back. "I have duties. The sick to attend."

"Then send someone you can trust," cried Meers impatiently. "Someone you can trust entirely. They mustn't merely find any old bobby, they are to get word to an inspector at Scotland Yard, Mr Charles Barré. Have you got that?"

"Yes. Yes."

"They must give him my name, and say that Clements and Polidori are mixed up in the Hobson case, he'll know what that means. He must come at once. Have you got that?"

"The Hobson case," she nodded.

"I cannot impress upon you enough how vitally important it is that the police are here as soon as possible. If Clements or Polidori are seen, in the meantime, please spread the word that I am to be informed at once, Nurse—I'm terribly sorry, I don't know your name."

"Leath."

"Nurse Leath. Thank you, now with all due speed, please."

She hurriedly retreated into the flow of staff and patients. While Dr Meers returned to the consulting rooms, Nurse Leath calmly fetched her overcoat and left the building. She walked out of the gates and through the darkened streets to the house on the banks of the Thames where she rented a room. She settled up with her landlady, thanked her for all the cake, changed out of her uniform, packed a small valise and caught an omnibus to Marylebone station. She never returned to London.

Meers and Maria continued their search. Meers grew increasingly despondent as he pieced together some of his erstwhile colleagues' activities. "They've been cutting up people who surely needed only minor surgery," he said, comparing papers he held in each hand. "Patients on the wards. I think they killed them deliberately."

"For what purpose?" said Maria, emptying one of the cupboards.

"It sounds impossible, but they were somehow using the dead to effect cures in their private patients. Using blood, perhaps? Is that what the reference to 'transference' means? It was tried at St George's, years ago, but it doesn't work. Although, it would explain the mystery of their results. How could they cover up all that killing? It's beyond belief."

"Until you met me, you'd have said what the von Frakkens did was beyond belief."

Meers sunk into a chair, his body slumped and drained. "Medicine has its limits. People die," he muttered to himself. "My God, how many? What happened to them?"

He was too entangled in his own thoughts, and Maria was too intent on finding more information, to notice the waiting room door slowly opening. The first they were aware of someone else's presence was the soft click of a revolver being cocked. Their heads turned to find Jabez Pell standing over them. With a glance over his shoulder, Pell shut the door behind him.

"Jabez?" cried Meers. "What are *you* doing here? And what the hell are you pointing a gun at us for?"

"I'm on an errand, for my business partner," said Pell.

"What business partner?"

Maria smiled to herself. "Wilhelm von Frakken." She tapped Meers on the arm. "There you are, Mr Pell was that link we were missing."

"You knew what was going on here, Jabez?" cried Meers. "You knew what Clements and Polidori were up to?"

"Only in the most general terms," said Pell. "They were never very forthcoming."

"Were? They're dead?"

"Not yet," said Pell. "I'll take you to them shortly." He eyed Maria with a vague antipathy. "My business partner will be delighted to get his property back. I've had an enlightening and prosperous morning, and now this happy circumstance. Am I having a lucky day? I think I may well be."

"Your errand?" said Maria.

Pell wagged the barrel of the revolver at the waiting room fireplace. "Burn all the papers. Leave nothing."

"What's become of you, man?" snapped Meers. "You were as opposed to von Frakken as any of us. I never had you down as treacherous."

Pell raised the gun a little. Meers and Maria set to work. "Treacherous? No, I'm merely a practical businessman. Safeguarding my assets, as you might say."

Meers took a lucifer from a box on the mantelpiece and struck it. "I'll have you know that, any minute now—"

Maria cut across him. "Someone might come in."

"I cannot lock the door. I brought the key with me," said Pell, "but I see it wasn't needed. You'd better hurry up and get on with it, hadn't you?"

The first handful of papers curled and crackled into ash, Maria and Meers crouched in front of the grate. The flames threw flickering shadows against the opposite wall, and across Pell's impassive face.

"You can't do this, man!" protested Meers. "This is evidence. Those two are cold-blooded murderers. And so is von Frakken, come to that! What could possibly induce you to take their side?"

"A prudent business decision," said Pell.

Twenty minutes later, the last of Clements's and Polidori's papers, appointment diaries and invoices were burned, among them the transcripts that Polidori had made of von Frakken's notebooks. Neither Pell nor von Frakken were sure what those two might have been up to, or what written records they might have kept. Better to burn everything. Their homes would burn tomorrow.

"Somewhere in here, I'm told there will be a small glass jar," said Pell. "Find it, if you would."

Maria and Meers exchanged glances, then Maria went through into the office. Pell moved to keep both of them in sight, holding the revolver at arm's length. Maria hauled up the lid of the refrigeration box and took out the jar.

"You'd already found it, excellent," said Pell.

Maria was about to hand the jar to Meers, but Pell flourished the gun. "No. I want *her* to burn it."

She took a deep breath, then slung the jar into the flames. It nestled on scraps of paper until the heat made it crack. The flesh inside spat and bubbled, curling at the edges, turning black and charred. The room was filled with a greasy, pungent smell.

"My carriage is waiting by the side entrance," said Pell. "I'm going to put the revolver in my pocket now, but I won't hesitate to use it if there's trouble. If either of you try to get away, I'll shoot the other."

Maria and Meers did as they were told. While leaving the hospital and climbing up into the four-wheeler, rain pattering at their backs, they managed to exchange whispers.

"He doesn't know about those organs, or they'd be burnt too."

"That's no good to us," said Dr Meers. It was fortunate for both of them that he was wrong.

CHAPTER XXXI

Pell was right. Von Frakken was indeed delighted to have Maria returned to him. He sprung from the armchair in which he'd been reading the moment she entered the parlour of Pell's apartment above the factory.

"The prodigal daughter!" he declared, throwing his arms wide. Pell nudged Dr Meers into the room too, tapping the barrel of the revolver into his back. "And another visitor!"

"This is Thomas Meers," said Pell. "He's another doctor at St Saviour's, I found the pair of them rifling through Clements's consulting rooms."

"You're Wilhelm von Frakken?" said Meers.

"I am. It's a pity we meet under such adversarial circumstances, Dr Meers, I'm sure we would have much in common, professionally."

"I doubt that very much."

Maria was rooted to the spot, her mind spinning with revulsion at what von Frakken had done to save himself. "Whose body did you steal?"

"You like it? As you may notice, one of the eyes is uncooperative and for some reason the hair has yet to begin regrowth, but all-in-all I'm happy with the work."

"Who did you kill?"

"Nobody of consequence, I assure you," said von Frakken. "This body is vastly more useful to me than it would ever have been for him. Really, there is no need to look so troubled."

"Are you claiming—?" began Dr Meers, his face contorting with confusion. "No. Utterly absurd!"

"Mr Pell's two associates carried out the operation itself, to my explicit instructions. They did a thoroughly competent job."

"Where are they?" said Meers.

"In the next room, my temporary laboratory."

Pell pointed to Meers with the gun. "What are you going to do with him, von Frakken? Put him with the others?"

"In that respect, Pell, we seem to have something of an embarrassment of riches at the moment. Most of our recent visitors are currently sitting quietly in the bedroom, he can join them there for the time being. Later tonight I'll take the majority of them down to the boilers."

Pell winced but was, since the triumphant success of his demonstration that morning, now firmly dedicated to his business partner's strategy. All that he wanted, or could ever want, was so close he could feel its kiss brush against his lips. If Meers, and the Prometheans, were sent to crawl obediently into the furnaces on the factory floor, their minds in a cataleptic lethargy, then so be it.

"Would you both like to see my laboratory?" said von Frakken. "I'm developing new products for the company. We'll expand into new premises soon, but for the moment we must do what we can. Our first product, our Restorative, is being manufactured now and will be on sale soon. Today's presentation at the Clanborough was pleasingly well received, Mr Pell informs me. Have you seen the evening papers? *The Examiner* is particularly effusive."

"I'm afraid I've not had the time," said Dr Meers.

Letting Pell keep them at gunpoint, he took them into the adjoining room. Standing in a row, naked and positioned up against the floral wallpaper, were Clements, Polidori and the Promethean who had died drinking von Frakken's spiked whiskey.

"My God, man," gasped Meers, "what the hell is all this?"

The dead man had successfully undergone von Frakken's revivification process. Controlled by an artificial enzyme similar to the one keeping all von Frakken's captives docile, the corpse swayed gently on its feet, its legs swollen from the settling of blood.

Clements had large geometric sections of his skin missing. Polidori's body, between stomach and pubis, had been removed entirely except for his backbone and spinal column.

"Two products are in development," said von Frakken. "Dr Clements is testing one derived from the same chemical base as our Restorative and which is designed to replace damaged epidermis. At the moment it is absorbed too quickly into the body and the effect is lost. A little more work is needed. Dr Polidori is testing a rather more ambitious project, a webbing on which artificial flesh can grow, to seal cauterised wounds or rejoin muscle which has become separated."

Involuntarily, Maria's hand slid to her sleeve, covering the dressing on her arm.

Meers spluttered. "Ghoulish, filthy insanity! This isn't scientific enquiry, this is the workings of a diseased mind!"

Von Frakken took the gun from Pell, keeping it trained on Meers, and plucked a filled syringe from a rack on his cluttered workbench. "Roll up your sleeve."

"I damn well will not!" cried Meers.

Von Frakken held the gun an inch from Meers's temple. Maria weighed up her chances of successfully snatching it away, but they were slim. "You prefer a bullet? It makes no difference to me. I'd prefer to avoid a mess. The girl Pell's assigned to attend me would then enjoy her work even less, I'm sure."

Meers glared and removed his cufflink. "What's in that? A sedative drug?"

"The effect is similar," said von Frakken, jabbing the needle into Meers's arm, "the chemical composition is rather more subtle than a common narcotic, this particular formulation producing a state analogous to hypnosis; it's a useful offshoot of the process that generates the artificial flesh from which your friend here is constructed."

Already, Meers's eyes were glassy and distant.

"I see I have the dosage exactly correct now," muttered von Frakken. "Mr Pell, you will take this gentleman to join the others for the time being."

Pell pulled at the sleeve of Meers's jacket and the doctor walked in uneasy steps, his mind drowning in the effort to think, held down under waters of fear and awe.

When they were gone, von Frakken beamed at Maria. He took a step towards her and she took a step back.

"There is much to be learnt from you," said von Frakken softly, "before you are dismantled."

"All you'll get from me is disgust."

"Aww, how sharper than a serpent's tooth—," he chuckled. "Is that Shakespeare? Or the late Mr Dickens? I cannot remember. You, on the other hand, I'd wager you know. You are a remarkable creature."

"My name is Maria."

"You have given yourself a name! Splendid! Your mental faculties operate far more efficiently than I dared hope, I was half expecting you to be an idiot. All my work was not in vain."

"But you'll still dissect me."

"The work must go on."

"Meers is right, this isn't work, this is atrocity. This room stinks of death. You stink of death."

Von Frakken went over to the reanimated corpse in the corner. It looked around itself vacantly. "Yes, this specimen is becoming a little over-ripe. Nevertheless, he's served his purpose and proved a point. I was absolutely right to abandon the approach pioneered by my grandfather, the re-assembling of the dead, and develop the new forms for which my mother laid the groundwork. An animated cadaver such as this soon reaches the limits of what it can do and the tasks it can carry out. Even when fully revitalised, the tissues become partly necrotic and in need of further electrical stimulus. These specimens do not last long. They can be given specific emotional states, but little more. They are inefficient."

He turned and thrust out his hands to Maria. "However, a being such as you, Maria—well, you are an entirely different proposition. You have become so much more than I imagined."

Maria's fingers cycled nervously at her sides. She stared at her creator, her thoughts tangled and knotted. "Why—why did you make me?"

Von Frakken smiled. "Because I could. You can't stop progress. You are the pinnacle of scientific achievement; you are man-made life."

"I didn't ask to be made."

"And I don't expect gratitude, any more than the engineer expects gratitude from the machine he makes, or the architect expects gratitude from the building he designs. You are what you are."

"But what am I? An object, to own? A thinking toy? My brain was made from thoughts that aren't mine, my bones grew in separate tubes. Is there even a *me* that exists at all?"

Von Frakken's voice dropped to a whisper. "Who wants to know?"

"I do."

"Then you have your answer. You will be part of the greatest change in history, the extinction of biological Mankind, the replacement of the human being. If you seek a purpose to your life, what better one could you choose than to have the whole world become like you?"

Maria spoke with slow deliberation. "I will end you, von Frakken. One way or another, I will end you."

"Will you, now?"

Von Frakken's expression suddenly altered, almost imperceptibly. His functioning eye narrowed a fraction and innate suspicion stirred in his mind, restless and questioning.

"Pell!" he called over his shoulder. "Come here!"

Footsteps thumped and the factory owner appeared in the open doorway. "What's the matter?"

"You say you found Maria, and her ally, going through the consulting rooms of our two friends here?"

Pell frowned. "Yes, indeed."

Von Frakken considered for a moment. "For how long had they been there?"

"I've really no notion," said Pell. "Why?"

"In how much disarray were those rooms? Think carefully, Pell."

He thought carefully. "Considerable, I would say. There were papers, in piles, all over the place. All of it was burned, every last item, exactly as you asked."

"Then they had been looking through those papers for some time." Von Frakken's face was gradually hardening. "You remember the purpose of my request?"

"To remove evidence of Clements's and Polidori's activities, in case they should become generally known," said Pell, unsettled, not entirely understanding what von Frakken was suggesting. "Also, to destroy any record they may have kept of your own activities."

"—And?"

Pell's frown deepened as he became more exasperated. "In doing this, to get rid of any record that might connect them to either of us. But everything is burned! Even if those rooms were stuffed full with Pell & Blight invoices, it wouldn't matter a jot!"

"It would, Pell, if a connection was discovered, and there was ample opportunity to communicate that discovery before you arrived."

"There was nobody else around."

"Nobody that you saw," hissed von Frakken. He turned to Maria. "Would you care to tell me the truth? Does anyone else know?"

Maria chose her words carefully, the faintest hint of a smile on her lips. "Dr Meers and I were surprised to see Mr Pell. Until that moment, we had no clue that he was involved. That is the truth."

Her gaze met von Frakken's. Mountain and immovable object. He weighed the odds, his lips pressed into a wriggling snarl. "You're a damned fool, Pell!" he spat at last. "This laboratory, and everything relating to my work, will have to be moved! Now!"

"This minute?" gasped Pell.

"Sooner! The police may be upon our doorstep at any moment!"

"We don't know that."

"Hence the need to move! *Think*, Pell! I will not allow my plans—our *business*—to be jeopardised because of some idiotic carelessness!" He raised his revolver, aiming it directly between Maria's eyes, and she tensed. "If I didn't want useful data from that brain, I'd put a bullet through it where you stand!"

He thrust the gun at Pell. "Watch her! Shoot her legs if she moves!"

"I have an idea," said Pell, stopping von Frakken in mid-step. "I know a place you can work, with few people about and very little effort needed to stay hidden."

"Where? Say nothing in front of *her*! I'll go and begin packing."

CHAPTER XXXII

"Sir, there's a Mrs Meers to see you," said the uniformed sergeant, his head poked around the inspector's door. "Says it's urgent."

Inspector Barré looked up from his desk. "Sophia? Show her up."

He sorted the paperwork he was working on into a neat pile, clipped it all together and placed it in the wooden tray to his left. He donned his monocle as Sophia Meers was shown in. He took her umbrella and gave it a shake.

"Delightful to see you," he said, with a polite nod. "Is something amiss?"

"I have a feeling it may be," said Sophia. "Tom may be in trouble."

"Please, sit down."

"Thank you, no. You'll probably be furious when you hear this."

"Oh?"

Sophia tapped her gloved hands together. "He went to St Saviour's, some hours ago. He was looking for a couple of colleagues."

"Yes," said Barré, "we'd discussed it. Asking if they'd seen Maria."

She paused, biting her lip. "No, to track down this von Frakken person. Maria was with him."

"What?"

"He said they wouldn't even be an hour, they were just going to ask a few questions. Something's happened, I know it."

"Where in blazes did he find Maria?"

"He didn't, she found us. Please, Charles, I'm sorry now I wish I'd—never mind."

Barré got to his feet and quickly opened the door. "Sergeant Otley!" he shouted, before turning back to Sophia. "They went to the hospital? Nowhere else?"

"No. These colleagues have consulting rooms there."

Sgt Otley appeared, out of breath from the run upstairs. Barré's men were finding it hard to adjust to the inspector's new habit-breaking decisiveness. "Sir?"

"Look after this lady and get me a couple of constables."

"I'm coming with you," said Sophia.

"No you're not, you're going home. Otley will arrange an escort and someone to wait with you," said Barré. By the clock on the shelf behind his desk, it was a quarter to nine. "If Thomas has got himself into difficulties, there's no knowing what we'll find."

With that, he left the office. A hair-raising ride got him and two of his men to St Saviour's by nine o'clock. Outside the hospital grounds, the huddled freak show caravans were dark and silent beneath the trees. Rain was falling harder now, from a jet black sky.

Barré, directed by one of the porters, marched up to Clements's and Polidori's consulting rooms and stopped dead when he saw the splintered lock. Hearing no sound coming from inside, he gave the door a push.

"You two, check everything," he said. His men spread out and began to rummage while Barré poked at the fireplace. Disposing of papers, from the look of it. Was that broken glass?

"Ugh! Inspector! In here, quick!"

One of the constables had found the refrigeration box and lifted the lid. He stood back with his hand across his nose and mouth.

"What's this thing?" said Barré.

"Not a clue, sir, but you look inside it."

Barré edged over the box. The human organs were unwrapped, with the liver sitting on top, dark and shiny.

"Is all that from people, sir?"

"The eyes certainly look human," muttered Barré, peering closer. Nestled beside the liver was a pen. "Odd thing to put there."

As he moved slightly from side to side, the light from the gas lamp caught the liver's smooth, glistening surface. The hard metal nib of the pen had been used to quickly scratch a single word into it: 'Pell.'

It took Barré only a few moments to put together the most probable scenario that would explain all they'd found. He couldn't deduce the fact that Maria had quietly picked the pen off Clements's desk, when she'd fetched the small jar of artificial flesh from the box, but the rest of it was reasonably clear.

"Constable," he snapped. "I want someone to go to the Pell & Blight factory in Whitechapel, not far from the Five Beggars, if memory serves. They're not to go in, they're to recce the place. If I've got this right, there's a dangerous man there and he's almost certainly got this missing Dr Meers with him. I want a report, back here, before the hour's up! Go on! I'm going over these rooms in detail."

"Sir!"

At a few minutes past ten, the breathless report that Barré received stated that equipment was being moved in the factory under cover of darkness, that said equipment was being loaded onto a cart, sir, and that none of it appeared to be of a regular commercial nature.

Barré pursed his lips. "Right, I want a dozen men there, out of sight, and I want them armed. They are not to make any move until I get there."

CHAPTER XXXIII

The rain had eased a little, but any loiterers in the street silently melted into the night mist at the first sign of a blue uniform. By the time Barré arrived at the gates of Pell & Blight Ltd, twelve men armed with pistols were waiting deep in the shadows, Sgt Otley among them.

They were unaware that they'd been seen, more than a minute ago, from a darkened window on the factory's top floor.

"Our scout saw lanterns moving about inside a while ago, sir," said Otley in a low voice, "and there was movement outside, near the cart they've been loading."

"Where is this cart?" muttered Barré.

"There's doors onto an alleyway, sir, down the side there and to the left."

"Right, two men—you, and you—watch that cart and if anybody attempts to leave, stop them. The rest of us will enter the building via the gates. Do we know how many are in there, Otley?"

"Only a handful, sir, if that. They've not made much noise. No workers about, at this time of night. Likely just this fugitive, along with Meers, couple of others."

"The owner lives on the premises," said Barré, "I expect he's in there. All of you, no firearms drawn except on my order. I want arrests, not injuries. We go in quietly, catch them off guard."

He paused to wipe raindrops from his monocle, then led the remaining ten men through the gates and across the factory's courtyard, their breath frosting in the cold. Away from the smog-suffused street lights, the darkness was almost total. Barré's fingertips tapped along a wall until they found the entrance. It was unlocked.

"Clearly, not expecting us," he whispered.

Quietly, they stepped inside. After a few yards, the narrow wooden stairs that led to the upper floors appeared out of the shadows. Barré leaned across to take a brief look, but there was no way to climb them without raising the alarm. He motioned for his men to continue at ground level for the time being.

They crept out onto the factory floor. Barré signalled to fan out and they moved among the vats and machines. A faint, softened roar came from the bellies of the two steam generators, the purr of sleeping dragons.

The rain outside suddenly began to pelt against the tall windows, quickening into streams that snaked down the glass. There was a long, low shudder of distant thunder.

Sgt Otley crossed the floor to speak to the inspector. "Sir, those doors, over at the far end. I think that may be the way out to the alleyway. It looks like they've got to come through here to get to the cart."

"Perfect," muttered Barré. "Send a man back to cover our route in. We'll have them trapped."

"Sir."

At that moment, they both looked up. The glimmer of a candle had flickered up at the counting office window. It moved at a steady pace, but they couldn't see who was holding it. Then it was extinguished as suddenly as it had appeared.

"Get everyone in position, Otley," whispered Barré.

Before Otley could reply, a second rumble of thunder came from outside. At the same moment, from the upper floor came a sound that froze the blood of every man on the factory floor. At first, they thought it might be a trick of the rain, a thunderous echo in the downpour, but it went on too long and it quickly became horribly distinct.

Somewhere above them, the combined scream of a dozen voices almost shook the building. A guttural, violent yell of rage, the deep banshee shriek of Hell itself, roaring on and on. Barré and the others flinched in terror.

"God almighty, sir, what's that?" cried Otley.

For a second, Barré's heart was racing too fast to speak. He was about to shout across the floor, telling his men to move in, when the howling war-cry began to descend the stairs.

It was unmistakable. Beneath the screams of anger was now the pounding of feet against the wooden steps. The unending, unnerving screech appeared to move at an angle down the wall, getting closer and closer. As it neared the factory floor, it got louder.

Barré had to shout to be heard above the screams and the lashing of the rain. "Draw weapons! Draw weapons!"

The continuous howl closed in. The police fumbled with the catches that kept the pistols clipped to their belts, their hands shaking, faces flushed with fear.

The scream suddenly burst out onto the factory floor, the people von Frakken had chemically subdued, now dosed into a murderous frenzy. Some were still intact, others were half dissected in various ways. Behind the rest staggered the corpse von Frakken had reanimated, screeching and clawing at the air.

"Fire at will! Fire at will!"

Barré and his men were only slightly outnumbered, but far outmatched in raw aggression. Shots rang out in the dark. Most of them flew wide of the mark, fired in panic from trembling hands. Those that found their target seemed only to goad the attackers, the pain spurring them on.

Von Frakken's drugged captives launched themselves at whoever was within their reach, their features contorted with blind fury. Dr Clements, his skin a patchwork, clamped his hands around the throat of a constable and barrelled him to the floor. Polidori's severed upper body flapped as he ran, supported only by his spine. He cornered Otley, who was yelling in horror, and dug his fingers into the sergeant's face, pressing and probing until there was a crunch of bone and cartilage and the yelling stopped.

Barré, teeth gritted, stood his ground and raised his gun at a captive charging towards him. He fired once, twice. Only at the third bullet, which put a hole in the man's head and shot a spray of blood out behind him, did he collapse like a puppet with its strings cut.

Several of the attacking captives broke pieces off the machines to use as weapons. Levers, metal plates and long handles were wrenched free and brought down on the police. The constables fought back, emptying their pistols, beating away flailing limbs and snapping teeth. A man whose left side had been snipped into exposed musculature limped at speed, holes where his eyes had been, until he collided with a terrified policeman and knocked him flying. The man stabbed wildly with an iron bar torn from a stamping mechanism, again and again until an agonised cry told him he'd struck home.

Polidori's backbone had snapped. Leaving his dead lower body behind, he hauled what was left of himself along by his arms. He found a constable cowering in shock behind one of the machines and crawled up him swiftly. The constable, wailing, leaped up and tried to run, but the additional weight toppled him forward. Polidori grasped his hair and bit into his neck, pulling out chunks of flesh, blood welling over his face.

Thunder shook the windows. A dozen fights to the death filled the factory floor with screams, the clang of metal, splashes of red.

Jabez Pell, who'd seen what was happening from the counting office, came clattering down the stairs. "Stop! For God's sake stop! Don't damage my machines!" he yelled frantically, arms waving, his face running with sweat and misery. "For God's sake, the machines! My money!"

Driven to panic, he grabbed at a figure crouching over a body. Clements reared up at him. His hands were covered in blood and his mouth gaped. He flew at Pell with a shriek.

"Clements! Clements!" croaked Pell, struggling to pull the hands from his throat. Clements pushed him backwards and his feet scuttered unsteadily until his back bumped up against a press, about five feet wide, used in making soap.

The sounds of the battle reverberated up the staircase to where von Frakken, revolver in hand, stood ready to depart with Maria and the still-docile Dr Meers. A scream from below distracted von Frakken for a split-second.

Maria seized him by the wrists, trying to twist the gun from his hand. A shot exploded, deafening in the confines of the staircase. They grappled furiously while Meers blankly stood by, Maria's greater strength gradually gaining the advantage.

Von Frakken kicked Maria's leg out from under her and she lost her balance. Keeping a tight hold on von Frakken, she pitched headlong down the stairs. They rolled and fell, over and over, pain lancing through Maria's body every time she hit a step. A sudden, bone-numbing collision told her they'd reached the foot of the staircase.

She tried to stand but her vision was swimming and her head felt as if she was still tumbling. She heard von Frakken call woozily. "Meers! Come here!"

She was on her feet, then on the floor, then sliding up a wall. She blinked and shook her head. Beneath her, von Frakken was slowly turning over, groaning.

With her hands held out to steady herself, she tottered her way to the factory floor. Instantly, the reanimated corpse was upon her. Its eyes rolled and the stink of bloated decay puffed from its ruined lungs. It slapped its hands to the sides of her head and squeezed, pulling her from side to side. She cried out.

Pell struggled to shake off Dr Clements. The doctor screamed into his face, eyes bulging, the artificial enzyme in his system wiping everything from his mind except the urge to destroy enemies, enemies, enemies.

The soap press, against which Pell was pushed, rattled as Clements throttled him. Suddenly, he grabbed Pell's waistband and hauled him up onto the metal surface of the press. Pell kicked and clawed wildly, but a hard slap knocked him flat. Clements quickly reached up to the handle of the counterweighted frame overhead, which was filled with a criss-cross of razor-sharp edges for cutting soap into bars. He brought it down heavily. Then again, and again, Pell's screams fading with each blow.

Maria felt dizzy. The corpse gripped tighter, violently twisting her neck first one way, then the other. Trying to stay steady on her feet, she took hold of the corpse by the skin of its sides and dashed it against the nearest machine. There was a crack as its arm broke. As soon as it let her go, she stumbled back out of its reach.

Barré's pistol shot Clements dead at point blank range. The body fell, revealing a dozen streams of blood that trickled down the sides of the soap press. He whipped around, gun raised, to find Maria staggering towards him.

"Where's von Frakken?" he barked.

"Look out!" cried Maria.

A bullet missed Barré by inches. Von Frakken, dragging the obedient Meers by his lapels, had reached the rear doors on the far side of the factory floor. He flung one of them open, letting in the teeming rain and a blast of cold night air.

He could barely be seen in the dark. His arm and leg suddenly contracted tightly for a second. "I leave now, or Meers dies," he shouted.

Fights were still in progress. A constable appeared close to Barré, thrashing to throw an attacker off his back. "Get von Frakken," he called to Maria. "I'll deal with this."

He despatched the attacker and rapidly reloaded his pistol. Maria made a dash for the door, but a hand grabbed her ankle and she fell, pulling something heavy across the floor with her.

The life was finally draining out of Dr Polidori. His hand grasped weakly at her leg and his head slumped. With a shudder and a flick of her foot, she sent his remains skidding into a corner and he was motionless.

Two more shots echoed outside. Maria bounded for the door and ran out into the freezing rain. The alleyway was empty except for the dead bodies of the two constables Barré had placed on guard, their pistols drawn but not fired.

There was no sign of the loaded cart. Maria ran to the end of the alley and up and down a couple of connecting streets, but there was no clue to which direction it went. The cart, along with von Frakken and Dr Meers, had gone.

CHAPTER XXXIV

And you let him get away?" gasped Sophia Meers. "With Tom!"

Inspector Barré bristled slightly and cleared his throat, smoothing his moustache. "I've got six of my men in the morgue," he said in a controlled tone, "and another three badly hurt, one of them with half the fingers bitten off his hand. Nobody *let* him do anything."

"The inspector did all he could," said Maria softly.

Sophia walked the warmly-lit sitting room, pausing to peer out across the rain-lashed street, into the night, every time she passed the window. "Tom will free himself, I'm sure of that," she said. "He sent a couple of ruffians packing in Leicester Square last year. He knows what he's about, he'll sort out this von Frakken madman."

Maria and the inspector exchanged looks. There were certain details of von Frakken's escape that Barré had insisted Sophia should not be told, for the time being, including the chemical sedation of her husband.

Maria had argued against it. She still felt damp from the rain and ran a finger around the inside of her collar.

The constable who'd accompanied Sophia home was standing guard behind Barré, shooting glances at this weird young woman with whom his superior officer seemed to have allied himself. Maria fixed him with a cold gaze for a few moments and he looked away suddenly, cheeks pinking.

"We must, and will, redouble our efforts to catch von Frakken," said Barré. "I've sent word to watch all roads out of London and all traffic on the river. I think we can be sure he was responsible for this." He nudged the evening edition of the *Examiner* that was lying discarded beside him on the heavily padded settle. A headline read, "*Sensational Incident At Clanborough Hotel – Wonder medication exhibited*".

"Will the factory close?" said Maria. "All work stop?"

"Until further notice," said Barré, picking the newspaper up. "At least, with the place shut up, this particular situation can be contained. Von Frakken won't want to abandon such plans, but he'll have to set up somewhere else, preferably a long way away."

"Wherever he's hiding until then," said Maria, "it's somewhere Jabez Pell suggested to him, I heard him say so, somewhere secluded. Probably quite nearby, he wouldn't try to leave London soon, he'll know we're watching."

There was a knock and the Meers's maid Edith entered, holding out a folded sheet of paper. "Madam, found this just now. Must have been pushed under the door."

Sophia took another look out of the window, craning her neck. "I didn't see anyone come to the house. Who delivered it?"

Edith shrugged and handed it over. Sophia caught her breath as she read the address on it. "This is Tom's hand! I'm sure of it!" she said, as she hurriedly unfolded the paper.

My dear Sophia

I write at the dictation of Wilhelm von Frakken. I am safe, but will be killed if any attempt is made to capture him. I will be killed if he

is followed or surveilled. He will leave the city in peace, if he is given
unimpeded passage. Once he is gone, I will be released unharmed.
   Dr Thomas Meers

"The hand is odd, as if written slowly, but it's his," said Sophia.

Barré examined the folded sheet then passed it to Maria. "This doesn't get us any closer to finding him. The only thing this note tells us is that he tore it from a journal, or the like. The rough edge."

Maria turned the sheet over in her hands. The paper was quite thick, heavier than you'd usually find in a notebook, but perhaps he'd got it—

A spark suddenly flared in her mind. She raised the paper to her nose and inhaled slowly.

"I remember this," she muttered. "Not a memory implanted or constructed, this is something I have actually experienced since—I know precisely where Dr Meers is."

"What?" said Barré. "How?"

"Where is he?" said Sophia.

"This paper is from a book, an endpaper. I've touched and smelt paper exactly like this in Professor Hobson's room at the museum. Pell certainly knew of that room, and it's hidden away."

Barré smiled. "That's it."

"You're sure of this?" said Sophia.

"I'm entirely sure," muttered Maria, feeling the paper between her fingers. "It's—it's a memory—*my* memory." For a second, she was reminded of the odd yearning that had drawn her back to the professor's boarded-up house, thoughts of her own past.

"We'll go at once," said Barré. "Constable, get back to the Yard, tell them where we've gone. This young woman and I will go alone, I'm not risking more lives and we'll need to approach him with the utmost dexterity. I am assuming here, Maria, that it would not be possible to dissuade you from accompanying me?"

"Of course not," said Maria. "Sophia, may I borrow a Mackintosh or something waterproof?"

"By all means," she nodded, and hurried from the room.

As soon as she was gone, Maria turned to the inspector and spoke in a low voice. "I don't believe a word of it, he'll kill Dr Meers as soon as he thinks he's safe."

"Undoubtedly."

"From the look of the note, Meers is still in a subdued state, doing as he's told."

"I agree, and we know how that state can change. Above all, we must not allow von Frakken the chance to make that change." He sighed to himself. "If I could dose up all the criminals in London with one of von Frakken's mixtures, I'd be in clover."

"You'd be as evil as he," snapped Maria, without a trace of humour. She reminded herself that everything von Frakken was doing, everything of which he was now capable, sprung from the very flesh that she was made from, and she felt a fresh twist of guilt.

"I'm afraid this is all I have," said Sophia, returning, "but it will keep the rain off."

Sophia handed her a darkly coloured hooded cloak, not unlike the one she'd worn when she first arrived in London. "Thank you," she said.

A heavy series of knocks at the front door made them suddenly start, and moments later Edith showed a bedraggled constable into the room, his cap and oil-skin cape dripping copiously onto the floor.

"Word from Division, sir," he said breathlessly. "Chap you're after. Man with the right description was at St Katherine's Dock half an hour ago. Booking clerk said he paid for two persons and three packing crates, under the name of Sloan, for the steamship *Lanchester*."

"Leaving?"

"First light, sir. Bound for New York. He took empty crates with him, said he's coming back."

"And we're sure it's him?"

"Clerk said he had a gimpy eye, sir."

Barré snorted. "He's cornered and he's running around in a panic. Excellent. He had the advantage, and in the span of ten minutes we've gained an upper hand like a ruddy Wilkie Collins melodrama!"

"I'll intercept him at the docks," said Maria. "You attend to Dr Meers, inspector."

"No, you're to—"

"I think she should go," interrupted Sophia, hand raised. "I think she has that right, Charles."

Barré hesitated, checking the time by the clock on the mantelpiece. "I still consider you a risk," he said. "But of late I can see some have to be taken. Constable, change of plan, you go with Maria."

"I don't want—" protested Maria.

"It's a precondition!"

"Then he's to consider himself under my orders!"

"Now see here—"

"Charles," said Sophia. "Every second we delay, my husband is in danger. I doubt even your own men have a greater motivation to see von Frakken caught than does Maria."

Barré's impatience showed in the thrust of his chin. "Very well. Go."

CHAPTER XXXV

Maria, wrapped tightly in her cloak, and the constable, wrapped equally tightly in a police issue overcoat that was slightly too small for him, made the journey to St Katherine's Dock in silence except for one brief exchange.

"What's your name, constable?"

"Frye, Miss."

The rain had set in for the night, dropping from the starless sky in a cold, dank curtain. The intermittent thunder was now accompanied by stark flashes of sheet lightning which lit up the sluggish, oily clouds from above. Puddles thick with the detritus of the roads swirled along the gutters. Londoners walked under umbrellas that shivered with the impact of raindrops, or with collars up and hats turned down to keep the weather out of their faces.

Maria and Constable Frye ran from the cab to the shelter of an overhang attached to the side of a large storage shed. From there, they saw a man ushering them to join him from a similar shelter thirty yards closer to the river, where a pile of stacked barrels formed a perfect shield for remaining unobserved.

"Our plain clothes man," said Frye. "He knows me. He'll be the one who talked to the shipping clerk."

They found they had a better view of the docks from their new position. The place was busy, even at that time of night. A long line of lights hung from tall poles along the length of the wharfs, and stubby cranes projected from wooden cabins raised up above ground level. Dozens of tall clippers and squat steam vessels were berthed in profusion, huge and ghostly, as far as Maria could see into the murky darkness. Workmen hauled goods up and down gangplanks, or heaved at sodden coils of thick rope. The masts of the clippers blended into the rain, making their furled white sails appear suspended, like rips in the fabric of the night.

"You see over there?" said the plain clothes man. "That's what we're keeping an eye on. That's where he'll have to go to leave cargo." He pointed to a flat-roofed hut, fifty yards along the wharf, with windows set in a line all around its walls. Lights, inside and out, illuminated the area in a soft shine. Despite the rain and the night, the faces of everyone who approached it were clearly visible and sharply defined.

The seconds ticked by. It was twenty minutes before Maria drew closer to the triangular gap between barrels through which she was keeping watch.

"There's a cart with three packing crates."

It was plodding towards the flat-roofed hut, its driver huddled under a canvas sheet and a broad hat. It drew up outside.

"He's not in any hurry," said Frye quietly. "He doesn't know we're onto him."

As the driver jumped down and took off his hat to shake the rain from it, Maria felt a twist in her gut. Von Frakken replaced the hat and went into the hut to talk to the shipping clerk.

"Might he give us away?" said Maria.

"Nah, seemed a decent young lad," said the plain clothes man. "In any case, I told him he'd be wearing devil's claws in stir if he said anything."

Von Frakken climbed back onto the cart while the clerk painted over the previous shipping details on the packing cases, then stamped and re-labelled them. The cart drove thirty yards further on, to the closest section of the wharf. A workman heaved the cases down and stacked them close to a line of others. The cart made a slow u-turn and went back the way it came, making for the road.

"Is he not boarding the ship?" said Frye.

"Probably wants to board at the last minute," said the plain clothes man, "especially if he's going to have a hostage with him. A ship's less easy to run from, if he thinks he's rumbled."

"I'm going to follow him," said Maria. "I don't want him out of my sight. Mr Frye, please go over to those three packing cases and dump them in the river."

"Eh?" Both men looked at her in astonishment.

"In the river," repeated Maria. "As soon as von Frakken is out of earshot."

"What the bloody hell for?" said Frye. "That's evidence, that is."

"That's his means of setting up again, and it has to be destroyed," said Maria. "Under my orders, Mr Frye."

"Being wagged by the tail, are we?" scoffed the plain clothes man.

"Don't tell anyone," muttered Frye. "Right? 'Cos I bloody won't."

"If someone questions your authority, constable," said Maria, "send them to Inspector Barré."

Reluctantly, Frye flipped up the collar of his overcoat and ran out into the rain. Maria pulled down her hood and hurried in the opposite direction.

Von Frakken was about to drive the cart out onto the road. A sheet of lightning suddenly flashed stark blue light overhead and a clap of thunder made the air shudder. Maria was sure she could keep up with the cart if it kept to its present speed, but the foul weather made that seem unlikely.

Parked on the road was a small, ramshackle open wagon with CLIVE O'CONNOR – FINEST OF BAKERIES hand-painted on its side, drawn by a sloping, skinny-looking horse. There was no sign of its owner. Maria quickly hopped up into the seat and flicked the reins. The wagon's back wheels were badly aligned and their grumbling was almost audible above the sound of the storm.

The pace of von Frakken's cart picked up and Maria followed suit, keeping back as far as she dared without risk of losing her quarry in the murky rain. Several times, she had to remind herself that she didn't need to clutch the reins quite so hard.

After a few minutes they entered Fleet Street, heading in the direction of The Strand. It was well lit and clustered with people going in and out of the hotels and public houses, or passing through on their way from the theatres nearby. There were a large number of cabs and other vehicles. Twice, von Frakken stopped for two-wheelers pulling out into the road.

Halfway down the street, a knot of cabs all but blocked the road entirely. Umbrellas danced around them. They elbowed each other at angles, some trying to move away, most trying to get close to the lights of a large restaurant.

Von Frakken steered to the right, to get around the jam, but moved ahead by only a few feet. He leaned over and looked down at the cart's wheels, to check their path.

Maria's heart raced. He had only to look up, to look back, and he would see her.

Cabbies shouted at each other. Umbrellas flapped as fares took their seats. One of the horses in the middle of the confusion gave a loud whinny, startled by all the close movement.

Von Frakken turned impatiently, to see if it was possible to retreat and find a different route. Maria froze. For several seconds, his gaze ran up and down the street. More vehicles were slowing down, further along. Seeing no way through, he faced ahead again.

Maria remained motionless, her breath hesitant. Too intent on his progress to notice her? she thought.

One of the cabs made a sharp manoeuvre and freed itself from the rest. The knot slowly began to unravel to a chorus of shouts and waved hands. Von Frakken veered right again and this time managed to steer clear. Maria followed, keeping her distance.

A bulky dray, low to the ground and heavily laden, began jostling to get past her. She pulled to one side and the dray rumbled ahead, its load tied fast under weatherproof canvas.

As it came up behind von Frakken's cart, the driver whistled loudly to get his attention. Von Frakken twisted around. After glancing at the dray sullenly, his gaze suddenly flicked in surprise.

He stared directly at Maria. Her stomach lurched.

Immediately, Von Frakken pulled a whip from beside his seat and snapped his horse into a gallop. With a sharp cry, Maria cracked the reins. She sped past the dray at a rapid pace, forcing it to swerve, and the driver's cries vanished behind her.

The speed of von Frakken's cart quickly increased. The rain stung at Maria's face and reduced the road in front of her to a blur, her grip on the reins becoming slippery. She heard a terrified squeal up ahead as someone jumped out of von Frakken's way.

The distance between the two of them started to lengthen. Von Frakken's horse powered on, whip striking across its back. Muddy rainwater sprayed around the wheels of both vehicles.

They were cannoning past Green Park now, thundering for Brompton Road at breakneck speed. Maria was almost lifted out of her seat by the violent juddering of the cart beneath her. She felt the blood ice in her veins as she flew headlong into the storm-blinded darkness, terrified of collision and of the cart skidding on the flooded streets, of losing the galloping shape ahead of her to the night. They careered on, street lamps pulsing a dim on-off across Maria's face as they sped past, people on the pavements shifting aside in alarm at the sudden burst of wheels and hooves.

Lightning flashed a split-second silhouette of von Frakken turning in his seat and the instant hammering of thunder made Maria flinch. Her hands skipped momentarily.

Turning?

There was a sudden splinter of light ahead and a loud crack. A bullet cut shards from the wooden seat at Maria's side.

She cursed herself. Why hadn't she asked Barré for his pistol?

Von Frakken fired a second shot and Maria's leg exploded in pain. As she cried out, one hand automatically yanked the reins and the wagon suddenly tilted at full speed. She felt two wheels leave the surface of the street by inches.

Panic bit into her. The horse galloped hard, its head dipping in time to the drum roll of its hooves, and the wagon regained balance with a shuddering bump.

Maria fought back the pain that pulsed through her and took a fresh hold on the reins. Her clothes were soaked through and her hood slumped, sending water down her back. Ahead, von Frakken's cart was forced to slow slightly by the curve of the road. Maria gritted her teeth and sharply urged her wagon on. It rattled as if to shake loose her bones. They tore past a small, neat patch of parkland, the gap between them narrowing.

Maria was only yards behind as they hurtled into Cromwell Road. She roared fiercely, spit and rain escaping the side of her mouth. The museum was somewhere up ahead, hidden in the storm. The street lights were fewer here, but the road itself was straight.

A pounding boom rent the air. A stark flash showed von Frakken raising his revolver once more, the jolting of the cart unsteadying his aim. Maria steered to one side.

Von Frakken fired at Maria's horse. The shot hit it in the neck. With a dreadful cry, the animal's legs buckled and it collapsed onto the road. The fall pulled down on the harness, and the back of the wagon bucked wildly. It flipped over, wheels spinning, its old wooden boards cracking and splitting under the strain.

With a scream, Maria tried to jump free, but the bulk of the vehicle swung up behind and knocked her flying. For a second she felt herself spin, rain swooping around her. The wagon was dashed against the road in a crash of timber and metal.

Maria scraped violently through mud and rainwater, skidding to a stop on her side. For a moment, she lay still as death, pain howling in every muscle. Her breath came in short gasps.

She opened her eyes to find herself half submerged in a deep puddle at the side of the road. A numb buzzing filled her brain and her limbs felt like molten lead, scalding and heavy. Wincing, she put her palm against the top of her leg, then turned it over. The pelting rain quickly washed away the coating of blood.

She raised her eyes, her head lolling. The road swayed sickeningly, and with it the cart von Frakken had been driving. Parked. Not moving. Where was—?

She found it hard to think. He was at the roadside. Behind him, towering in the night, the museum. Was he—? Motionless, for a second. Rain. Turned away. Through the gates.

He could have shot her. Why hadn't he shot her? Wanted her living, still. If he could. Unless he had to.

Or—? Left her. Left her here to die.

Hurts. Everything hurts. Leg.

He was going for Meers. To get Meers.

Maria slowly eased herself into a sitting position, groaning loudly with pain. Get up! Get! Up! If von Frakken were to disappear into the night now, she would lose him, almost certainly forever.

She crawled onto her hands and knees. A crack of lightning lit up the road in front of her. A thousand drops of rain—a million—falling, falling, falling from way up in the sky, dashed into tiny explosions in the mud, joining the mass of water, all individuality gone.

Grunting, she lifted herself onto her feet. Her legs shook and her hair was matted into wet veins across her face. She limped a few steps and staggered suddenly to one side, her balance still wayward.

With a rolling shudder of thunder sounding overhead, she passed the gates and followed von Frakken through the immense, arched entrance of the Natural Sciences Museum. One of them would not leave the building alive.

CHAPTER XXXVI

The cavernous entrance hall of the museum was a cold mass of shadows. Still all but unoccupied, and still not completely built, the museum's vacancy felt like a silent, empty mind, waiting to be filled with knowledge, waiting for time and experience to accumulate within its walls.

Maria stood dripping, breathing hard. She sloughed off her sodden cloak and it slopped to the tiled floor.

There was no sign of von Frakken, already on his way up numerous flights of steps to what had once been Professor Hobson's room. Maria followed as fast as the bullet in her would allow, her mind beginning to clear, her leg leaving a drip of blood every few yards. The continuous rumble of the storm muffled the sound of her boots against the stone steps.

She was still two staircases away from the room when a sudden, angry yell tore through the air above her and echoed along the vaulted corridors. Von Frakken had missed Meers and his rescuer Inspector Barré by several minutes. At that moment, the two of them were heading south in a cab, Barré attempting to draw the doctor out of his induced catalepsy with *sal volatile*.

Maria hesitated, one hand poised on the wide stone balustrade beside her. His hostage gone, she reasoned, von Frakken now had nothing with which to bargain. His only course of action would be to escape without detection. He'd surely prefer to kill her now, tear off one of her limbs, or remove her head. Considerably less trouble to him, and almost as useful.

No further noise came from the floor above. Maria strained to hear anything above the storm. Dazzles of lightning pulsed through a skylight high above the stairwell.

He would realise she was pursuing him. He would pursue her.

She looked about her for some sort of makeshift weapon, but builders hadn't worked in this section for weeks and nothing had been left unattended. Although she remembered the way up to the professor's room, she didn't know if it was the only way back down to ground level. Most probably, it was not.

She took a few steps up, intently watching the darkness beyond an archway up ahead. She advanced very slowly, making no sound, listening for a footstep or the clicking of von Frakken's revolver. Her leg throbbed and she flinched every time she put weight on it. She felt her heart thump and her hands jittered with nerves.

Creaking. Somewhere behind her.

She turned, holding her breath.

It may have been the wind, through an open window? Or the building, settling in the cold?

A shape flew at the periphery of her vision. She hurried back down the steps, in time to catch a glimpse of von Frakken racing to the foot of a staircase running parallel to the one she'd ascended and vanishing from sight across a tiled landing.

She ran after him, ignoring the burning ache of her leg, expecting a shot to ring out from the darkness at any moment. Crossing the landing, she found herself in an immense store room.

It was filled with items which would soon form part of the museum's exhibitions. Some were still sealed into boxes, but most were unpacked and crowded around the room at random. There were chests of shallow drawers filled with pinned beetles and butterflies, tall glass cases holding varieties of a particular species, and reptile eggs from around the world.

Above all there were dead animals, stuffed and mounted. Birds posed in mid-flight or with their wings spread, beaks open as if snatching food from the air. A leathery rhino, with head dipped and jutting horn, was stacked beside a large tiger which stood with a savage, frozen snarl, its fangs bared and polished. A brown bear reared up on its hind legs, roaring, about to lash out with sharp claws. A crate was topped with snakes, cobras and puff adders, several with heads raised to strike.

Maria made her way around one after another. She could see a tall arched opening at the far end of the room, but only its ornately carved upper edge was visible behind fur, feathers, scales. The din of the rain was louder in here, and she detected no sign of von Frakken.

Suddenly, as if in answer to her thoughts, his voice echoed. "I would regret your death."

It seemed to come from everywhere and nowhere. Maria scanned the room slowly, her eyes wide, conscious of her every breath. "But still you would kill me," she called. "Abandon me. Am I not your warped child?"

"I am nothing if not pragmatic, I'm sure you've come to understand that. I do whatever is necessary, but I am not without sentiment. You are a creature made from desire, of love for knowledge and progress. I wish to offer you a last chance."

Maria hesitated. "To do what?"

"To join me." His voice was low, almost unsteady. "To be the good shepherd of the future, its redeemer, its divine sacrifice. You are the mother of a new world, whether you accept that or not, you are the progenitor of a new Mankind, who admits his weakness and turns to something more rational, more resilient."

"More standardised."

"Exactly! Biology has had its day, it has failed to deliver intelligence and longevity to the levels that must be attained in the centuries to come. We commoditise the human body, and thus it is reborn. Biological life upon this planet is as cheap as dirt, it crawls in every hole and gutter. It generates no profit, therefore it is worthless. You are a higher form of life!"

"Higher? To one who looks down, perhaps."

Maria moved slowly among the boxes, feathers and fur, alert for any glimpse of von Frakken, listening for an echo that would locate him. Gradually, she worked her way across the room, getting closer to the tall arch.

"Days ago," called von Frakken, in a tone that might have been pitiful, "upon our first meeting, you expressed a wish for death."

"And you said I am no more than you made me," said Maria. "That isn't true. I know that now."

"Your last chance. That brain! It could be on show for all time, in a museum like this, or inserted into a machine of calculus and organisation! Are you really going to force me to waste it with a bullet?"

"You'd waste your most successful experiment?"

"If you won't do as you are told, then the experiment has failed, no matter how successfully completed. Less free will next time, that is the lesson learned here. You, as you are, are a failure, and only I understand you. You don't belong with humans."

"They're better than you."

For a moment, there was only the teeming of the rain outside. "You have made your choice."

An ear-splitting shot suddenly shattered the glass case at Maria's side. Shards burst across the room. Instinctively, she ducked down. Between stuffed birds of prey, a shadow blinked. Crouching, she sped after it.

How many bullets had he used? she wondered. How many did he have?

In the darkness, von Frakken bumped against a set of drawers. The sound of it scraping on the stone floor told Maria that he was past the arch and into the room beyond.

This one was even larger, a long, broad gallery punctuated by skylights through which lightning flickered. Maria gasped when she saw what rose, almost to ceiling height, at the gallery's far end.

Half the gallery, closest to the arch, was as randomly crammed full of objects as the store room. The other half contained exhibits assembled from among bones carefully arranged on tarpaulin sheets. The skeletons of dinosaurs reared up out of the darkness, stark and dominating, posed to imitate life in the same way as the preserved animals over which they towered.

To one side was an immense arboreal beast, clawing high up a plaster tree trunk, and a horned creature with a skull that spread into a petrified fan above its shoulders. To the other side was a huge carnivorous predator, the claws of its atrophied forelimbs dwarfed by the huge frame of its head and the width of its ribcage. It was held up by two metal rods, one beneath its neck, the other halfway along its knotted spine. Behind them all, hung on the walls, were the outlines of prehistoric cephalopods and giant fish, frozen in rock.

Maria's momentary distraction was broken by a sharp click. Von Frakken, barely visible in the shadows, aimed his revolver directly at her. She dropped with a cry and scurried away. Von Frakken lowered his aim and slowly retreated towards the skeletons. For a second, his left arm twisted involuntarily and his head twitched to one side.

How many bullets? Crouched behind a crate, Maria looked around for a loose object, something with which she could draw his fire and make him waste ammunition. Finding nothing, she tore a couple of buttons off her coat. She peered around the edge of the crate, into the space between the jumble of exhibits and the monstrous skeletons.

A shadow glided slowly. Von Frakken crept towards the looming carnivore, but Maria couldn't tell which way he was facing. Holding her breath, she flung one of the buttons way off to her right. A second later, it struck something hard and rattled noisily as it rebounded.

The shadow instantly reacted, but fired no shot. The stillness in the gallery was broken only by the low, tumbling throb of the storm. Von Frakken merged into the pitch dark beneath the ancient predator's bones.

Was her first try too distant? Would he shoot at something nearer?

There was no lightning to guide Maria's aim. She held the button between two shaking fingers and raised her arm, then threw it blindly into the dark towards, to her best guess, von Frakken's position.

The button hit something metal. Von Frakken swung sharply and fired, spinning himself off-balance. The bullet hit the supporting rod under the dinosaur's neck and there was a sudden, loud creak. Von Frakken grasped the rod to steady himself. His arm pulled in a spasm. Something broke at the base of the rod.

The predator's entire skeleton suddenly lurched and shifted in mid-air, as if reanimated into life for the first time in millions of years. As it twisted, the wired bolts that joined it together groaned and screeched like a cry across the primaeval swamp. It dropped, a huge dead weight, its upper jaw and vacant eye sockets jutting ahead of falling ribs and spine.

Von Frakken looked up as lightning flickered through the gallery. For a fraction of a second, he was rooted to the spot in horror. The dead creature's upper jaw pounded him to the floor, its giant stone teeth biting deep into his chest, the weight of the skull pinning him down. A deep burst of thunder shook the room.

He struggled uselessly, blood welling up from his mouth, his limbs shaking. His head thrashed from side to side. A ragged puddle of blood spread rapidly beneath him.

He looked up at Maria, now standing at his side. His functioning eye blazed, with an intensity she'd never seen before, and she suddenly recoiled. It was the Eye of her nightmares. The watching, judging Eye, that followed her in the dark, had always been his. The glaring, critical eye of her creator.

His expression changed. It became filled with regret. Words bubbled through the blood that lapped around his lips. "We could have made a world. Now, you are truly alone."

His fingers clawed uselessly at the floor, and then he was dead.

CHAPTER XXXVII

Tuesday 18th November 1879

Inspector Barré's discomfort in social situations prompted him to announce, for the third time in half an hour, that he really ought to be going.

"Nonsense, Charles," said Dr Meers. "You can finish your tea, surely?"

Barré eyed his half-empty cup. He adjusted his monocle and chased a speck of dirt from his sleeve.

A hazy, blue-grey daylight filled the Meers's comfortable sitting room. Barré and Sophia sat opposite the doctor and Maria, tea tray between them. A crackling fire blazed in the grate.

Barré searched for conversation. "You've no lasting ill-effects, Tom, from your drugged state?"

"No, but it left me with a devil of a headache," said Dr Meers. "I can barely recall those hours, it feels like some horrible dream."

"One never to be repeated," said Sophia.

"Provided von Frakken's research never turns up," said Meers.

"It's—gone?" said Maria, eyebrows raised.

Barré straightened his collar. "My men swear they know nothing, the captain of the *Lanchester* swears it never came aboard. The Yard have got Whitehall clamouring for its recovery."

"They don't subscribe to the tall tales of hoaxes?" said Sophia.

"They wrote them," said Barré. "I'm afraid poor Jabez Pell will find nothing but shame and infamy in his grave."

Edith poked her head around the door. "Clear the tea, Madam?"

"Not yet, Edith," said Sophia. "Could you bring us some of the fruit cake? Thank you."

Edith paused a moment, her nose wrinkling. She left the door ajar behind her.

Barré glanced at the clock. "That sounds delightful, I'm sure, but I really should be going."

"By the way, Maria has decided to accept our offer," said Meers.

"Offer?" said Barré.

"To live here permanently," said Maria, "with Dr and Mrs Meers. I thought I might be Maria Hobson, from now on."

"He'd have been very pleased." Meers smiled and sipped his tea.

"Weren't you rather against hobnobbing with the likes of us?" said Barré.

"Well," said Maria, "that's an opinion I must leave behind, isn't it? My jigsaw puzzle existence has been short, but I do have experiences and memories which are mine alone. In the end, perhaps that does amount to a life, be it human or otherwise."

The inspector rose to his feet, replacing his tea cup on the tray. "That's all fine and dandy, but what are you to do? We're rid of von Frakken and his ilk, so where does that leave you?"

"I was rather hoping that you might have the answer to that, Inspector," she smiled.

"Me? In what way?"

"There must be police matters—like those involving me—which can't be pursued like regular thefts and murders. Instances requiring an unusual discretion."

Barré's frown narrowed his eyes. "What exactly are you proposing?"

"I could work for you. Unofficially, of course."

"Entirely unofficially," said Barré. He walked slowly back and forth, his frown wavering in time with his thoughts. For a second, he looked as if he was about to speak, but changed his mind.

He paused in the doorway on his way out. "I'll let you know."

THE END

ABOUT THE AUTHOR

Richard Gadz was bolted together in the late 1950s, in a laboratory hidden deep in the Carpathian mountains. For a number of years, he worked his way across South America and Antarctica as a freelance guillotine salesman, but following a series of bizarre gardening accidents he now lives permanently in the UK at Warwick, not far from the famous castle, although he spends most of his time in a world of his own. Richard Gadz is the pen name of Simon Cheshire, author of the highly acclaimed horror novel Flesh & Blood.

richardgadz.co.uk

ABOUT DEIXIS PRESS

Deixis Press is an independent publisher of fiction, usually with a darker edge. Our aim is to discover, commission, and curate works of literary art. Every book published by Deixis Press is hand-picked and adored from submission to release and beyond.

www.deixis.press

Lightning Source UK Ltd.
Milton Keynes UK
UKHW012337291221
396350UK00003B/822